Hiding Behind The Couch Series

I0670925

Crying in the Rain

SECOND EDITION

by
Debbie McGowan

Beaten Track
www.beatentrackpublishing.com

Contents

Author's Note

Why have I released a second edition of *Crying in the Rain*?

To be clear, I didn't hate the first edition, but seeing the things I didn't like about it crop up in reviews…well, there's an argument there for not reading reviews, I suppose, but those readers weren't wrong. There was too much 'head-hopping'. *Crying in the Rain* is essentially a romance novel, and modern romance novels are usually written from one point of view at a time rather than the 'psychic fly on a very nearby wall' omniscient narration I most often use in the Hiding Behind The Couch series.

So I've fixed the head-hopping. What I haven't changed is the overall story or the characterisation, but I have developed both further, expanding some scenes and deleting others, including the original epilogue, which was from Fergus's point of view.

Ade and Kris are imperfect men whose fictional experiences are inspired by real experiences of real people. Their story also slots into the overarching saga of Hiding Behind The Couch, and while *Crying in the Rain* can be read as a stand-alone, there are references to other events and characters important to the series.

Content Warning: *this story deals with issues of domestic violence and past childhood sexual abuse.*

With special thanks, love and hugs to AS.

"I know too much and not enough."

Allen Ginsberg

1: Always on Sunday

Ade

A DE WAS AWAKE, had been for hours, waiting for a reasonable time to get out of bed. He'd settled on 5:15, a full forty-five minutes to shower and dress and be ready to leave when his alarm went off at six. He could say he needed to be in work early to prepare the studio, even though they'd likely spend most of the morning rehearsing and wouldn't record until after lunch.

Why should I need to say anything at all? But the tiny spark of resistance found nothing to ignite because the excuse itself didn't matter, only that it worked.

5:14

His heart pounded double time to the flashing colon between the numbers, and he tried to slow it, concentrate on the day ahead instead of whatever might happen next.

Whatever might happen next.

It had to end somewhere.

Easing onto his back, he bit hard on his lip to stop the hiss escaping as he lifted his arm and pushed away the duvet, slid his leg off the side of the bed.

Paused.

No response to that, he shuffled to the edge of the mattress and eased the other leg out, remaining as close to horizontal as he could. A half-snore in the dark; he froze, waited.

Nothing.

He resumed breathing, quietly through his nose, every sound amplified in the early morning silence, every movement a chore. He felt a hundred years old, doddering and woozy from last night's wine and the throb in his face, sharp as an ice pick to the teeth, jaw, cheekbone…he couldn't pinpoint its exact origin. It was probably all over.

God, I wish it was.

In the sanctuary of the bathroom, he set the shower running, taking a minute to prepare himself for the ordeal of brushing his teeth—in the dark. He'd been here before, in front of that mirror. The pain was bad enough without his reflection deriding and sneering. *You coward. You didn't have to go through this.*

The toothpaste stung like acid where it frothed onto his lips, the brush whacking into his teeth over and over as he circled in the tiny space of his barely open mouth. Any more and he'd have been yelling. As it was, he couldn't spit, could only let the foam dribble down his chin and into the sink. He was almost tempted to switch on the light, see if the foam was tinged pink, but he honestly didn't care.

The shower was cold, at first like shards of ice slicing at his back, but after a while, he became indifferent to it. The sponge rasped, chafing his skin, but his pain receptors were already overloaded, so it tingled rather than stung. Like repeatedly pinching a bruise. Barely aware of his teeth chattering or the numbness of his extremities, he turned off the shower, clinging to the wall as he climbed out and then stood, quaking and dripping and listening for anything other than his short, shaky breaths.

Still nothing, but for how long?

He towel-dried vigorously everywhere but his face, which he dabbed gingerly, flinching with every touch. Naked and dithering, he crept into the bedroom, snatched up the first clothes he touched in the curtained darkness and fled to the living room to dress. The boxer shorts and socks were old and grey, the shirt was crinkled with frayed cuffs, but that was fine. Fitting, actually. Old and grey was how he felt. The trousers were OK—there were bleach splashes up one of the legs, but who would notice? Of course, he'd forgotten his shoes, and his hairbrush and gel were also in the bedroom. It would take too long, and in any case his scalp felt like it was burning. He'd just go in, grab his shoes and leave, buy coffee on the way. By the time he got home from work, his *guest* would be gone.

Ade made it into the bedroom and out again with his shoes, grabbed his jacket from the hook and his keys from the hall table, clutching them tightly to his palm to mute their tinkling. He was enjoying the cut of the sharp edges a little too much and squeezed harder, smiling grimly, imagining the heat and the smell of the blood as it oozed between his fingers and dripped from his clenched fist. It was sick, macabre, both triumph and failure and just for him, but he couldn't allow himself to think like that. He needed people, company, right away, before the craving for self-destruction pushed any further through his flimsy defences. Hands shaking, he locked up and sped down the stairs, out of the apartment building—no, *MY apartment building, MINE*—and onwards to the commuter coffee bar in the train station, the only place open this early in the day.

"Morning, sir. What can I get you?"

"Vanilla latte, please—large, to go."

The barista set to work, every clang and button push ringing scorn in Ade's ears. Definitely too much wine last night, or that was part of the problem. The rest? The rest was just too much.

"Would you like anything to eat? Almond Danish, perhaps?"

"No, thanks." He probably ought to eat something, but it hurt to speak, so there was no way he was getting a pastry past his lips. He noticed the barista kept looking at him; caught in the act, she smiled, and he smiled back. It wasn't a wise move. His whole face felt stretched and undone, his tattered pride seeping through the cracks. *Oh, don't mind me, the poor little queer who deserves everything he gets.* It was in his mind to say it, just to see her reaction, but they exchanged cash and coffee and all he said was thanks and then left, trying to go slowly because he was way too early and people would ask questions. With some effort, he dropped to a stroll and cautiously lifted the cup to his lips, choking back a laugh at the impossibility.

Even the coffee's mocking me. Tilting his head to get any of the liquid out of the sippy hole and into his mouth was a non-starter—unless he was prepared to share his agony with all the early commuters marching by.

Discarding the lid in the next bin he passed, he took a moment to gather his thoughts and whatever else he could. He'd escaped, unnoticed, and for the next ten hours, theoretically, all he had to worry about was his work.

In an ideal world, it would have been a more taxing day with plenty to keep him preoccupied, perhaps a futuristic drama in need of custom effects or a documentary—experts were wafflers and always needed a ton of editing. But a contemporary play with a cast of four was what he had. On the plus side, the writing was decent, and he'd checked the roster of actors in advance. The two women he'd worked with before. The two guys he'd heard of but not met, although both were experienced radio actors, so there'd be no hand-holding. If they arrived on time and had given the script at least a cursory look over, Ade would be happy. Or not happy, but the recording should go well and keep him busy enough to partially shut the door on the other.

Except the other never took no for an answer and would kick the door down. There'd be no escape next time. No escape now, if he answered that incoming call. He pulled his phone from his pocket, dismissed the call and stepped off the kerb, a horn honk away from killing himself.

Idiot. Get a grip. He waved an apology at the cabbie and safely made it across the road, pausing to make the most of the adrenaline rush. He even managed to take a decent mouthful of coffee. The voicemail icon popped up. He switched off his phone, pocketed it and continued on his way, paying better attention to his surroundings, snatches of muffled music from passing cars, the streetlights' glitter across the wet tarmac. It had rained heavily overnight, leaving the city fresh with only the slightest breeze— quite mild for October—and the sky was slowly brightening.

Mornings like this, Ade missed joining the other nicotine addicts for a quick puff outside the studio. It would've been an easy means to while away the hour and a half early he was. Maybe it would help him feel part of the world again?

At the door to the newsagent's, he slowed and seriously contemplated purchasing a pack of Marlboro and a disposable lighter. He could see Gavin—the news producer—standing by the studio's side entrance, lit cigarette poised between finger and thumb, hidden inside his hand, the other hand holding his phone. Ade gave in to the temptation, bought the cigarettes and went to join his fellow producer.

"Hi, Gav," he called, attempting cheery but sounding like his jaw was wired shut.

The other man looked up from his phone screen and frowned, failing to hide his disgruntlement at being disturbed, but quickly replaced the frown first with a smile and then with another frown. "I thought you were off the ciggies."

"Social smoking," Ade said lightly, focusing his attention on peeling the cellophane from the packet and breathing, aware of Gavin's appraising gaze passing over his face and of the bone-jarring throb that became more intense with every word uttered. Well, the adrenaline had been nice while it lasted.

Gavin returned his attention to his phone. "You're in early. What you working on today?"

Ade flipped the lid, the scent of new cigarettes wafting wonderfully up into his nostrils. He teased one free and lit it, taking far too big an inhalation for his first smoke in six months. He suppressed the cough—barely. "A play," he wheezed out, slowly letting the smoky breath wisp through his lips. "Kitchen sink makeover."

"Yeah?"

"Mm." The nicotine-induced dizziness was quite delightful. "It's a contemporary interpretation of *It Always Rains on Sunday*— the script's excellent." He felt like a bad ventriloquist, squeezing the words through clenched teeth, and must've sounded that way too, as it took Gavin a moment to respond.

"Sounds like one of Sal's," he said dryly.

What started as a laugh was strangled by Ade's inability to stretch his mouth into a smile and emerged as a breathy grunt. "It is," he managed to push out.

Gavin nodded. "Should be good."

"Yeah." Ade was confident it would be. Sally O'Connor was one of those playwrights who could churn out a quality script once a week, every week, but they were all much the same, which wasn't a bad thing. Listeners loved them; actors loved them, especially as Sal gave both actors and producer free licence to improvise, and if she liked what they'd created more than what she'd originally written, she'd incorporate the changes into her script. She got paid, whatever. She'd also known Ade a long time, and he was dreading her turning up today almost as much as he was dreading going home.

"I'm heading in," Gavin said. "Catch you later."

"See you." Ade watched him leave, yet still jumped as the door banged shut. He'd thought he was past that. This time yesterday, he'd been certain of it, yet here he was, jacked up on nicotine and pain endorphins and not giving a shit about the state of his clothes or his hair or the damp seeping through his jacket from the brick wall he was leaning against. A poster boy for abject failure.

It had to be the cigarette making him feel sick. He stubbed it out half-smoked and shoved his hands in his pockets, his phone warm and silent against his chilled palm. He'd have to turn it on again soon, deal with that voicemail and however many more awaited him. Soon, but not yet.

2: Early Birds

Kris

THE MANCHESTER TRAIN was as empty as the platform had been, for the time being at least. Their hometown station was so small, Kris had rarely seen anyone else boarding the first train even when he'd taken it regularly, but the commuters wouldn't be far behind. He kind of missed being one of them, if only because he'd had a travel permit and wouldn't have been worrying about accidental fare evasion since there was no longer a staffed ticket office. Nor was there an automated machine, so Kris took his seat, fare in one hand, script in the other, and kept a lookout for the guard.

He didn't need to leave this early. He wasn't really sure why he had. This job was no different from any of the other plays he'd worked on, other than it being the first decent role he'd picked up in a while, and it felt like a step in the right direction, a real move away from ads and voiceovers. Not that he regretted the fourteen years he'd been doing that. After all, how many actors secured long-term, salaried positions straight out of college? Admittedly, he'd shared his classmates' mindset in thinking radio acting was an old man's game, but unlike his classmates, he'd had responsibilities to people other than himself.

It might not have been a glamorous road to stardom, but it had paid the mortgage, and, despite his friends' over-the-top imitations of more or less every ad he'd ever recorded, he was glad for the experience. He had a solid repertoire of accents and a 'very agile register'—his agent's contribution to his CV. Kids with bikes, young dads at the pub, middle-aged car salesmen, oldies wowed by their stair lifts, Kris had played them all. If not for the upheaval of the last couple of years and the awkwardness of seeing Jack at the studio every day, he'd have still been playing them, and happily, but he couldn't deny it felt good to have a role with some meat to it.

Kris flicked through the script, carefully, as the stapled top corner was barely holding. Even though they weren't highlighted or marked in any way, his lines leapt from the pages. He knew the entire script—he'd printed it as soon as he'd had confirmation the part of Tommy was his—but there were still bits that surprised him. Not the story itself. His drama class had watched the original black-and-white movie, their tutor selling it to them as 'the ultimate 1940s British noir', which as young, pretentious students they'd *adored* because the movie was avant-garde, but it was only when Kris read Sally O'Connor's script that he appreciated how complex the characters were…and how much of a challenge it would be to capture the danger, the sexiness and the ordinariness through sound alone.

The train slowed and stopped at the next station, and a couple of office workers boarded Kris's carriage, taking a seat at either end. One put in earphones, the other took out their ebook reader. The doors closed, and the train moved off again. Kris watched out the window until the platform was no longer in view and returned his attention to his script as best he could. The money for his ticket was sticking to his palm; no sign of the guard yet, he took a chance and put it back in his pocket, exchanging it for his phone so he could go over the email and double-check he was heading for the right studio, wondering if the other actors were doing the same. Probably not. He was a worrier by nature. As Shaunna had pointed out the previous evening, *after* she'd gasped in mock horror when he'd sat down for dinner without his script, he couldn't be any more prepared than he was—than he'd been for a week already.

Remembering that didn't stop him fretting, but he did put his phone away and, for a few minutes, sat back and managed to take in the scenery along the side of the track, mostly fields, a few houses, a single car waiting at the level crossing. The train slowed again; Kris didn't see how many passengers boarded, and none joined his carriage, but they were still a way out from the city with plenty more stops before his. He waited for a minute or so after the train took off again, still no sign of the guard, and chanced running through his final scene one more time—without his script—the scene when Tommy finally showed his true colours, the violent nature underlying his seeming heartbreak over abandoning Rose. True, there were clues littered throughout, and Kris would be taking his lead from the producer over how much he pushed those. Too obvious and the ending would be trite and predictable, too obscure and it would feel inauthentic.

"Tickets, please."

The call startled Kris back to his surroundings. He hadn't noticed that the train had stopped, never mind taken on quite a few more passengers, all of whom flashed permits as the guard moved swiftly along the aisle. Kris had to stand to get the coins out of his pocket, and he had them in his hand before the guard reached him, but he still apologised.

Presumably, the guard had seen where he'd joined the train, as he dispensed Kris's ticket without comment and continued on his way, through to the next carriage. Soon after, they reached the next station, and the train filled considerably. A woman talking on her phone took the seat opposite Kris's and continued her conversation. It wasn't loud, but it was distracting, so he tucked his script back into its folder and, not wishing to eavesdrop, though it was impossible not to, took out his phone again.

~ *Be amazing today! x*

The message was twenty minutes old, which surprised him. Shaunna wasn't an early riser, and she wasn't in work today.

He sent back: *Thanks. Hope I didn't wake you. x*

She hadn't mentioned having any plans. Since they'd told their friends they'd separated, neither felt compelled to share the details of every little thing they got up and with whom, but it was virtually impossible to keep secrets from each other when they still shared a house.

~ Nope. Forgot to switch off my alarm. Made a cuppa and came back to bed. x zzzz...

Kris didn't reply to that and instead passed a little more time scrolling back through their texts, most consisting of one of them asking the other to pick up bread or milk or something on their way home. It probably was weird that they still lived together—some of their friends had blatantly said as much—and they had talked about selling up and moving into their own places, but after so many years, first as friends, then co-parents, then spouses, neither of them wanted to. It was comfortable, easy, and it worked for them. If that ever changed, if either of them met someone else...well, they'd deal with it when the time came.

The train drew into the next station, the one before Kris's stop, and a few more passengers boarded, most airport-bound and lugging along large suitcases. He contemplated moving to stand by the door: the stations were only a couple of minutes apart, and the thought of being stuck on the wrong side of someone's luggage, unable to leave the train, was giving him minor palpitations.

He needn't have worried, or not about that, because several minutes on, the train was still standing at the platform. Leaning against the window, Kris could just about see the front of the train, where the guard was talking to the driver. The guard glanced along the line and with a shrug reboarded. The announcement came a second later.

"Due to a points failure, this service will be delayed by approximately fifteen minutes. We apologise for any inconvenience."

*

The hydraulics hissed as they powered down again, the tick of the idling train like a stopwatch counting up to the moment when Kris would have to concede he was too late to make it. Perhaps he should give up now, switch platforms and head back home. Except it wasn't in his nature to quit, even when that was the best option, and in any case, given how early he'd left, he wasn't actually late yet.

The woman sitting opposite leaned forward and wriggled out of her jacket, smiling apologetically for invading Kris's space. He smiled back.

"It's stuffy in here, isn't it?" he said.

She nodded and blew out of her mouth, directing the breath up towards her hair, which had flopped in the humidity. "Mind if I open a window?" she asked.

"Not at all."

She stood up and slid the narrow vent open a few inches, letting in a waft of cool, damp air. Leaning towards it, she took a few deep breaths. "That's better."

Kris had to agree. He was one of those always-cold people, so the heat didn't bother him, but with the outside world obscured by condensation and the growing impatience of the passengers, the atmosphere in the carriage had become quite oppressive.

The woman sat down again and fished a compact mirror out of her bag, eyeing her reflection in dismay. "God, I'll be fit for nothing by the time I get to my interview."

"New job?"

"Yeah." She smoothed under her eyes with a fingertip. "Head of Physics. I'm a high school teacher…and beginning to wonder if I should take this as a sign." Frowning, she put the compact away and explained, "It's a big step up for me. I've only been teaching for three years."

"It's always struck me as a really tough job."

"It is, but I love it."

"Well, break a leg," Kris said.

She laughed. "Thanks. How about you? What do you do for a living?"

"I'm an actor."

"I thought so."

"Did you?"

"*Break a leg*?"

"Ah. Yeah." Kris chuckled.

"And wasn't that a script you were reading?"

"It was. I'm recording a play today. That's assuming this train ever moves."

"Sod's law, isn't it? Will they start without you?"

"Probably." Kris hoped they wouldn't. There were plenty of scenes that Tommy wasn't in, but he liked to listen to the other actors, get a feel for the dynamics between the different characters.

"So have you been in anything I've seen?" the woman asked.

"No, but you might've heard me. I'm a radio actor."

"Oh, really? I'd swear I've seen you on TV."

Kris shook his head, while she tilted hers, studying him intently. He had a good idea what was coming next, although maybe she was a little too young to make the connection. Whether she would've done so in time, he'd never know, as that was the moment when the hydraulics powered up and with a very welcome judder and a sarcastic cheer from the passengers, the train slowly but surely left the station.

3: Empty

Ade

THE BUILDING WAS somehow colder and more formidable without the bustle of delivery drivers and admin staff. Ade hurried along the windowless service corridor, pausing to calm his nerves before he stepped through the door into the public foyer, where a lone security guard sat behind the desk. The sign above him was still dark, but light from the computer monitor flickered across the guard's face as he glanced up to see who was there.

"Morning, Mr. Simmons."

"Morning, Abdul." Same bad-ventriloquist act.

"Did you wet the bed?"

Ade made an amused grunt in his throat. "Something like that." He wanted so much to enjoy a few minutes' conversation with someone he knew was safe but who didn't know him well enough to ask awkward questions.

"Want me to put that in the bin?"

"Mmm?"

Abdul nodded at the takeout cup Ade was holding by its rim.

"Mmm! Mmm-mmm." He tried to unlock his jaw, by some miracle keeping the scream silent as he took a sip to prove he wasn't done with it. "Nicer than the coffee here."

"You're not wrong. I bring my own." Abdul raised a shallow plastic Thermos cup above the desk. "Cheaper too. Cheers," he said and slurped a mouthful, grimacing. "Bit cold by now, mind."

"When do you finish?"

"Another twenty minutes."

"Not long, then."

"No, thank goodness. I'm ready for my breakfast this morning. Actually…" Wheeling his chair a few feet along the desk, Abdul grabbed the signing-in book and wheeled back again. "I think one of your actors is here already." He tapped the last entry on the page.

"Guess I wasn't the only one who wet the bed," Ade muttered to himself, but Abdul heard him and chuckled.

"I sent him up to the cafeteria."

"OK. Thanks. See you later."

Ade continued past the reception desk to the lift and pressed the call button, pondering while he waited. Should he find his early arrival or head straight for the studio? On the one hand, he was in no fit state, mentally or physically, for small talk with strangers; on the other, he might keep his precarious hold on his sanity if he had company, and other than the breakfast show and news teams, upstairs would be a ghost ship.

The lift arrived; Ade stepped in and automatically pushed the button for the fourth floor.

Studio it is.

Now he was alone and somewhere he wouldn't be heard if he did scream, he poked experimentally at his face, hitting a couple of spots that made him swear. He stopped prodding; the pain once again dwindled to a miserable ache, which was bearable but would dog him all day. *Should've bought painkillers instead of cigs, idiot. Failure number three of the day, and it's not even eight o'clock.*

The lift stopped and the doors opened onto yet another empty corridor. Ade set off, concentrating on the warning jolts from his jaw that accompanied his every step. Better that than listen to the destructive thoughts. People saw the bruises; they didn't hear the voices ridiculing, undermining.

To-do list. Those helped. They didn't silence that whining, sneering chorus of insults and judgements—nothing did—but there were things he needed to do before the actors arrived. *The rest of the actors*, the voices sniped, seeing as one was sitting upstairs in the cafeteria. *Who was it again?*

Jotting 'revisit CVs' as point #1 on his mental list, he veered off into the toilets, tipped the rest of his coffee into the hand basin and ditched the cup in the bin, then took it out again.

Well, that's a stroke of luck.

It was a bit slummy, but he fished the discarded hair gel tub out of the bin and unscrewed the lid. Scraping what little remained from the sides with his fingertips, he spiked his hair, all the while aware of his failings reflecting back at him in the wide mirror running the length of the wall...but not of the person in one of the cubicles until a toilet flushed. Ade launched the empty gel tub at the bin and fled before the door opened. It was probably only Gavin, but Ade felt unworthy enough without forcing his ugly mug and bad breath on to someone else. If his luck held, there'd be some mints or gum in one of the desk drawers so he could get rid of the cig-and-coffee stink. Not much he could do about his face.

Studio Three was in darkness, as he'd expected; he'd told his engineer not to bother coming in until after lunch. He switched on one set of lights and the air conditioning, breathing the cool, fresh air in deeply through his nose, releasing it through narrowed lips, easing them apart. Another breath; another couple of millimetres.

"OK. Let's see if proper talking is a possibility. 'She sells seashells on the seashore.'" So far so good. "'The raging rocks and shivering shocks shall break the locks of prison gates, and Phibbus' car shall shine from far and make and mar the foolish Fates.' Well, at least my Bottom is still in good shape." He snorted a laugh at the irony. Excruciating waves of hot pain raced over and through his head. "Shit!" *Too much!*

He sank down, not even thinking to check if the chair was there first and honestly, would it matter if he dropped humiliatingly to the floor? He wasn't the most talkative of producers at the best of times, having to plan the words in advance as much as he did. Now he couldn't even smile without swearing or sobbing his guts out.

But something else was brewing in the midst of all the misery and self-pity. Anger, and it was no longer directed inwards.

He picked up the folder containing the actors' agency profiles and flipped it open but couldn't see the words through his tears.

Anger. Yet he never lashed out.

He shut it again and rooted through the drawers for mints, chewing gum or anything that would make him remotely less disgusting. Pens, pencils, stray paperclips, spent staples. No mints.

Anger that he couldn't just get on with his work, the one thing he absolutely knew he was good at.

He slammed the drawer and sat back, squinting at the overhead light, the pretty prisms dancing on his lashes. He felt dizzy, not surprisingly, as his last meal was lunch the previous day, and he had a headache—the tailing edge of the hangover, perhaps. That was definitely the least damaging way to think of it.

Anger…subsiding.

"List." They were his saving grace, stopped him forgetting the important things when the other stuff was shredding his thoughts. He had apps and paper notebooks full of them, checked off or crossed out, never deleted, records to remind him he wasn't really a…what was it again? *Useless airhead. Everyone knows it, but it's cheaper to keep you on than fire you.*

"Shut up."

Unlocking his tablet, he opened a new checklist.

1.

Nothing. He stared at the blankness, trying to recall what it was he needed to do, but despite his determination, his mind was a fuzzy mess, meandering towards dark, haunted alleys that all led to the same place. *Where was I? Coffee...Abdul...did you wet the bed—got it.*

Sitting upright again, Ade made a second attempt with the folder, flicking through the pages until a name jumped out at him. *Kristian Johansson. That's the one.*

And evidently, his head had been up his backside for the past month because he recalled nothing about Kristian's CV. Like, for instance, that he'd been on a retainer with their rival local station, which Ade used to listen to, not that he'd ever admit it to his bosses. They'd rejected a series about a small-town GP that went on to become their rival's most successful show, with the lead role played by none other than Kristian Johansson.

You should've known that, but of course you didn't. You're a hack...

Ade ignored the accusations and kept reading, through the other actors' CVs, taking an interest, committing details to memory. When he was done, he thumbed back and studied Kristian's cover photo: pale complexion, light-brown hair with blondish tints, very Scandinavian—an easy assumption to make, given his last name was Johansson. The smile, while fake, showed a man who was also happy in front of the camera.

Ade closed the folder and set it back on the desk, drumming his fingers in time with the thrum in his jaw. If he moved carefully, didn't do anything too stupid...

"List."

1. Don't do anything stupid.

He almost smiled at that but stopped himself, backspaced, started for real.

1. Revisit CVs.
2. Buy mints.

He had an hour, plenty of time to pop out and get back before the rest of the actors arrived, so that was what he did, taking the stairs down to the service corridor, out the side door, past Gavin, smoking again, and Abdul, cycle helmet on, about to head home.

A mob of schoolkids had descended on the newsagent, who ignored their clamour to take Ade's money for a packet of extra-strong mints. Ade immediately slotted two into his mouth, groaning in relief...pleasure?...as the sharp menthol paradoxically soothed and aggravated his aches.

Back in the building, safe and maybe a little sounder than before, he booted his phone on his way up the stairs so he could check off item #2, wavering when he reached the studio floor. His stomach clenched, begging to be filled. Could he stand the pain? The scrutiny? He wasn't sure, but this was going to be a long day.

2. ~~Buy mints.~~
3. ~~Delete voicemails.~~

Pride glimmered in his periphery. He hadn't even listened to them, but for safety, he overwrote item #3 with:

3. Breakfast.

Low-level chatter interspersed with clangs from the kitchen greeted him at the cafeteria entrance, and he slowed his pace, trying to appear casual and normal as he passed by the cleaners grabbing a quick cuppa mid-shift. A few of the clerical staff were in too, he noticed, but no management yet. No presenters, either; most came in, did their show and left.

Reaching the counter, Ade dragged up as much of a smile as he could. It wasn't perfect, but it was the best he had.

"Morning, Pip."

"Good morning, Ade."

He scanned the breakfast stuff on offer, fried eggs, sausages, bacon, shrivelled and unappealing, same as him with Pip's glare burning into him. She wouldn't say anything, but she'd know, and he hated that she'd know. Her concern hovered like a warm blanket, so close, yet he couldn't reach it, didn't dare try, so utterly ashamed.

"What would you like?" she asked coolly. "Coffee and a bagel?"

There was no chance of him chewing his way through a bagel. "Porridge, I think."

"You hate porridge."

"The one with—" Someone queued up behind him and he reworded on the fly. "—Tate and Lyle is OK."

"Are you sure? I could do you some scrambled egg."

Ade nodded. "Thanks, Pip. You're the best."

"I'm *your bestie*, and don't you forget it," she said sternly, and he nodded again but couldn't look at her. She was the best friend he'd ever had, so kind and supportive, always there when he needed her whether he'd asked for her help or not. Still, it was hard to remember sometimes that she wasn't angry with him.

"Go sit," she prompted, her tone gentler now, which was somehow worse.

Obediently, Ade set off towards his usual table but then stopped mid-step when he spotted the man sitting alone in the back corner of the cafeteria, his poise relaxed as he watched distantly out the window, very much the chilled Scandinavian. He picked up the cup in front of him, glancing around the room as he sipped, not entirely coming off as someone amenable to company, but in the second or less that they made eye contact, Ade knew he had to take a chance and went over to introduce himself.

4: Company

Kris

"MR. JOHANSSON?"

"Yes?" Kris startled, though he wasn't overly surprised, given he'd met the man's gaze, briefly and by accident, but he couldn't recall having met him before.

"Ade Simmons," the man said and held out his hand. "I'm working on the play with you today."

"Ah. That makes sense." Kris shook Ade's hand and gestured to the seat opposite by way of invitation. "I prefer Kris, if that's OK."

"Got it." Ade sat. He seemed a cool operator, very formal. *Maybe they use last names here.*

"Sorry." Kris backpedalled. "Mr. Johansson is fine, but...he's my dad, not me, if you see what I mean."

Ade's smile was very controlled, almost fake. "My dad passed years ago, but I'm just the same."

"Sorry about your dad." It was a silly thing to say, and Kris felt foolish. Ade didn't seem to notice.

"Thank you, although he didn't live with us, so..."

One of the serving staff appeared next to the table. "Your coffee and eggs, sir," she said, placing the mug and plate in front of Ade.

"Thanks, honey."

She hovered until he looked up at her but said nothing further, just gave him a sad smile and, with a courteous nod for Kris, returned to the counter.

"My mate," Ade said. "Pip."

Kris hadn't planned on asking.

"We go way back." Ade lifted a minuscule amount of egg to his mouth, knocked most of it back onto the plate with his top lip and swallowed with a grimace.

Kris averted his eyes, no desire to watch Ade eat, particularly as he seemed self-conscious doing so in front of someone else. The script was a handy tactical retreat, and it wouldn't hurt to go through his lines…yet again. He'd never forgotten them during a performance, but that didn't diminish his fear that he might, which was higher than usual. For some bizarre reason, it mattered to him that he didn't embarrass himself in front of Ade.

I'm working on the play with you today, Ade had said. *One of the other actors?* Kris's script only indicated his part, not who was cast in the other roles. *Production team?* He couldn't very well ask the question when the guy was eating—or trying to eat was a more accurate description, and the little progress he had made with his breakfast came to a complete stop when he realised Kris was looking at him again. Rumbled, Kris blushed.

"Sorry. I was wondering…" His explanation petered out when Ade flinched and pressed his hand to his cheek. "Toothache?" Kris guessed.

Ade tilted his head from side to side—a 'kind of' response—and pushed his plate away. He gestured to the script. "What do you think?"

"It's fab. I've been in one of O'Connor's plays before—the one about the air crew and the passenger who gives birth during the flight. I can't remember what it's called. I think I've used up all my memory on my lines." Kris smiled nervously.

"You've learnt your lines?"

"Yeah. I always do, and then I forget them all again, until I have to perform them for real. Like now? If you were to ask me to recite any of the script, I'd fluff it within about three words. Once I get into the studio? No problem."

"We have digital editions in the studio, so no page-turning…"

"I know, I know. I just prefer to learn them beforehand. It gives me a better chance of getting properly into role. So would I be right in thinking you're part of the production team?"

"Yes," Ade confirmed. "As in it's my team."

"You're the producer?"

Ade nodded.

"Cool." That did nothing to settle Kris's nerves. He sidetracked. "I wish I could remember the name of that play."

"The one about the plane?"

"Yeah. Do you know the one I mean?"

"I do. And you'll to kick yourself when I tell you."

Kris made one last concerted effort to remember and shook his head.

"*Air Born.*"

"Of course!" He laughed at his temporary stupidness. "I wouldn't mind, but it was only a couple of years ago."

"I don't think I caught that, but I have heard you as Doctor Derbyshire. You're a talented actor."

"Thanks, although it's an easy role..." Kris sighed and reconsidered his comment. "I probably shouldn't say this to someone from a rival station, but it's not a good work environment there, which is why I auditioned for *On Sunday*. I'm considering going for some TV auditions too."

Ade nodded in approval. "You'd go far, especially with the obsession with Scandinavian shows at the moment. That's a guess on my part..."

"You guessed right," Kris said. "I'm Swedish, but I grew up in England."

"Hence no accent."

"No, but I can fake it if I have to."

"Like a Swedish *'Allo, 'Allo!*" Ade mused.

Kris laughed. "Can you imagine?"

"A BAFTA winner, for sure."

"Oh, totally."

"Plus, if you don't mind me saying, you are a handsome man."

Kris smiled, bashful but flattered. "Why would I mind you saying that?"

"Some people don't like it—a man telling another man he thinks he's good-looking?"

"Hey, I'll take compliments however they're packaged."

Both of them laughed at that, until Ade drew in breath sharply and squeezed his eyes shut. Whatever was going on with him, he was clearly in a lot of pain.

"Have you taken anything for that...toothache or whatever it is?" Kris asked.

"No. I meant to buy painkillers on the way in but forgot."

"I've got some." Kris picked up his bag from the seat next to him and rooted out the packet. "They're co-codamol. Is that OK?"

Ade took the offered pills, poking them between his lips with his fingertip and following up with the smallest slurp of coffee.

"You probably know already," Kris said carefully, "but you have bruises."

"Have I? Where?"

Kris indicated on his own face, positioning his fingertips and thumb either side of his chin.

A flash of pure horror passed over Ade's features, so quick Kris would've missed it if he hadn't been staring straight at him, but then Ade rolled his eyes. "That's the last time I down so much wine on a work night."

Never mind BAFTAs or ARIAs. Ade should've been starring in the play, not producing it, because that performance was award-winning. Kris might've been mistaken, but Ade didn't seem the type to get into drunken brawls, and those bruises, four on one side of his jaw, one on the other, were from someone who'd got up close and very personal.

"Anyway, I disturbed your rehearsal," Ade said, standing. "I'll leave—"

"No, don't," Kris interrupted. It was a fight not to reach out and offer comfort, lay a hand on Ade's, something he'd never do without permission even with people he knew well, but...

He couldn't explain it, and now he'd made the situation more awkward by pressuring Ade to stay.

"I mean, don't go on my account."

"If you're sure…"

"Really."

Ade sat back down and took out his phone. "I'll take a look at my checklist for today. Give you some peace." He winked.

Kris smiled, though his heart was still racing from the total hash he'd made of what should've been a casual coffee with the producer. The trouble was it felt more than casual, and he was staring again. He put a stop to that right away and dug into the script, but the words were a nonsense blur, so he reverted to looking out the window, pretending he wasn't aware of every little move Ade made. Typing on his screen. Scrolling. A sip of coffee. Another sharp inhale when he touched the biggest of the bruises on his jaw.

Inevitably, Kris's gaze drifted back to Ade, who immediately put his phone face down on the table and attempted a smile.

"I need to tell you about the thing," he said.

"The thing?" Kris shook his head. "It's none of my business."

"No!" Ade's eyebrows shot up in alarm, a coppery auburn, same as his hair. He grunted and bashed his forehead with his fist, flattening some of the short, gelled spikes. "I didn't mean…" He held up his hands, gesturing to himself. "It's a me thing. Nothing sinister."

"OK?"

"I always tell new people…well, not *always*. But…" Ade rolled his eyes again. This time, he wasn't hamming it up.

Kris sat back and folded his arms, still a little worried what Ade was about to reveal, although it was refreshing to meet someone who shared his gift for cocking up conversations.

"I mean, I don't bother if I'm just buying a coffee in a new café or, I don't know, exchanging hellos with someone I'll never meet again or…" Ade stopped rambling. "I have a speech impediment."

"You do?"

"Yes."

"Sorry. I wasn't doubting you. I just didn't notice."

"No. You wouldn't, because I'm careful with how I speak. It only affects one letter. Well, the sound of it."

"Would it be weird if I try to work it out?"

Ade shrugged. He seemed amused that Kris would want to.

"It is weird, isn't it? Never mind."

"It's kind of funny, but a nice change. Most people get all edgy and shifty-eyed when I mention it. Anyway, you go ahead."

Kris accepted the invitation at face value and replayed what Ade had said so far. "OK. Your 'S's are fine. 'Th'? No—you pronounced 'thing' correctly." He was unpicking their conversation like it was a script, looking for something that wasn't there while trying not to cringe at his own contributions, including this one. "Is it…'R'?"

"Yep."

"Woohoo," Kris cheered quietly. Ade laughed and made a decent show of hiding that it was killing him. "That's a pretty common letter. It must be hard to avoid."

"Like I say, it's the sound of it but only in certain words. There's a name for the condition, which I can't say because guess what? It contains that sound! I can usually…circumvent with cunning use of synonyms."

"That's brilliant!"

"Thanks?" Ade's eyebrows rose again, but this time in definite amusement. "However, faced with communicating with an actor whose name contains that letter…"

"Ah. Sorry." Kris felt terrible, as if he was to blame for choosing his given name. "If it's easier, you can call me K or KJ or even Mr. Johansson."

Ade smiled. "Thanks, but I have to get it over with sooner or later. It's just a little less of a nightmare doing it this way. And now I can see you analysing what I say."

Kris blushed. "Sorry. And I seriously need to stop apologising."

"I don't mind you analysing *or* apologising, but so you've heard me say it, let's start again." Ade held out his hand for it to be shaken. Kris accepted. Looking him right in the eyes, Ade said, "Hi, Kris, I'm Adrian Simmons, but I prefer Ade. I'm the producer."

Kris held the eye contact, enthralled. He couldn't stop the smile as he said, "Hello, Ade. I'm very pleased to make your acquaintance."

"The feeling is mutual, but I'm afraid I really do need to go and start setting up." Ade rose to his feet. "You're welcome to come with me."

"I will," Kris said. "And on the way, you can tell me how you came to be working in radio production."

5: Out of Excuses

Ade

THE MORNING WORE on, and the pain in Ade's jaw wore off, as he'd known it would once he had the distraction of work, and the studio downlights meant his bruises were in shadow. Not that it made the situation any less dire, but it would've been worse still if he'd had to spend all day with people asking him what he'd done. There was a small but loud part of him that might actually tell them.

At lunchtime, he followed the smokers outside and lit a cigarette, realising the second he inhaled that he didn't want it, but the lure of company, being able to stand by and listen to their mindless chatter, was a welcome escape from the feeling of cold dread, the icy tide that rose as they edged closer to finishing the recording.

Mid-afternoon, they were on a third take of the pivotal scene in which Rose admitted to Tommy that she had loved him once but wasn't sure of anything anymore. In the movie, the scene ended with her crying out his name and throwing herself on him in a passionate kiss, but there was something about it in its contemporary, audio-only form that jarred, and it took Ade reading in as Rose for him to figure out what it was. The words weren't his, yet as he spoke them, Rose's despair became one with his. The man she'd loved was brutal and selfish, and she stood to lose everything by harbouring him. The idea that, in modern times, she would make that choice was unthinkable to most, but not to Ade, and by the time he was done, his actors looked somewhat unnerved.

31

Nonetheless, it had the desired effect, as on a fourth take, the actor playing Rose nailed it, after which the cast headed up to the cafeteria for a well-earned coffee break.

Ade took the opportunity to listen back through his headphones, really pleased with what they'd got so far. He exported a thirty-second clip and sent it to Sally O'Connor, not realising he still had company until he heard Kris clear his throat. Smiling, Ade removed the headphones and swivelled around to face him.

"Hey."

Kris smiled back. "Hey, I just wanted to compliment you on your acting. You're amazing."

"Thank you," Ade accepted bashfully, his cheeks warming. "So are you. I love what you and Ella did with the scars scene."

"Really?"

"Really. I just sent the writer a raw clip, it's so good." That and he hoped it would put her off turning up at the studio. "TV would be lucky to have you."

Kris bowed his head. "You're too kind. I wouldn't even know where to begin with your job, whereas you can do mine without breaking a sweat. Have you ever considered an acting career?"

"Ha. Yes. As a matter of fact, I used to do a lot of stage stuff, but the speech thing got in the way. Writers get very precious when a jumped-up thespian asks them to amend their well-considered words."

"I hope that wasn't a jibe at me," a husky female voice said from behind Kris. Ade's heart sank. So much for pre-empting her visit.

Ever the eye-catcher, even now in her early sixties, Sally wore a vibrant tie-dyed kaftan over deep-purple crushed-velvet culottes. She drifted past Kris, her gaze fixed on Ade, her cheery smile holding for now, as she wasn't yet close enough to see any fine detail. Ade tried his best not to shrink into his seat. He loved Sally to pieces, but he really didn't want to face her today.

Kris must have picked up that they knew each other, as he started to back out of the room, making his excuses, but Ade needed him to stay and so quickly introduced them.

"Kris, this is Sally O'Connor, Sal, this is Kris Johansson. He's playing Tommy."

"Riiiight," Sal said, eyeing Kris up and down as if his physical appearance offered a valid indication of his ability to take on the role. She took a lunge-step towards him, and her hand shot out from within the folds of fabric. Kris recovered quickly from his astonishment and accepted her greeting.

"Good to meet you, Miss O'Connor. I love your work."

"Riiiight," she said again. "OK. Good."

Ade would've intervened, but his nose was itching from the pungent, perfumy cloud that always accompanied the playwright and would no doubt linger for the rest of the afternoon. He couldn't risk a sneeze, but the way Sally was drawing out every syllable, it was clear she thought Kris was sucking up and was preparing to test him.

"Which work exactly? Just *On Sunday*, or…?"

"Well, it's a beautiful reworking, and I love the modern voice you've given Rose, although I hope you won't be offended if I tell you I prefer…" Kris's eyes widened in panic, and he looked to Ade. He'd forgotten it again. Ade mouthed the words at him.

"*Air Born*," Kris repeated aloud, with a subtle grateful smile to his co-conspirator. Ade gave him a wink to say *you're welcome*.

"Oh, do you?" Sal gushed airily, suddenly convivial. "It's my all-time favourite, though I dare say it's not the done thing for one to adore one's own work. And may I ask which part you played?"

As Sal commenced interrogating Kris, Ade used his eyes only to try and signal to Kris not to leave him on his own with her. Luckily, Kris was good at reading facial expressions. That or it was the connection between them that had been growing stronger all day. Either way, it meant Sal didn't get the chance to lecture Ade, despite making it obvious she'd noticed the bruises. He was only delaying the inevitable, but today he wasn't up to being told he was a fool. He knew he was a fool, and it changed nothing.

Sal stayed just long enough for the rest of the actors and crew to return from their break, share a few pleasantries and listen to the next scene before bidding farewell and floating away, leaving a flowery wake strong enough Ade wouldn't have been surprised to discover rose petals littering the corridor all the way to the lift.

"OK," he said, once she was gone. "Final scene." With a sigh of relief that at least one trial was over, he put on the red light and hit record.

*

"We're going for a drink. Would you like to come?"

Again, Kris had hung back; the rest of the cast were already on their way to the lift, and Ade was alone at the control desk. The question paralysed him, took the power of words from him, because he so desperately wanted to go for a drink, be normal, socialise with his colleagues, but was it worth the risk?

"I don't think we'll be staying out late," Kris added. "And I'd love to hear more about your acting experiences. There's such depth to your characterisation. Want to give me some tips?"

Ade smiled at the compliment. It warmed him right through—not that he didn't get complimented. He was good at his job—efficient, well-organised, and he made sure his cast and crew knew how much he appreciated their efforts. They, in turn, were grateful and very kind. Kinder than he deserved, he suspected, because he was just doing what he was paid to do. But for all of that, Kris's words had struck a long-silent chord in his soul.

"And I'd really like some interesting company." Kris smiled hopefully.

A battle raged in Ade's head, the answer hanging in the limbo of his existence—*yes…no…yes…no…yes…*

"I don't know that I can." He picked up his tablet and glanced over his checklist. *Everything's done. I'm out of excuses.*

"I'm sorry," Kris said.

At the same time, Ade said, "Yes, OK." He turned to face Kris and nodded. "I'll come for a drink."

"I didn't mean to be pushy."

"You weren't. I was being indecisive." Ade put on his jacket as he followed Kris out of the door and caught Kris's ear with his cuff. "Oh God. Sorry!" Ade gasped and backed off. Kris rubbed his ear and laughed.

"It's OK. I have two."

In what was clearly a valiant attempt to put Ade more at ease, Kris struck up a conversation about Sally O'Connor's other plays, which carried them along the corridor, down in the lift and out onto the street. It was a neutral topic familiar to them both, and it was working because by the time they reached the pub opposite the radio station building, Ade was back in his fully-in-control producer persona and joked and chatted with the actors, no trouble at all. Every so often, he glanced Kris's way, and they shared a smile, but they didn't get the chance to talk until later in the evening, after the crew had gone home and the actors decided to go out for a meal. Kris waited to see what Ade wanted to do before he too declined their invitation.

"I hope this isn't because you feel sorry for me," Ade said as they laid claim to a couple of bar stools vacated by the others.

"Not at all. Aside from the fact that I'm still eager to know more about you, I'm severely allergic to shellfish, so I tend to avoid going to restaurants I'm not familiar with."

"Ah. So you carry an EpiPen?" Ade asked. Kris nodded in confirmation and took it out of his pocket, handing it to Ade. He'd never seen one before and handed it straight back, terrified he'd drop it and leave Kris without his life-saving medicine. "How does it work?"

"It's really easy. You pull the tape off the top, press the other end to your thigh and hold it there for ten seconds."

"That's clever." Ade wasn't watching Kris's demonstration, still with the tape in situ, he hoped. He was actively staring at Kris's profile. The Nordic slope of his nose, the defined angles to his temples, cheekbones and chin...the puzzled amusement in the inquisitive blue eyes that met Ade's. He blushed. "It's quite a common allergy, isn't it?"

"So I'm told. That and peanuts, but I don't have a problem with those. I do have a problem with cats, though."

"Because they eat fish?" Ade asked innocently, but the corner of his mouth twitched, giving him away.

Kris shook his head and chuckled. "I actually have no idea if they eat fish or not."

"They do. We used to have a cat. Well, I say we...when I was a kid. My mum called her Tiddles, but I don't think that was her real name. She belonged to one of our neighbours, an old lady who died, and Tiddles was always at ours, so Mum took her in." Ade smiled to himself. He hadn't thought about that cat in years. Hadn't visited his mum in a while either. He should probably rectify that...once the bruises were gone.

Realising he'd hijacked the conversation, which was absolutely not his intention, and that Kris was waiting for him to say more, Ade said, "Anyway, we were talking about you."

"We were," Kris agreed, "but I'd much rather hear about your early career on stage."

"Really?" Ade pulled a face, making out it was a tedious chore, though a quiet fluttering had started up in his stomach, and it wasn't the fear-born kind. "It's not very exciting, I'm afraid."

"I'd still love for you to tell me."

"Well, OK, then..." Ade took a long suck of the straw in his G&T in preparation, but it was such a novelty having someone pay an interest in what he had to say, he didn't know where to begin, so he went right back to the start, his uni days as an English Lit. undergraduate, his friends talking him into joining the drama society, discovering how much he enjoyed acting, getting the first role he auditioned for after graduating, and then another and another and another...until his run-in with the director who'd refused to cast him because of his rhotacism. What he'd told Kris earlier was true—he *had* suggested that some of character's lines could be rewritten if his 'R's were that much of a problem—and he had Equity behind him, but there'd been other things going on by then, and his self-confidence was, he'd thought, at an all-time low.

He'd since learnt it could sink a lot lower, but at the age of twenty-four, he'd known nothing. He'd given up acting, taken on an unpaid internship with a national radio station and built up huge debts paying his living expenses. If his dad hadn't died, he'd have ended up on the streets. Instead, he'd been able to pay off his credit cards and go back to college to retrain.

"So that's it, really," Ade concluded. Kris wasn't to know he'd skipped most of the past eleven years. "Told you it wasn't exciting."

"Not action-packed exciting, no," Kris said, "but you've achieved so much!"

"And failed a lot too."

"Tripped over and picked yourself up. I mean, you're a producer for the second-most popular talk radio station in the country. And that's your second career!"

"OK, if you put it like that…" Ade conceded with a smile. And yes, he'd maybe become a little bit animated talking about the roles he'd undertaken when he was a young actor with the world at his feet. Between the alcohol and attention, he felt like he was glowing. "But that really is enough about me. Another drink while you regale me with your life story?"

Kris laughed. "Better make it a coffee or you'll fall off your stool with boredom."

"I doubt it." Ade waved to get a bartender's attention and ordered their drinks, then turned back to Kris. "So you…oh. Problem?" Kris was on his feet, putting on his jacket.

"I didn't realise the time. I'm going to miss my train."

It prompted Ade to check what time it was. "No way!" He couldn't believe they'd been chatting for so long. Well, he'd done all the chatting.

Kris tucked his folder under his arm and smiled apologetically. "Sorry to abandon you, especially as I hassled you into coming in the first place."

"Don't worry about it. I need to head home soon too. And anyway, you didn't hassle me."

Kris didn't look so sure about that.

"I've enjoyed it," Ade said sincerely.

"Yeah. It's been so good getting to know you." Kris held out his hand, Ade reached out to shake it, and the moment they made contact, everything changed.

It was different from their handshake earlier in the day, as if the physical connection somehow cemented what had been building between them, and now they couldn't release each other.

It was, eventually, Kris who broke free first, mumbled something about Ade having a pleasant rest of evening and left. Dumbfounded, Ade watched him walk out the door and pause to fasten his jacket. Kris glanced back, locking gazes with Ade. Then he smiled, waved and was gone.

The sound of glasses being set down on the bar snapped Ade back to reality.

"You did order this beer, right?" the bartender asked.

"Yeah. He had to go for his train." Ade checked the time again, admonishing himself for not keeping track. Quarter past ten was too late to convincingly claim he'd only just finished work, too early to have any chance of sneaking in undetected. *And why should I have to? You know what? Screw it.* He paid for both drinks and knocked back Kris's beer while the bartender was getting his change.

Kristian Johansson, what did you do to me? He examined his hand and clasped it with his other, re-imagining the sensation of the soft palm that had warmed his, the lightest squeeze of his fingers. Everything about it had been gentle, unthreatening, but there was another power at work, and it had awakened Ade's long-dormant response to consensual physical contact. That one simple handshake had thrown his world completely off its axis.

6: Crush

Ade

> TOMMY: *You startled me.*
>
> ROSE: *Shh. He's asleep downstairs. How are you feeling?*
>
> TOMMY: *Fine.*
>
> ROSE: *You don't look fine.*
>
> TOMMY: *Well, I am. Perfectly fine.*
>
> ROSE: *When I think of how you used to look, with your wild hair, and your bright clothes... When did you stop wearing the designer blazers? They were so you.*
>
> TOMMY: *When I turned twenty-five. They made me look like a kids' TV presenter.*
>
> ROSE: *When you met him. And what have you got to show for it apart from broken bones and bruises?*
>
> TOMMY: *I was unlucky.*
>
> ROSE: *Maybe... Don't do that. Don't touch me, Tommy. We mustn't. I thought you loved me.*
>
> TOMMY: *Why do you think I'm doing this?*

ADE WOKE IN a sweat, shaken up by the dream. He threw off the duvet and turned on his side, so tired, yet every time he neared sleep, his brain fired up again, searching for meaning. And then he was too cold. He gave up and stumbled away to the shower even though it was, once again, only five in the morning. More galling still, he was missing out on having the bed all to himself.

Under the soothing jets, he closed his eyes and replayed the day before, getting straight in his mind what was real and what wasn't. The play. That had happened. Kris. Drinks after work. Also real. And Kris had noticed the bruises—pointed them out, in fact—but hadn't mentioned them again or so much as looked at them, not in any way that was obvious. Sadly, as the suddenly soaring pain reminded Ade when he washed his face, the bruises were all too real.

The attraction was real too, at least on Ade's part, and it did seem at the pub that Kris was interested, not to mention whatever it was that happened when they touched. But...could he trust his instincts? If his life wasn't so difficult right now, he'd have considered Kris viable dating material from the moment he set eyes on him, but there was no escaping the truth that he was in this situation because his instincts had failed him before.

I thought you loved me.

Why do you think I'm doing this?

Those weren't even the right lines, and in any case, it was just a dream. But he couldn't deny he liked Kris. So he had a bit of a crush on an attractive guy who'd paid him the right kind of attention. It didn't have to mean anything more than that. Kris was an actor; of course Ade would find him attractive. Actors were his type. Over-emotional, self-absorbed, indulgent, dangerous...

Except he hadn't got those vibes from Kris. Or maybe that was wishful thinking.

Oh, come on, Ade. Wishing for what? Shouldn't you know better by now? He switched off the water and got out of the shower before the daydream carried him any further away from reality. He didn't want a relationship with anyone. Not yet. Maybe not ever. They only ended in disaster.

Keeping his eyes averted from the mirror, he brushed his teeth, carefully. It hurt less than it had yesterday, which was something. Shaving was a non-starter, but when he did catch his reflection, he realised it was better that way; even with just a day's stubble, the bruises were less noticeable, and less noticeable meant less likelihood of inquisition.

Half an hour later, running five minutes behind, Ade was at the door, ready to leave, when the sound of the key in the lock made him freeze in terror. He couldn't do this. Not now. He had to go to work. The door opened.

Fergus smiled disarmingly. "Hi. I didn't think I'd catch you."

"You mean you were hoping you'd missed me."

"Not at all."

It was no coincidence that Fergus had arrived right after Ade would usually have left for work.

"You need to leave your key," Ade said coolly, although his heart was pounding so hard he was starting to think he might have a heart attack from the stress.

"My stuff's still here."

Then take your stuff, give me my key, and get out of my FUCKING LIFE! That was what he wanted to say, what he *needed* to say, but it was stuck inside, languishing in the stack of unsaids from every other time. He shuffled soundlessly past Fergus, staring straight ahead of him at the door, his escape route, grasped the handle, breath held in hope, and started to press down.

"Ade."

He closed his eyes in shame, but this was so normal he barely saw it as such. The familiar pattern slipped over him like prison bars, invisible yet cold and strong as steel. He refused to turn around and somehow kept his tone measured to say, "I'm late for work."

"I'll give you a lift. Just talk to me."

"I'd rather walk." Yet he wasn't walking anywhere. The power over him, the fear that stilled him—it didn't matter about work or success or earning his own way because it always came back to this.

"Please?" Fergus tried, turning the word into a pathetic whine.

Playing the 'poor little me' card. Don't fall for it. "Later," was all Ade could utter. *Just. Leave.*

"There won't be a later."

"Ferg…" Ade turned part way to face his ex-boyfriend. "I don't want—"

"Didn't I do what you asked of me?"

Ade didn't answer.

"I stayed away, gave you space. I can't help it if I still want to be with you."

Still Ade said nothing. Whether it was fear or sense or simply weary resignation that stopped him, he didn't know, but nor did Fergus know what to do with it, and it was working to Ade's advantage.

"You want to be with me too," Fergus stated.

Ade made a sound of disbelief under his breath. Fergus heard it.

"If you don't, then what was Sunday night all about?"

Ade shook his head, feeling the anger and defencelessness swell, trying to suppress both with the few reserves he had left. This was how it started, how it always started.

"I'm going to work," he said. He wrenched the door open and fled his apartment, down the stairs, through the entrance hall without stopping, bursting out onto the pavement breathless and panicked, but he couldn't stop. He needed to get to the radio station, get past security to where Fergus couldn't reach him, or not physically, but it wouldn't end there. The mind games would take over, going where the punches, kicks and jaw-crushing restraints could not.

He didn't stop until he reached the lift and flung himself inside, trying to breathe and not cry as the doors closed, carrying him upwards to his sanctuary. He couldn't live like this. Not anymore. But what choice did he have? How many times had Fergus walked out on them, with lies of how Ade was spending too much time with his friends or flirting with *him* or *him*, as if Ade would dare to risk another punch, another bottle smashed over his head. Months would pass, and Ade was so damned angry with himself for missing Fergus, wanting everything to be right between them, how it used to be. *How it used to be?* No. It had always been hellish. What he remembered was his imaginary relationship, the 'if only' for all that was missing from every 'if I can just get through this'. What he missed had never been.

The lift doors opened, and Ade drifted along the corridor towards studio three. It wasn't being used today, and the prospect of just sitting in the dark, silent room propelled him, though his legs were dead weights and his vision was blurred and tunnelling. Peace: he needed peace. He reached the studio door and turned the handle.

"Ade!"

He jumped so violently he took the skin off his knuckles on the doorpost. *No, no, no!* He was going to vomit. He swallowed it back and turned to face his pursuer.

"Kris? What are you doing here?"

Kris slowed as he reached Ade's location, keeping his distance. "Hey. Are you OK?"

"Fine," Ade said, attempting bright and breezy through clenched teeth.

"You don't look fine."

Ade laughed somewhat hysterically and wasn't sure he could stop.

Kris's eyes crinkled with concern. "What did I say?"

"You, er…" Ade scratched his head in confusion. "Why are you here again?"

"Ah, well." Kris cleared his throat and blushed. "My plan was to lie and tell you I'd lost my wallet and called in to see if I'd left it here."

"But?"

"I don't even own a wallet."

"Right. So?"

"I wondered if you'd like to go for a drink with me again."

"Now?"

"I meant after work, but we could go for a coffee now...if you'd like to, that is."

Before Ade had time to think about it, the words left his mouth. "Yes, I would."

They both laughed lightly—Ade was almost certain Kris was in on whatever was happening between them—and stepped off, side by side, making their way back to the lift.

"Is there anywhere in particular you'd recommend?" Kris asked.

"Would you mind if we just went to the cafeteria?"

"Not at all." Kris bashed his palm on his forehead. "You're working. Do you want to leave it till later?"

The lift doors opened, and they stepped inside. Ade pushed the button and glanced at Kris. "No. I'd really like to have coffee with you. I have nothing scheduled for this morning."

"But you still have to come in to work?"

"Not necessarily. I'd rather work here than at home, though."

"Is that a boundaries thing?"

"Er...no. I have an unwelcome visitor, but hopefully he'll get the message and have left before I get back this evening."

Ade made it sound casual, like he'd picked up a guy after Kris left him in the pub the night before, and he must've been convincing because Kris's stance changed, becoming more rigid, less open, and his expression... If Ade wasn't very much mistaken, he was trying to hide his disappointment. His gaze dropped, straying dangerously close to the bruises, and Ade quickly intervened to save them both.

"I enjoyed your company last night."

"Likewise. I wish I could've stayed longer."

"I drank your beer. After you left."

"Did you? Sorry."

"And another two G and Ts. I don't usually drink that much— don't usually drink at all during the week. I got home at midnight and totally crashed out!"

Kris's smile was back. "I don't drink much either."

Phew! Not all in my head.

In the cafeteria, they queued together, neither speaking. It felt natural, comfortable, as if there was no need to fill the silence with small talk, yet Ade needed to know he wasn't making another horrible mistake. Could he ask? *Are you single? Interested? The sort of person to kick the living daylights out of your partner and then beg for a chance to do it again?*

They bought lattes and took them over to the same table as the previous morning. For a while, they sat, quietly sipping and watching the activity around them, but anticipation hung in the air. Several times, Ade caught Kris doing the same thing he kept doing—taking a breath to speak and then releasing it. Maybe he was reading too much into it, but the longer it went on, the harder it became. There was so much he could have said that it seemed safer to say nothing.

Ade had just tipped the last of his latte into his mouth when Kris, bravely and devastatingly, broke the silence.

"If you ever want to talk about the bruises, I'm here to listen."

The latte almost came back out. Ade swallowed and glared, but he couldn't hold the eye contact. It was too probing.

"Or not," Kris added. "You just seem so…"

When Kris didn't finish the statement, Ade chanced looking up at him again. "So what?" he asked.

Kris shrugged. "On edge, I guess. Like when I called your name earlier… I'm sorry I startled you."

"It's OK. I was miles away." Ade studied the frothy remnants of his drink. "You know that section of dialogue, after Rose wakes Tommy? I had a dream last night about that scene."

"Understandable. We ran it four times yesterday."

"True. But in the dream, it was you and me. And you were Rose."

Kris made a sad face. "Was my Tommy that awful?"

Ade laughed. "You know it wasn't, but you also make a wonderful Rose."

Kris bowed his head in exaggerated thanks.

Ade rolled his eyes. "The lines were switched at the end, though. In my dream, I mean." He felt his cheeks heat up. Why was he telling Kris this? It was one thing flirting and passing compliments, another entirely sharing his dream or any of his other thoughts, because this was already way deeper than physical attraction. For all Ade knew, Kris offered a listening ear to everyone and got hit on all the time. With the loud shirts and snug-fit pants, he didn't exactly dress to blend into the background. That was a big part of the attraction, Ade realised. That Kris was permitted to dress however he liked.

Permitted. How ridiculous that anyone should need permission to wear the clothes they wanted to.

"I used to wear bright colours." Ade quickly covered his mouth with his hand, wincing at the pressure on his bruises. He hadn't meant to say it, but there was no taking it back now.

7: Bottle

Kris

KRIS DIDN'T COMMENT, or not in words. By the time they'd finished recording yesterday, he'd been completely captivated by the contradiction that was Ade Simmons, assertive producer, cool, calm and in control, versus the nervous, almost meek man he became away from his domain.

Watching Ade now, it was like those two sides were at war with each other. The set of Ade's jaw, tensed shoulders and clenched fists said he was ready to flee, yet that defiant glare was back, challenging Kris to ask why, but he already knew. He'd picked up on it almost at the start, even before he'd seen the bruises, but he hadn't been sure until Ade's reaction in the corridor.

So no, he wasn't going to ask why because it was dishonest and voyeuristic and would block Ade's only escape route—

"Of course," Ade said, matter-of-fact, "I have to attend a lot of meetings with management."

—and he'd taken it.

"There are...expectations." He gestured to his attire, today a plain navy shirt open at the neck, black brushed-denim jeans and black suede loafers. Casual and stylish, but very plain and middle-aged, completely at odds with the boyishly handsome face with a sprinkling of freckles across the nose and hairstyle straight out of *GQ*.

Kris zoomed out, taking in the whole person again, and discovered he wasn't the only one having a good look while they could.

"If you don't mind me asking, how old are you?"

"Thirty-six. You?"

"Thirty-nine in January." That sounded so much older than thirty-six.

"Ooh! My birthday's in January too," Ade said. "The twentieth."

"Mine's the thirteenth."

"Oh…" Ade seemed disappointed, but then shrugged and added, "Well, that's exactly a week apart."

"We were obviously destined to meet," Kris teased.

"Without a doubt!" Ade smiled, zapping Kris with the same spark as last night.

"I don't feel nearly forty."

"No, me neither, but what does that mean? Feeling nearly forty?"

"Older and wiser?" Kris speculated.

"Ha, I wish I was wiser." Ade shook his head, briefly retreating into himself before shrugging it off. "You're right, though. I dress like my dad."

"Hey, I didn't…mean… It was just you said…" Kris pursed his lips, hearing his mum's voice in his head. *Stop, take your foot out of your mouth, and try again.* "Your dad had excellent taste."

Ade bowed demurely. "A sideways compliment, but I'll take it."

Kris laughed. "And I suppose at my age, I should be dressing a little more conservatively."

"Why?" Ade nodded at Kris's shirt. "That's *so* you."

Kris pulled his shirt out a bit so he could see it. Shaunna had picked it out for him, claiming the swirls in multiple shades of blue, turquoise and green perfectly complemented his complexion and drew out the blue of his eyes. He'd taken her word for it, to save himself another half an hour of indecision that might've meant missing Ade. Still, he was curious.

"How is it so me?" he asked.

"Based on yesterday, and your CV. And…" Ade blushed so deeply his freckles all but disappeared. "Your online agency profile, reviews, interviews…"

Kris narrowed his eyes. "Are you stalking me, Mr. Simmons?"

Ade nodded. "I'm afraid so."

They both laughed but quickly fell quiet again. Their cups were empty, their coffee date over. This could be the last time they saw each other, because even though Ade had just admitted he had all Kris's contact details, they hadn't officially exchanged them, and Kris didn't want to impose.

"I'll let you get back to work," he said as Ade said, "I'll walk you out."

Kris had walked himself in, but he wasn't going to argue against a few minutes more in Ade's company.

As they travelled down in the lift, he watched Ade's fuzzy reflection in the steel walls, observing that they were both doing the same thing again. They shared a smile but didn't speak until they reached the ground floor, where Ade stood by while Kris handed back his visitor's pass, then followed him outside.

"Might as well have a smoke while I'm here," he said, pulling a cigarette packet from his jeans pocket. He thumbed towards the side street that ran next to the radio station building and moved off. Kris moved with him. "You don't have to stay—oh! I haven't given you my number!" Switching the packet to his other hand, Ade took out his phone and unlocked it. The packet slipped upwards out of his grasp and tumbled down onto the pavement. "Damn it."

"I've got it," Kris said. He picked up the packet and kept hold of it while Ade dealt with his phone.

"What's your number?"

"Not a clue!" Kris took out his phone and unlocked it…and dropped the cigarette packet.

"Oh God!" Ade started laughing. "Are you OK with me taking your number off your CV?"

"Yeah, totally."

"I'll text you later if that's all right?"

"Perfect." Kris handed back the cigarette packet. Ade immediately took one out and lit it. "Mind if I hang around while you have that? I've got to re-record a set of ads I did last year, but I'm not due there until ten."

"Sure!" Ade replied tightly before coughing out a spluttery blue cloud. "I don't really smoke," he said.

Kris raised an eyebrow.

"Honestly, I don't. I gave up ages ago, but I bought these yesterday, so I figured I might as well finish the packet. Oh, who am I kidding?"

"Hey, no judgement here." Kris had never smoked, but Shaunna had when she was younger. Jack was a smoker too, and while Kris couldn't say he enjoyed kisses that tasted of cigarettes, it wasn't a turn-off. "So…about this drink. Would you like to meet me later? About seven o'clock?"

"Seven o'clock…" Ade tapped ash from his cigarette, took another drag, tapped the ash again.

"Or whatever time suits you," Kris added.

"Seven should be fine, I think."

"You can say no," Kris assured him, praying he wouldn't.

"It's not that I don't want to…"

"Rain check?"

Ade considered for a moment. "No. It should be OK, but can I call you later if it's not?"

Kris couldn't help grinning at that.

"What's funny?" Ade asked.

"I've never been stood up in advance before."

"Ah." Ade's chuckle was bittersweet. "That's what I'm trying to avoid, as I won't know if I can make it until I get home from work."

"OK," Kris accepted. "Is there anywhere in particular you like? Anywhere you don't?"

"Maybe somewhere near you, in case I don't make it?"

"It's a forty-minute train journey."

"I have a car."

Ade stubbed out his cigarette and fished a packet of mints from his pocket, offering them to Kris. He took one for the sake of politeness, and thank goodness he had, because the next minute he and Ade were hugging and kissing cheeks.

"See you later," Ade murmured close to Kris's ear.

"I hope so," Kris replied.

"Text me the details." Ade released him and went back inside. Kris stared after him a moment longer and set off for the rival station a few streets away.

*

"Did you see him?"

Kris hadn't even made it as far as closing the front door.

"Yep. This morning."

He walked through to the kitchen, pausing to accept the gift of a tea towel from Casper on the way. Very pleased with himself, the nutty golden Lab went bounding ahead and did a couple of circuits of the table, almost knocking Shaunna's legs from under her. Boiling water overshot the mugs she was filling.

"Casper, pack it in!" she shouted. It made no difference whatsoever. The dog always acted like they'd been gone for weeks.

"Have you just got in?" Kris asked, letting the dog out into the garden.

"About ten minutes ago." She padded past him, barefoot, and collected the milk from the fridge.

Kris sat at the table and picked up the post, thumbing through the envelopes, flipping each to the back of the pile. Nothing exciting. A mug appeared in front of him. "Thanks."

"Welcome."

Casper charged back in, and out again.

"I'll take him for a W-A-L-K in a minute," Kris said.

"He can wait." Shaunna thunked down on the chair opposite, tea in one hand, a packet of biscuits in the other, preparing to get the low-down on All Things Ade.

"Well?" she said.

"Well what?" Kris asked, trying to keep his expression serious. His mouth was having none of it. He stuffed a biscuit in it.

"Aha!" Shaunna grinned. "So he *is* single?"

Kris chewed quickly and swallowed down some tea, burning his tongue in the process. "I didn't get the chance to ask, but I'm guessing so. He's agreed to meet up for a drink tonight."

"That's promising."

"Yeah, it is…"

"You don't sound too sure."

"I'm not. There's something not right."

"Is this about the bruises?"

"I think so. Maybe he's got kids with emotional problems or a relative with dementia or something, because he said he wouldn't know if he could make it until after work."

"Or he's in an abusive relationship?" Shaunna speculated, and she wasn't being spiteful, though she'd have every right to be, seeing as a married man was part of why they were separated—only a very small part. They'd already been sleeping in different rooms when it happened, and Kris had been struggling with depression. Jack had made a move on him, and Kris had kind of fallen into it. The result: a short and meaningless fling that he was so ashamed of he'd kept it from Shaunna and even temporarily moved out to avoid facing her.

Jack was Kris's only indiscretion, but he still felt like a cheat. He and Shaunna had been together for twenty years, and she was his best friend. She knew everything about him. They lived together, ate together, did their laundry jointly, shopped for groceries, went to the cinema, to dinner—everything they'd always done as husband and wife, and that was the problem. However excited she was to hear about Ade, it felt wrong to talk to her about seeing someone else.

"I know you're worried," she said. "But it's not the same as with Jack."

"It isn't?"

"Good God, no! He was a manipulative piece of…work. There again, I know what you're like. You take people at face value and go all in."

"You mean I'm gullible," Kris said.

"Trusting," Shaunna corrected. "And there's nothing wrong with that, as long as you're not setting yourself up for heartbreak."

"Should I cancel?"

"No. But you should probably ask Ade straight up if he's involved with anyone else."

Kris suspected it was already too late, as regards saving himself from heartbreak, but at least he'd know where he stood. Still, he didn't relish having that conversation.

"Hey, maybe you could come along as my chaperone," he joked.

Shaunna rolled her eyes. "Or maybe I should stop trying to mother you."

Kris laughed and got up. "I'm going for a shower."

"OK, hun. You want a shirt ironing?"

"What was that about not mothering me?"

She grabbed the tea towel the dog had nicked earlier and flicked it at Kris's behind as he passed.

He dodged away and ran upstairs, returning half a minute later. "Are you sure you don't mind?"

"Not at—" Her eyebrows arched in surprise as she took the plain black shirt from him. "It's a date, not a funeral!"

"I know! It's just…Ade mentioned he used to wear bright colours, and…well, I should start toning it down a little. I'm nearly forty, after all."

"So?"

Nothing to add in his defence, Kris started back up the stairs, listening to the clanging of the ironing board being set up.

"He must be pretty special," Shaunna called after him.

He stopped and glanced over the banister, giving her a hopeful smile. "Yeah. I think he is."

8: No Entry

Ade

A DE CLIMBED THE stairs to his apartment, clinging to his
good mood like a drowning man to flotsam. Ten hours
ago, he'd been racing down these very stairs, trying to outrun
the shitstorm that was his life with Fergus Campbell in it. He'd
genuinely believed it was futile. In a stupid moment of weakness,
he'd let the emotion vampire back in, been seduced by his lies of
getting help, trying harder, doing better, and what was the point
in running when all you were doing was running around the
same circle? It was easier to lie down and submit than fight to
break free again.

But then Kris had shown up, and the shock seemed to have
jolted Ade's heart back into its old rhythm, reminding him: he'd
had a life before Fergus; surely, he could have one *after* Fergus
too. Whether Kris would be a part of that life in the longer term,
Ade didn't care to predict, but he was certainly persistent—not
in a pushy way. He'd given Ade plenty of chances to back out of
their date, which Ade had no intention of doing, and he really
wished he could have given Kris an unqualified yes, but he didn't
know what he was coming home to or if he'd be able to get out of
the apartment without causing a scene. *THE apartment? YOUR
apartment, for God's sake! What happened to your backbone?*

Slowing his steps, he tiptoed the last few yards to his front
door and halted, listening for noise within.

Nothing.

Fergus usually had the stereo blasting and the TV on at the
same time.

He's gone.

Sagging in relief, Ade pushed his key into the lock. It wouldn't turn.

"The absolute…" Ade knocked on the door, irritated he had to. He was so done with the mind games, but of course, he got no answer. He knocked again, harder this time. "Ferg? Open the door, please."

Still nothing and getting angrier by the second, Ade called Fergus's phone and heard it ringing inside the apartment. He hammered on the door. "Fergus, come on!"

But along with the anger, he was starting to worry. He'd been here before, when Fergus had taken an overdose after Ade finished things the second time and then sat sneering at Ade in A&E, knowing he'd won. Then he'd threatened to electrocute himself—*I'm taking a bath with the toaster. Goodbye, Adrian*—the fourth time, or maybe the fifth. Ade had lost count by then, along with any sympathy for Ferg's mental health or supposed lack of. It was emotional blackmail, pure and simple, and it had worked until now.

Ade gave it one last try, banging with his fist and even with the edge of his phone, but all his hammering achieved was to disturb his neighbour Mary, who opened her front door and beckoned him with a crooked finger.

"He's on the balcony," she whispered, tilting her head back for Ade to follow her inside. She led him through the living room and out onto her balcony, from which Ade could see his own, where, sure enough, Ferg sat with his back to them, an empty wine bottle upright on the table, another on its side on the floor and a third bottle, still half-full, in his hand. He swayed back in his seat, completely off his face and in a world of his own. Ade felt the tears rise in his throat and bit down hard on his lip to stop them. Mary gently touched his arm, and it broke him.

"Come and have a sit down for a while, lovey," she said and steered him back inside, shutting the French doors behind them. "It's a bad do, this."

He nodded behind his hands. A tear squeezed between his fingers.

"Oh dear. Right, you sit here…" She nudged him sideways and backwards until he felt the edge of the sofa behind his knees and sat. "I'll fetch you some water, give you a chance to pull yourself together, lovey."

A chuckle slipped its way past Ade's hopelessness and escaped as a snotty bubble into his palm. He lowered his hands but kept his eyes closed, listening to Mary pootling around. They'd been neighbours since he moved here twelve years ago, so she'd witnessed a lot of what Ade had been through with Fergus, or heard it at least, and called the police so often it was a wonder they hadn't blocked her number. They'd turn up, tell Ade and Ferg to tone it down and leave again because the few times when Ade was visibly injured and they'd charged Fergus, Ade had refused to testify and the magistrates had had to let him go.

"Here you are." Mary squashed a clump of toilet paper into his hands and set a glass down on the table beside him.

"Thanks." He blew his nose and dried his eyes, still sniffling. "Sorry about this."

"Eh, no need for a brave face here, lad, Sometimes we just need to let go, get it all out. Did he hurt you again? The other night?"

Ade couldn't bring himself to answer, not consciously, but to his horror, he felt his head move up and down in a nod. Cat out of the bag, he touched his jaw.

Mary bent in front of him, squinting through her glasses. "Oh, Ade." She straightened up and tottered off again, returning with an ancient-looking brown jar.

"What's that?"

"Muscle balm. Smashing stuff, this. Takes the swelling down in no time." She unscrewed the lid and held out the jar. "Scoop some up with your fingers, rub it on."

Reluctantly, Ade poked a fingertip into the greasy gloop.

"That's it. Get a good dollop," Mary encouraged. Ade complied and rubbed the balm over the bruises, catching a whiff of menthol and eucalyptus. It would all be stuck in his stubble, but he wasn't sure it mattered.

"Thanks, Mary." He wiped the residue on the toilet paper and looked around for a bin.

"Here." Mary took it from him and handed him the glass of water, watching him drink as if she expected him to refuse or choke on it. He swallowed and smiled glibly. She sighed and sat next to him. "What are you going to do, lovey?"

"I...I don't know." He felt so defeated. Admittedly, his hope that Fergus would be gone by now had been a long shot, but he really hadn't expected this. At worst, he'd thought he'd have to lie, say he needed to go back to work but could drop Fergus at home first, which was why he'd suggested meeting Kris near where he lived. Fergus had followed him out before and caused an almighty scene in a restaurant. In retrospect, it was almost comical, as the chef had come out of the kitchen, wielding his cleaver and yelling in Cantonese until Fergus left the premises.

That was the last time Ade had tried dating, nearly four years ago, because it had been easier to cope with living half a life if he ignored the missing other half. But that connection he'd felt with Kris, sharing a drink, chatting...it had him remembering and hoping and wanting. And it gave him courage.

Ade wiped his eyes and blinked a few times to clear his vision.

"I'm going to talk to him," he told Mary and stepped past her, out onto the balcony, where he had a clear line of sight.

"Fergus."

He had his back to Ade, but he'd have heard him. *Ignorant bastard.*

"Fergus!"

He lifted the wine bottle to his lips and swigged. Ade's hair bristled with anger. *How dare you drink MY wine!*

"I'll be at the front door in thirty seconds. You need to go and open it."

The response was delayed by Fergus's state of inebriation, but he did finally twist to look in Ade's direction, his head wobbling as he tried to focus. He looked like a haggard old drunk, a life gone unrecoverably wrong.

"I'm coming now," Ade said, his voice calm and emotionless. It was hard reining in his anger, but any love he'd been clinging to had been crushed with this morning's cigarette. "Did you hear me, Fergus?"

"Fuck you," Fergus spat and turned away again.

"You will open the door."

"Or what?"

"Or I'll call the police."

That seemed to get through, as Fergus leaned both hands on the patio table and swayed up onto his feet then swung, almost gorilla-like, to the doorjamb and flung himself inside the apartment.

Ade turned back and saw Mary's worried expression. "He won't start anything," he assured her. "He's too drunk."

"Even still," she said, not at all reassured. She followed Ade to the front door. "I'll wait here."

He moved off, towards his own front door. He could hear the key moving on the other side and glanced back at Mary, steeling himself for the encounter.

"If it sounds like it's getting out of hand, I'll call 999," she said.

Ade nodded his consent, not that it made the slightest difference whether he gave it or not.

The door handle moved and the door slowly opened, just a few inches. Ade waited. He heard Fergus shuffling away and stepped inside, removing the key from the inside of the lock and leaving the front door ajar before he followed Fergus along the hallway and into the living room. It was a shambles, the contents of Fergus's pockets scattered along the sofa, presumably where he'd started off, dirty plates, dishes and mugs on the coffee table, a broken glass on the floor; the TV remote was in two pieces at the base of the far wall.

"Going for a piss," Fergus announced and staggered away to the bathroom.

Until then, Ade had had no idea how he was going to get Fergus out of the flat, and he'd need to work quickly if he was going to pull it off. Grabbing the landline phone with one hand, he scooped up all of Fergus's pocket junk with the other and went out onto the balcony, from where he ordered a cab and shoved the junk into the pocket of Fergus's jacket, still hanging on the back of the patio chair. The toilet flushed. Ade took a few deep breaths to steady himself and held position.

Fergus emerged from the bathroom and looked around him in a daze, his mouth twisting into a leer when he spotted Ade on the balcony. He meandered out and cupped Ade's face, brushing his thumb roughly up his cheekbone, dragging the skin with it. The pain was nothing, but the stench of Fergus's breath, heavy with wine and garlic, almost had Ade retching. He breathed through his mouth and hoped it didn't show as he said casually, "That was the taxi firm to say the car's on its way."

Some of Mary's muscle balm must've transferred onto Fergus's fingers, as he was scowling at them but looked up when Ade's words registered. "Taxi?" he slurred, his eyes wandering and stupid as he tried to stare Ade down. "Did I order a... I don't think... I don't..."

Ade edged sideways and picked up Fergus's jacket, holding it open for him. Miraculously, Fergus was going along with it and after a couple of attempts managed to get one arm in each sleeve. And there was the honk of a car horn.

"That's yours," Ade said, using his body to steer Fergus back inside and through the apartment. As he reached the door, he sensed resistance, and Fergus groped at the empty keyhole, but Ade kept him moving, past the door and out into the communal hallway. If he could just persuade him to leave the building, it would be all right. He could do this. That was what he was telling himself, anyway.

He heard Mary cough to reassure him that she was still there. Fergus looked her way and then back at Ade, realisation dawning in his eyes. For a horrible second, Ade thought Fergus was going to shove him back inside the apartment, but then he just sneered and leaned in, swaying forward until their noses were pressed together. Ade stayed as still as could be. Still was invisible; still was safer.

"Don't ever think you're cleverer than me, cos you're not. You're nothing without me." Fergus staggered back and eyed Ade up and down in disgust. "Skinny ginger runt. Who'd want anything to do with you? You vile little fuck."

Ade was shaking with fear and rage, but his anger was draining away, leaving an empty void into which self-doubt poured. It wasn't true. None of it was true. But he didn't really believe that anymore. If you heard it too many times, it became the truth.

It took all his strength to stay in one piece as he waited for Fergus to disappear from view, his uneven shuffled footsteps on the stairs slowly becoming distant, a rumbling storm that could turn and come back at any moment. The door downstairs slammed shut, and Ade fell against the wall, sliding down until he hit the floor and sat, openly sobbing, not for Fergus but for himself—for the man he had become.

"All right now," Mary murmured, wrapping her arms around him. "You let it all out. I've got you." He had no doubt about that. Sweet little old lady she might be, but she was a force to be reckoned with.

"Did you..." Ade sniffed and swallowed down a ton a snot. "Did you call the police?"

"I did, lovey. They'll be here in forty minutes, they said. Forty minutes." She shook her head. "You could be dead by then..."

Ade turned and gave her a look.

"I didn't mean you in particular, you daft bugger. But while we're on the subject, are you going to change the locks again?"

Ade shook his head and, before she got in another chance to tell him he was daft, plucked Fergus's key from his pocket. "Ta-da!"

"Oh, thank God!"

He held the key out to her. "For you," he said. "Just in case."

She took it from him and dropped it into her pocket. "Here, you'd best give me a hand up."

He did so, carefully, wincing with her as she straightened to her full, tiny height.

"You know what else, Mary?"

"What?"

He was smiling—quite feebly, but smiling, nonetheless. "I have a date."

"A date?" She beamed back at him. "Oh, I'm so pleased for you, Ade!"

"Thank you. For everything. I honestly don't know what I'd do without you. You've been so kind and patient."

Mary tutted dismissively, but he saw her wipe her eye before she gave him a gentle shove towards his apartment and said, "Well, what're you standing out here for? Go and get yourself ready!"

Laughing, he pushed the door open and turned back to look at her. She flapped her hands to shoo him inside.

"You have a lovely time, do you hear?" she said sternly. "You deserve it."

"I will," Ade promised, albeit with a trembling lip.

9: Scripted

Kris

KRIS FINISHED THE last inch of his second beer and scrolled distractedly through the script he'd loaded onto his phone so he'd look less like a man who had been stood up, which he wasn't…yet, but he was convinced that every notification would be from Ade saying he couldn't make it. Given he'd called twice, first to say he was going to be half an hour, then an hour late, Kris didn't think he was being pessimistic in preparing himself for disappointment.

"Can I get you anything else?" the bartender asked as she picked up Kris's empty glass.

"Will you kick me out if I say 'no, thanks'?" He didn't want to spend the evening sozzled or running to the gents' every five minutes.

"Depends how busy we get." She winked and continued her circuit of the few occupied tables. "Hot date?"

"Hopefully." Quiet as it was in this bar on a weeknight, he kind of wished he'd picked somewhere he'd never been before because he was blushing brighter than the recording light above Ade's studio door, and not out of embarrassment that his 'hot date' might not turn up. Just thinking about Ade had Kris's heart leaping around like a cartoon heart on a spring, and he was sure everyone could see it boinging against the inside of his shirt.

Feeling terribly conspicuous, he checked for messages—no new ones—and tried the script again, but it wasn't holding his attention, so he resorted to watching the bartender flirt with a guy at the bar. She was so laid-back and natural, leaning in to listen, a subtle flash of cleavage, a smile, always in control...the total opposite of Kris, who, when Ade walked in a minute later, gave himself hiccups and almost fell over his feet getting up to greet him.

It went from bad to worse, as Kris hesitated, unsure if they should embrace, exchange a quick peck on the cheek, or lips, or shake hands. They both danced from side to side for a few seconds before Ade laughed and initiated the same kind of hug and air kiss they'd shared earlier in the day.

"Mm," he murmured against Kris's cheek. "Love your aftershave. You smell really good."

"So do you." Shower-fresh with a subtle woody cologne.

They released each other, and Ade took a step back. "And you look great, although I was expecting...more colour? Is that my fault? It is, isn't it?"

"Not at all," Kris assured him. "I do wear plain shirts sometimes, and...I don't know. I just..."

"Dressed down for my benefit? You didn't have to do that."

Kris shrugged. He felt he did. Whatever Ade's reason for no longer wearing bright colours, it hadn't sounded like a freely made choice.

"Are you OK with this table or would you prefer to sit somewhere else? Or move on?"

"Here's fine," Ade said, looking amused but flattered when Kris pulled out a chair for him. "Why thank you, kind sir!"

Kris smiled—couldn't seem to stop smiling—and resumed his seat. "You're welcome." He waved to garner the attention of the bartender, who nodded to acknowledge she'd seen him.

"They have table service here?" Ade asked.

Kris nodded. "For regulars." That made him sound like a barfly. "Not that I'm in here all the time. We come here maybe once or twice a month at most. What would you like? They have Coke and juice and mixers—not sure about non-alcoholic beers. A tonic water?"

"Erm...sorry?"

"Well…you're driving, aren't you?"

"I drove here." Ade sounded defensive. Kris cringed.

"Sorry, that came across as bossy and judgemental."

"A little, but I know that wasn't what you meant. To be honest, I need some gin in my tonic water tonight, even if I have to abandon the car and hitchhike home."

The bartender arrived as Ade was speaking. "A G and T?"

Ade glanced Kris's way before he answered. Kris shrugged—externally. Internally, he was banging his head against a wall.

"I'm having another beer, so…"

Ade smiled at the bartender. "Yes, please."

"Ice and lemon?"

"Fab, thanks."

"And a beer, Kris?"

"Yes, thanks."

She returned to the bar to prepare their drinks, leaving them in an uneasy silence. Kris couldn't believe how badly he'd screwed up. He wasn't a drinker, and the two pints he'd had was usually his limit, but he'd never police other people's alcohol intake. He tried to come up with something to say that wasn't yet another apology, but they knew almost nothing about each other. The little he had picked up from Ade told him they'd both had more than their fair share of trauma, and it didn't make for good first-date material, especially as Ade's seemed to be ongoing. Not that Kris had any real idea of what *did* make for good first-date material, seeing as he'd been on precisely three, including this one.

Perhaps that was a good place to start.

He peered across at Ade, who was immediately attentive and seemed to have forgiven Kris's latest faux pas.

"I was thinking…we should get to know a bit more about each other?"

Ade nodded, though he had that same look about him as this morning, the one that suggested he might bolt at any second.

"I'm happy to set the ball rolling," Kris offered. "I have a feeling it might be easier for me than for you?"

Ade nodded again, still a little uptight, but he adjusted his position, so he was turned towards Kris, and settled back against the seat.

"OK, well…" Kris paused for their drinks to be delivered, along with a knowing grin from the bartender. Kris thanked her and gave her a tip even though he had an open tab and usually tipped when he settled up. "I've always been an actor, which you probably know already from my CV. I moved to England with my family when I was three. I have an older brother, Lars, and we have nothing in common whatsoever. He and my parents moved back to Sweden when I was in my twenties."

"They left you here all on your own?" Ade looked horrified.

"It wasn't a moonlight flit or anything. We came here for my dad's work, and it was always the plan for us to move back when he retired, but by then I was in a long-term relationship with Shaunna, and we have a daughter…well, she's my stepdaughter, but my parents always accepted Krissi as their granddaughter. They offered to pay for the three of us to resettle in Gothenburg, but we decided to stay in England."

"Wow, OK. So you and Shaunna settled down pretty young."

"Er, yeah, you could say that." Kris chuckled. He'd come back to that, assuming he hadn't chased Ade off before he got that far.

"Were you together a long time?"

"Twenty years. We only separated last year, and…" This could be make or break, but he wanted to be honest with Ade. "We still share a house."

"Oh!" Ade blinked a few times in surprise and picked up his drink, half-emptying the glass before he said, "I guess if it works for you…"

"It has until now." Even though he and Shaunna had discussed what they would do with the house when it stopped working, it had been more of a technicality, an *if…then* rather than a *when*, and Kris could feel the foundations shifting beneath him. He was no longer on solid ground, and it was disorientating but also exhilarating.

"Hey," Ade said, resting his hand on Kris's. "It's not a deal breaker."

That smile…

Kris vented a breath and followed Ade's example, taking a less-than-sensible glug of his beer. He'd been so worried how Ade would react, and he honestly couldn't have wished for a better response.

"Can I ask…if Krissi's your stepdaughter…"

"Why is she named after me?"

Ade nodded.

"The short version—I was the first person Shaunna told she was pregnant, and we came up with this mad idea to tell our parents the baby was mine. We couldn't keep up the lie, but we were always together, and I got to see this bump growing and feel first kicks, so by the time she was born, she felt like she *was* mine."

"You were at the birth? Amazing!"

"Yep. As was Krissi's biological father, although we didn't know back then. But that's a whole other story." And absolutely not one for a first date.

"I need pics!" Ade snapped his fingers bossily. Kris laughed.

"I think I can oblige." He opened his photos on his phone and passed it to Ade. "There're a few on here from the summer. That's Krissi." He pointed to her. "And that's Shaunna."

"Is this your garden?"

"No. Dan and Adele's—friends of ours. Don't tell them I said this, but our garden's much nicer—completely Shaunna's doing, I hasten to add."

"I won't say a word."

Ade spent a long time examining the photo, zooming in on Shaunna and Krissi, occasionally nodding or sipping his drink. He flipped through a few more of the photos, all of them much the same—Shaunna and Krissi laughing at something or other,

Shaunna and Krissi drinking from their glasses at the same time, Shaunna and Krissi smiling at the camera… If it hadn't been clear already from what he'd said, the photos confirmed that Shaunna and Krissi were Kris's life.

"They're very alike," Ade said eventually. "Other than their hair and skin tone. I'm guessing Krissi's dark complexion comes from her biological father?"

"Yeah, and she's a lot like him personality-wise too. She's one of those roller coaster fiends, and he's into extreme sports."

"Risk-takers," Ade mused. He handed the phone back. "I may be a little biased, but Shaunna's hair is gorgeous."

Kris's eyes strayed to Ade's gelled copper spikes, which were a few shades darker than Shaunna's 'ginger-nut orange', as she called it. "It is. It's beautiful."

Ade smiled, acknowledging the compliment applied to him too. "You still love her a great deal," he observed. Kris nodded. "So why are you separated?"

"It's hard to explain…" Kris wasn't sure he knew himself, and his rehearsed answer of *we just grew apart* wasn't going to cut it. "We maybe should have just been best friends all along. I think that's all it is. We're really good together as friends and parents. We always have been. And Shaunna is the most amazing mum— she's one of those people who looks after everyone else, you know? Including me. Last year…" He paused, knowing if he went any further, Ade would probably be out that door in five seconds flat and never look back. But what other option did he have? Build another relationship on half-truths and have it blow up in his face twenty years from now? This felt like the start of something important, and he wanted to get it right, but Ade also deserved to know what he was letting himself in for if they did take it further.

"I had a breakdown a couple of years ago," Kris said before he bottled out, although that was only the prelude. "Krissi decided she wanted to find her biological father, and it put a lot of strain on us all, but Shaunna…she's a lot tougher than me. She took care of me, made sure I took my antidepressants, picked up extra work while I was sick. Then I went back to work, and I'm ashamed to say…I had an affair, which I suppose only brought things to a head because we were no longer living as husband and wife, if you see what I mean.

"Even now, our friends question us because they say we act like we're still together, and on one level, I get it. We've got everything we had before, bar the sexual intimacy. But on another… I don't know. Something changed between us, or we're not who we used to be. Maybe that's all it is—we're different people now."

"You grew apart," Ade said, though he seemed lost in thought, a little pensive, staring into the mid-distance. He blinked and looked back at Kris. "Can I ask you a personal question? Or should I say *another* personal question." He rolled his eyes, and Kris laughed. "You don't have to answer."

"Go on."

"Are you bi?"

"Yes, I am."

"OK. I wasn't sure. I've always known I'm gay, but some people don't for a long time, and I wondered if that was why things ended with Shaunna or if I missed something."

"Missed something?"

"This isn't meant as a criticism, but it sounds to me like you pretty much had the perfect relationship."

"We did."

"But it was a closed relationship?"

"Yeah. I mean, we never discussed it, but I never wanted to be with anyone else, and I don't think Shaunna did either."

"Yet you had an affair."

"I don't know why I didn't just say no when he made his move, which isn't me saying I'm without blame. I guess I was missing the intimacy—not necessarily the sex. Being physically close to someone. But in a new relationship, you don't usually get one without the other, and he was in the same situation as me, or so he said."

"He was cheating on his wife," Ade stated. Kris nodded.

"When I told him we were done, he claimed theirs *was* an open marriage, apparently forgetting he'd previously said he was in the middle of a divorce."

"What an arse."

"Yeah." Kris smiled ruefully. "In conclusion, I screwed up my marriage and threw away my job, and he just carried on as usual."

"Wait—" Ade held up a finger. "It's not Jack Malton, is it?"

Kris somehow kept his groan to himself. He felt like such an idiot. Of course Ade would know Jack. They worked in rival radio stations a couple of blocks apart, although Jack was a show host, not a producer.

"I'm going to assume by your silence, and the fact that you look like you want a black hole to suddenly appear and swallow you whole, that's a yes."

Kris nodded. He couldn't even meet Ade's eyes.

"I can see why you fell for him. He can be very charming. And very...controlling."

Kris glanced up. Ade smiled gently.

"I'm sorry you went through that."

"Don't be." Kris didn't want sympathy. He didn't deserve it.

"Just remember, we all make mistakes," Ade added cheerfully. "Now..." He glanced around the bar. "How do I summon your admirer?"

"Who?"

"The bartender."

"Oh!" Kris laughed and blushed. "She flirts with everyone."

"Uh-huh. If you say so," Ade teased. "Ooh, there she is!" He waved and caught her eye. "Same again?" he asked Kris.

"Just a Coke, please. I'm a lightweight."

The bartender arrived for Ade's order. Kris listened to their interchange, feeling vindicated when she proved his point by flirting with Ade, although all traces of smugness were wiped out when Ade turned back and dazzled him with the most incredible smile. Kris's heart leapt back onto its spring. He wanted this, more than anything, and he wanted to make sure Ade knew that.

"I hope telling you this doesn't scare you off…"

"Nothing has so far," Ade said.

"I know we've only known each other for two days, but I think I've fallen for you already."

10: Bar

Ade

ADE INTERNALLY CHEERED, a hint of self-belief creeping around the edges of his obliterated self-confidence. He didn't say *I feel the same* because he wasn't sure he did yet. Nor did he run away, but he was going to keep the conversation focused on Kris a while longer. Or Kris and Shaunna, at least. After ten years with Fergus, it was far too easy to fall into the trap of believing all relationships, however well they started out, eventually turned sour, yet here was Kris saying his and Shaunna's marriage had ended but they were still friends. The best of friends. Ade felt a twinge of jealousy, which he took as a good sign that he did indeed feel the same as Kris, but it was also ridiculous. He pushed it to the back of his mind and moved on.

"Tell me more about Krissi. How old is she?"

"Twenty-two. Twenty-three a week on Sunday, actually."

"Oh!" *Twenty-two?! How?* Ade was glad he'd kept his exclamations of surprise mostly to himself. It didn't compute, and the best he could come up with for why Kris had a stepdaughter of that age was that Shaunna was older. *But he was there at Krissi's birth. A teenage boy in a relationship with a grown woman?* Judging by the way Kris was watching him, arms folded and a smirk on his face, essentially saying *I'll give you a minute*, Ade was way off the mark, on some aspects anyway.

"You were fifteen?" he asked, adding as a distractor, "My maths is appalling."

"No, that's right," Kris confirmed.

"And Shaunna?"

"Was also fifteen. I'd have told you if you'd asked."

"Wow!" Ade couldn't get his head around it. "At that age, I couldn't even manage a part-time job on top of school, or work the washing machine or…well, anything! How did you cope? I mean, you went to drama college. How did that work?"

Kris shrugged. "I went to drama college, came home for the weekend whenever I could and every holiday. Bear in mind Krissi was at playschool by the time I left sixth form, and Shaunna still lived with her mum and dad, so they helped out a lot. But as I say, Shaunna was—is still—a brilliant mum. A brilliant woman. I think you'll get on really well with her."

"I will?" Now Ade folded his arms, loving how quickly Kris became flustered after he'd described so matter-of-factly being *a parent at fifteen!* Ade could honestly have listened to him all night, and that second G&T was clearly working its magic too. He'd hardly given Fergus a thought.

Leaning forward, Ade rested his elbows on the table and balanced his chin on one hand, ready to indulge in some serious flirting, but as he held Kris's gaze, the intensity hit him like a tidal wave, frightening and unexpected and breathtakingly wonderful, and all he could utter was, "What are we doing?"

Kris shook his head. "I don't know, but whatever it is, I think it's fabulous. I'm so glad I auditioned for *On Sunday.*"

"Me too. And yes, I'd love to meet Shaunna." Ade picked up his glass, peering demurely over its rim. "We're endangered, you know."

Kris rolled his eyes drolly. "I know."

"Us redheads need to stick together." Ade pouted, selfie-style, which he doubted looked in the least bit attractive, but still Kris sucked in breath sharply, their stifled laughter confirming the almost out-of-control physical attraction was one hundred percent mutual. It was too fast and yet not fast enough, but Ade was terrified they'd mess it up by moving it to the bedroom so soon.

He was also aware that Kris was done talking about himself—had been done some time ago—so Ade could either prolong the agony by probing for any more details Kris was willing to share… or he could just get it over and done with. An involuntary sigh escaped, capturing Kris's full attention and leaving Ade with no choice. Well, he could still run, but he wanted to stay, see where this went.

"It's not a nice story," he said.

"Hey, you don't have to tell me."

"You've been so honest and open."

"Mmm…that was kind of the edited highlights. I can tell you more, though frankly, I'm surprised I haven't bored the pants off you already."

"God, not at all! You've done so much with your life." *And I've done nothing. Achieved nothing.* Ade toyed with his glass, empty other than the lemon slice and a couple of slivers of ice, melting away before his eyes.

He'd once been like Krissi, drawn to the thrill, not so much of roller coasters but of illegal raves—waiting for the call to say where and when, then racing off through the night—although he'd kept away from mood-enhancing drugs and couldn't say he'd ever been tempted to try extreme sports. Danger with safety rails had been his limit, and then Fergus had come along and ripped the rails off; Ade had been dangling off an emotional precipice ever since.

If there was to be a future for him and Kris, he had to open up, however painful doing so might be. Fergus could not be allowed to spoil this for him.

"OK," he began, still unsure how much to say. He feared that he might start and never stop.

"I have an arse of an ex-boyfriend who doesn't get that it's over."

He paused. Kris nodded, encouraging him to go on.

"That's why I was late tonight. He turned up at my place this morning, just as I was going to work. I was hoping he'd have left before I got home, but instead, he drank all of my wine, ate all of my food and trashed the place. So I packed him into a taxi and sent him home, but it took a while."

"Ah. That makes sense."

"Does it?"

"As an explanation for why you were late."

"That's something." Ade fished the slice of lemon out of his glass and squeezed it gently, then harder. "He's a very angry person with a lot of issues."

He didn't say the words; he didn't need to because he saw the moment Kris put it all together—the bruises, Ade's freak-out this morning. Or maybe the stricken quietness that had dulled the bright, colourful man beside him was simply because Ade was confirming what had been obvious all along.

The lemon was a dry husk in Ade's aching fingers, and his lip hurt from sawing it between his teeth. He was waiting for the questions—the same questions his sister, Pip and the few other people who knew had asked when they first found out. *That's not just everyday angry, Ade, and so what if he has issues? Does that give him the right to take them out on you?*

But the questions didn't come.

Kris reached out and took Ade's hand in his, nothing more. A simple, instinctive gesture offering comfort, no judgement, but so rare and precious it felt like a warm bed with arms around him, a vision of future happiness that for just a fleeting moment was more than a distant, impossible mirage.

Ade kept his face down and his eyes trained on their hands, focusing on the gentle rub of Kris's thumb along the edge of his own. A stray tear spilled, and Ade wiped it away in shame. "I'm sorry."

Kris squeezed Ade's hand, not hard. Just enough to signal he'd heard. The silence resumed, but the conversation played out in Ade's head.

"Why are you sorry?"

"*For messing you around this evening, for making you feel you have to wear that boring shirt, for driving all the way here for a date because I'm shit-scared of Fergus coming after me, for being too much of a coward to stand up in court and tell them what a violent, abusive bastard he is.*"

"I'm going to the gents'," Ade said, hanging on to his control by a thread as he eased his hand out of Kris's. "I need to blow my nose and..." The words crumbled away as the tears engulfed him, and he fled across the bar without looking back. He was humiliated enough, and Kris would be halfway to the door already if he knew what was good for him.

***

Kris

KRIS STARED AFTER Ade, feeling as if a ton of rocks had dropped on him, pinning him to his seat. Now he understood everything—the bruises, the lack of bright colours, the uncertainty about making it for their date, the agreement to come to Kris's hometown rather than meet up in the city where they worked and where there were a lot more venues to choose from for a night out.

He understood that there was so much he did not understand, and he was sliding too, but it wouldn't help Ade if he returned to find Kris bawling his eyes out, so he ordered more drinks and opened the script on his phone...and worried...and wondered if he should go and check on Ade. He must have read a hundred lines or more, not a single word registering, before Ade sat down, eyes averted, and took a long drink from his replenished G&T.

It seemed to take a great deal of effort to do so, but eventually Ade looked up and met Kris's gaze, searching...for understanding? For forgiveness? For someone he could trust? Kris held the eye contact, allowing Ade access to his emotions, letting him know he was wide open and unafraid. Ade smiled weakly.

"I'm really sorry I've ruined our evening. It's very poor dating etiquette."

Kris shrugged. "You haven't, and anyway, dating etiquette is just a play with a terrible script. All those shallow questions and answers—'What do you do?' 'Do you come here often?' 'What's number one on your bucket list?' 'Can I see you again?' If you have to ask, you probably already know the answer."

"God, you're so right!" Ade laughed, not quite back to his bubbly pre-talking-about-the-abusive-ex self, understandably. "Not that I've been on the circuit recently. I imagine it hasn't changed much. Have you dated anyone since you and Shaunna separated, apart from…you know?"

"Jack? No." Ade had flipped the conversation, but Kris was fine going along with it, wherever it took them. "I went on nights out with people from work a few times—there are a couple of gay guys I got on well with at the station, both quite a bit younger than I am, so we used to go out in Manchester, clubbing. They were always trying to fix me up, but I'm not into one-night stands. I tried all that when I was at college, and it wasn't that much fun then."

"So there's only been Shaunna for you?"

"And George."

Ade's eyebrows rose, and he shuffled closer. "And who's George, other than someone who puts a smile on your face and turns your cheeks rosy?" He picked up his drink and waited to be regaled. Kris sighed wearily, but he honestly didn't mind talking about George.

"He was my first boyfriend. We went to the same high school and were together on and off until Shaunna."

"Did you break up with him for her?"

"No, actually. He dumped me."

"Outrageous! How dare he!"

Kris laughed. "George wasn't out, and I was. Very much so. But that was just one of many things we didn't agree on. I tried to get him to see that we were paving the way for other gay and bi kids, but he couldn't do it. He's very sporty—he played for the school football team—and he's kind of a typical man. Not like alpha male or anything. Just into lots of things that are traditionally very masculine and heteronormative. Like, for instance, he studied agriculture at uni, then moved to Colorado in his twenties and ran a cattle ranch."

"That is pretty manly," Ade said. "And impressive. Should I be worried that one day you'll drop everything and go join him?"

Kris shook his head. "Definitely not. For a start, he's back in the UK now."

"A threat even closer to home!" Ade was mock aghast, or Kris hoped he was laying it on. "Are you still in touch?"

"Yeah. There's a group of us who've stayed friends since school. We're really close. We pop in to visit each other all the time and celebrate birthdays and go on holiday together—we went to visit George while he was in Colorado. That was…eye-opening."

"I've never been anywhere like that. What was it like?"

"The scenery was incredible, surrounded by snow-capped mountains and so much space, it's hard to picture, living here. The ranch, though…well, it wasn't as if George had misled us, but I guess we all imagined a huge homestead with a porch like something off *Dallas*, and it turned out to be a broken-down shack in the middle of nowhere, surrounded by hundreds of cows and horses. Really not my thing. Or George's. Although some of those cowboys were really, really hot."

"Go there often, did you?" Ade teased.

"Not often enough!"

They both laughed and clanged their glasses in a toast to 'hot cowboys'.

"This is nice," Ade said.

"Yeah, it is," Kris agreed. Ade looked so much happier than he had, and that made Kris happy too, even if he was feeling a certain amount of pressure to keep the stories coming.

"Last month, one of our friends got married, and believe it or not, we had a group honeymoon."

"Kinky!"

Kris laughed. "There was definitely nothing kinky going on. Ellie and James—the couple who got married—have a baby, and James has a son from his previous marriage, so their kids were there, and Dan and Adele's daughter—"

"And Krissi?"

"Not this time. She says she's too old to go on holiday with the parentals. I think what she means is we're too boring, and to be fair, there's not much for a town girl to do in a cabin in the Welsh mountains. On the plus side, it meant Casper could come with us." There were entire subplots Kris could've gone into, but some of those weren't his to share, so he finished with, "Casper's our dog—a golden Lab. Quite big, moults all the time, generally a bit on the dozy side."

"No offence to Casper," Ade said, "but I think you've just described every golden Labrador, ever."

"Hey, I'll have you know he's named after one of the three *wise* men."

"Oh, so he's Casp-*ar* rather than Casp-*er*?"

"Nope, I was kidding. Krissi chose the name because he's always 'pleased to meet ya' like Casper the Friendly Ghost, but I felt I should say something in the poor dog's defence."

"Ah, OK." Ade chuckled. "I've no idea what that is, incidentally."

"A cartoon Krissi used to watch on TV when she was little. She made us record every episode."

"My sister's kids are like that. She goes mad because they ask to watch something and then leave the TV playing to itself. Or they used to. I haven't seen them in a while." Ade's focus drifted, and he sighed and closed his eyes for a moment but once again shook off whatever it was. "Does your brother have children?"

Another tiny insight, another switch back.

"He does. Two daughters, eighteen and fifteen. They're beautiful girls, both stereotypically blonde Swedes, even though Lars is darker than I am. Lena—his wife—is fair. And she's stunning. Fragile, like an ice crystal."

"An interesting description."

"Hmm." Kris hadn't meant to imply his sister-in-law was cold, but both she and Lars were emotionally quite restrained, even for Swedes. "They're right for each other. He's a businessman, and she's a former model who loves hosting dinner parties. Very conventional and sensible, and their home is immaculate." Kris frowned. "I can't imagine what they think of us with our clutter. Shaunna insists the house always stinks of dog. Honestly, someone only has to sniff and she whips out the incense. Potpourri and scented candles everywhere!"

"Sounds very cosy to me," Ade said.

"Oh, it is, but it's a far cry from that functional, minimalistic style us Swedes are famed for."

"What matters is that you like it."

"I do. I love it." Kris shrugged. "But then I look at Lars and Lena with their big house, daughters at private school, fancy new cars... Even if I was as successful as Lars, I don't think I'd want that lifestyle."

11: Classic

Ade

KRIS EXCUSED HIMSELF to go to the gents', so Ade didn't get a chance to say so, but from what he'd heard and seen, Kris was way more successful than his brother. He was a brilliant actor, a loving father, never mind being in a relationship for twenty years *and* coming out the other side still friends. Those were things that Ade could only dream of. Or they had been until this evening.

It was so easy, sitting and chatting like normal people. At no point had Kris put pressure on Ade to talk, just filling the gaps, giving Ade glimpses of all the important people and animals in his life. Of course, Kris was used to performing, but he was off the clock. He could still be playing a role, Ade supposed, but that wasn't his impression. Indeed, he'd learnt more about Kris Johansson in thirty-six hours than he'd ever know about Fergus, who was presumably still sleeping off the wine. No texts, no calls; it was bliss.

"Can you believe it's gone ten already?" Kris asked, sliding back into his seat.

"Is it?" The evening had gone so fast, yet all the stress and trauma of getting Fergus out of his flat seemed like days, not hours ago. What *had* been days ago, though, was Ade's last proper meal, and his appetite was back with a vengeance, as if his body had suddenly turned back on and was urging him to take whatever was on offer. He pressed on his belly to ease the emptiness, but it merely served to draw attention to the loud, hungry grumble. Kris's eyebrows rose.

"I was going to suggest we have another drink before last orders, but would you like to go for some food?"

Ade screwed up his nose, embarrassed, but God, he was hungry, and he was fairly sure the G&Ts had anaesthetised his face enough that he'd have no trouble eating everything put in front of him. He was only delaying answering because Kris was looking at him—the phrase 'drinking him in' sprang to mind because he was doing either a very poor job of disguising his attraction or an excellent job of making it obvious.

Emboldened by the alcohol and attention, Ade blinked slowly and wet his lips. Kris's gaze immediately fixed on the gap between Ade's front teeth—according to the orthodontist *not* the cause of his rhoticism but something he'd always been ultra-conscious of and kept concealed behind tight-lipped smiles. Not so on this occasion, however; he teased the gap with the tip of his tongue, feeling both silly and fluttery with desire. Then Kris's Adam's apple bobbed with his gulp, and Ade giggled, as did Kris—hiding behind his hand.

"I'm sorry, but you're very attractive."

"Thank you," Ade said. "I think you are too. I thought so from the minute I saw you yesterday morning. But to answer your question, yes. I'm absolutely famished."

"In that case..." Kris took out his debit card and waited for the bartender to look his way, waving the card at her.

"I'm not sure what to do about the car," Ade said. He hadn't intended on drinking over the limit, but if he'd been in any state to plan ahead, he'd have booked into a cheap local hotel and left the car there.

"Where did you park?" Kris asked.

"In the car park out back."

"I'm sure they won't mind you leaving it there. Want me to ask?"

Ade nodded hesitantly, half-hoping the bartender would say no, but she was at their table already.

"I can't see it being a problem," she said. "Just overnight, right?"

Kris looked to Ade to confirm.

"That's right," Ade said. "I'll come back for it first thing."

"No worries then." She handed Kris his receipt. "Enjoy the rest of your evening." She smiled at them both but followed up with a wink that was without question just for Kris.

"Told you so," Ade said as they stepped out onto the pavement. Kris waved his hand.

"She knows we're on a date, that's all." He paused to fasten his jacket. "Did I do the wrong thing?"

Ade frowned. "When?"

"Suggesting you leave your car in the pub car park."

"Oh! No. Which way?"

"Towards the town centre." Kris pointed along the street, and they set off at a slow stroll.

"It seems a nice area." Ade tried to make it sound like he was making a general observation.

"It is," Kris confirmed. "Your car should be safe enough."

Ade chuckled. "I'm not a petrol head or anything. But it was my dad's car."

"What is it?"

"An MGB GT. He bought it new in the early seventies, and he took such good care of it. Waxed it every Sunday, full service every year…"

"Vintage or classic? I've never really understood the difference."

"You know more than most. Vintage refers to the really old cars, before production lines. Mine's a classic slash antique."

"Can I see it?"

"Now?"

"Why not? We don't have a reservation anywhere, and it'll put your mind at ease."

Ade grinned. "OK then." They about-turned and headed back. "I should warn you it's nothing flash or fancy, and it's not worth much to anyone else…"

"But it's priceless to you," Kris said.

"Yes. And here it is." Ade gestured and stepped aside, beaming proudly. Under the bright blue-white of the car park's floodlights, his little maroon MG was positively gleaming.

"Wow, it's gorgeous!" Kris said. "That chrome is like a mirror. It must take a huge amount of work to keep it like that."

"A couple of hours a week. I love it. Mind you…" He buffed a watermark off the bonnet with the inside of his sleeve. "If it wasn't my dad's, I'd trade it for an E-Type in a heartbeat."

"That's a Jaguar, isn't it?" Kris asked.

"It's *the* Jaguar! My dad took me a trade show when I was fifteen—well, he took me to loads, but that was the one I remember vividly because there was a Series 1 E-Type on display, British Racing Green, green suede interior, absolutely stunning. I've wanted one ever since, but they're far too expensive, and I don't drive that much. As it is, this little beauty spends more time in the garage than on the road." Although if he could stop boring Kris with car talk for thirty seconds, that might change. "Sorry! I get carried away."

Kris shook his head, smiling. "Your enthusiasm is infectious. That friend I mentioned—Dan? He's always been mad about cars, but not this sort. The showy new ones that look like they should be on a racetrack."

"Supercars," Ade said. Kris shrugged. "Like Ferraris and Lamborghinis?"

"Yes, that's them."

"I can see the appeal…"

"I can't, but your car is different. It has personality."

"By the gallon!" Ade said. "Anyway, thank you for convincingly feigning interest. Shall we go and eat?"

"Let's do that, but for the record, I'm not faking it."

Ade needed no further encouragement and chattered all the way to the restaurant—an unpretentious place with a soul kitchen vibe and multicultural menu, which, Kris explained when he squeezed a word in edgeways, was one of a handful of places he could trust not to cross-contaminate his meal with shellfish. Ade was more than happy with Kris's choice, regardless of the reasons for it. He was enjoying the company and being somewhere Fergus wouldn't think to look for him even if he were sober enough to do so.

They were seated at a table near the back and both accepted a glass of the waiter's beer recommendation whilst they decided what food to order. Ade tried to ignore the seafood section of the menu, but his eyes were instantly drawn to the prawn Kashmiri. He loved sweet curries and seafood and would usually have gone for that by default, but the last thing he needed was his date going into anaphylactic shock.

"It's fine, you know," Kris assured him. "It's only if I ingest it that it causes a severe reaction."

"How much would you need to ingest?" Ade asked, chancing some rare optimism and thinking ahead.

"Not much. But the chefs here are super careful."

"Say, for instance, if someone who'd eaten prawns was to…lick your face or something…"

"Well…" Kris bit his lip, fighting a smile. "If I knew they were planning to, I'd take antihistamines in advance, but I can't say it's a situation I've come across."

Ade blushed. Flirting didn't come as easy to him as it used to, but it was fun practising and not worrying that he'd be ridiculed or told he was an embarrassment.

"I'll go with the chicken Kashmiri to be on the same side," he said, meeting Kris's gaze. "Leave my face-licking options open."

Soon after that, the waiter returned and took their order, and then they were eating and chatting and laughing like old friends, and Ade knew he wanted more of this. So much more. But it would mean sending Fergus packing once and for all, and he'd never been strong enough, always letting him worm his way back in. Tonight was a glimpse of an alternative reality, of his life without Fergus in it. Whatever happened, wherever it went, he'd hold it in his heart for always.

12: Dessert

Kris

"NEXT TIME, I'M having one of these all to myself," Ade grumbled playfully, withdrawing his spoon from the sundae glass.

Laughing, Kris scooped up the last of the chocolate sauce marbled with melted vanilla ice cream, of which Ade had eaten almost all, but Kris didn't mind in the slightest. "You're really not a fan of sharing dessert, are you?"

"I shared!" Ade protested. In a flash, he grabbed Kris's wrist and, locking eyes with him, closed his mouth around the spoon and slowly pulled back, sucking it fully clean. It had exactly the intended effect, sending a rush of heat to Kris's cheeks and other places.

"If I didn't know better, I'd say you were seducing me," he said.

Ade smiled coyly. "It's just flirting. There's plenty of time for seduction on our next date. I hope that's not assuming too much?"

"Definitely not. I've had a wonderful evening." He didn't want it to be over, but it was getting late, so reluctantly, the next time the waiter came their way, he asked for the bill. "How are you getting home? Or have you booked into a bed-and-breakfast?"

"No. I was going to call a taxi."

"Won't that be expensive?"

"No more so than a hotel room. Is there a local firm you'd recommend?"

"Kind of. There's only one in town. They have an office around the corner."

"That will do nicely," Ade said, smiling up at the waiter, who left the bill on the table and retreated while they figured out who was paying what. Or, rather, Ade figured it out, and Kris handed over his card and absently keyed in his PIN when prompted. He was torn between offering Ade a place to stay and worrying that doing so was too forward. Shaunna would be fine with it, he was sure, but he'd hate Ade to feel he had to accept if he didn't want to.

There were no free cars when they arrived at the taxi office, so they had to wait. Kris watched Ade out of the corner of his eye. He seemed agitated.

"Are you OK?"

"Hmm? Oh, yes. I'm fine. I just…I was figuring out my plans for tomorrow, so I could come and collect my car." It was a subtle hint that Kris might have missed were they not already on the same wavelength.

"I was thinking about that. You're at work in the morning, I'm guessing?"

"I am."

"And we haven't drunk so much that you'd be incapable of driving back first thing, so…what about staying at my place?"

"Won't Shaunna mind?"

"Not at all. Like I said, we're best friends, and she'll know…" Kris paused, but then decided to go for it. "Tonight has been amazing, Ade, and if you didn't come home with me, I'd only spend half the night jabbering to her about you and then no doubt lie awake for the rest of it, concocting reasons to call you tomorrow."

"Oh," Ade said quietly. "Heavy."

Kris grimaced. "I'm sorry. I wasn't planning on telling you that."

"I'm glad you did." Ade pondered for a moment. "OK. I'll come back with you, but I haven't done this in a long time."

"This as in…?"

"Dating. I tried once, and it didn't end well. So if I act like a naïve teenager, that's why."

Kris nodded and smiled. "OK. I'll bear that in mind, but I'm no gigolo either." A taxi drew up in front of them, and he moved towards it, opening the door and gesturing for Ade to get in. "I should also warn you…I *hate* people sleeping on the couch, so you can have my bed, and I'll go in with Shaunna."

"Or we can share?" Ade suggested.

Kris's heart leapt, and off it went again, bounce, bounce, bounce. "It's a possibility," he said, shakily pulling the door shut behind them.

They didn't talk on the way back. Ade spent most of the ten-minute journey watching out of the window, and if Kris had had his wits about him, he'd have been a better tour guide, not that there were many features of interest in their hometown. He was in a quandary over whether he should send Shaunna advance notice, and by the time he reached a decision, they were pulling up outside the house. The living room lights were on, confirming she was still up.

"I hope she likes me," Ade said so quietly Kris suspected he wasn't supposed to hear it, but he couldn't pretend he hadn't. Shaunna's approval was important to him too.

"She'll love you, I promise." He didn't know where it came from, but all of a sudden he was confident everything would be OK. Surely, something that felt this right had to work out.

They had no chance of making a stealth entry; Casper's little woofs heralded their approach up the path. Kris paused outside the front door.

"Ready?"

Ade nodded.

Kris pushed down on the handle and opened the door a few inches, until the Labrador's muzzle, tea towel in mouth, poked out. "Hey, Caspy." Kris pushed the door fully open, shaking his head at the loony dog's jiggling, his tail a waggy blur. Ade gasped.

"Oh gosh! He's so lovely!" He crouched down to Casper's level. "Hello, handsome." Casper shoved his nose into Ade's hand and released the tea towel. "Is this for me? Thank you very much!" He let the dog have a good sniff of him—a dog person, without a doubt—and straightened up, grinning. "I'm officially smitten."

Grinning back, Kris stepped past, patting the dog on the flank to get him to move. "You can have him," he said, beckoning Ade inside. At the same time, the living room door opened, and Shaunna stepped into the hall. Both she and Ade stopped dead and stared at each other. After a beat, as if mirroring each other's actions, they tilted their heads, taking in each other's hair— Shaunna's fiery curls cascading messily from a sprung comb clip, Ade's gelled copper spikes—leaned left, leaned right, nodded approval and, finally, smiled broadly.

"You must be Ade," Shaunna said, stepping forward.

"And you must be Shaunna," Ade said, moving in for a hug.

"I've heard so much about you," they both said at the same time and giggled.

Shaunna hooked Ade's arm and led him through to the kitchen. Kris followed in their wake. "It's lovely to meet you. Here, let me take that…" Casper's tea towel gift. She handed it off to Kris. "Sorry about the dog hair. If I'd known you were coming, I'd have thrown the hoover around."

"Who cares about a bit of dog hair?" Ade said, picking a clump from his jeans. Shaunna took it from him and handed that to Kris too.

"Do you have a dog?" she asked.

"No, but we had them when I was young. My mum used to take in all the old stinky mutts no-one else wanted."

Discarding the tea towel and dog fluff, Kris edged past to reach the kettle. He was feeling a little surplus to requirements, for which he had only himself to blame. Listening to them chattering away like they'd known each other for years, he was overwhelmed with affection for them both. This could've been an absolute disaster, and his relief was immense, but everything was racing ahead of him, and his stomach was churning with nerves, with excitement, with possibilities for the future.

It was madness. He and Ade hadn't even kissed yet. True, the attraction was undeniable and, from what Ade had said, mutual, but who was to say it wasn't a short-lived infatuation? What if they kissed and discovered it did nothing for them? And if that happened, would Shaunna and Ade stay friends? In the few minutes they'd been acquainted, they'd bonded over the trials of being a *ginger* and losing a parent—Kris now knew Ade's dad had died the same week his ex had moved in with him—and already that bond seemed so much stronger and more permanent than the connection Kris and Ade had spent two days nurturing.

The trouble was, after Jack, Kris was wary of jumping without looking. Shaunna was right about him going 'all in', but in his previous relationships, it had taken him a long time to reach the point where he let go and allowed it to happen. He still had no idea how Jack had sneaked past his defences, and while intrinsically he knew Ade was a totally different and altogether better person, Kris felt the same loss of control now as he had two years ago. It was, honestly, terrifying.

"Kris?"

Shaunna was suddenly next to him, her voice hooking him out of his thoughts.

"Are you all right, hun?"

"Yeah. Why?"

"Are you making tea?" She looked pointedly at the kettle, still in his hands and empty.

"I am!" He took it to the sink and filled it. "Tea or coffee, Ade?"

"Tea, please. Too late for coffee. So, Shaunna, do you work?" Ade was still looking at Kris as he asked and gave him a wink that said *I've got this.*

"I do," Shaunna answered. "I'm a hair stylist."

"Oh, how glam!"

"Ha! Hardly." She paused to drop teabags into the mugs Kris had set out, smirking at him because that was as far as he'd got. He made a quick getaway to the fridge for the milk.

"Well, it sounds glam to me," Ade said.

"Standing on your feet all day, wearing latex gloves and inhaling chemicals and other people's hair?"

"Ew!"

Shaunna snorted a laugh—not at Ade, who kept catching Kris unawares. The way he'd wrinkled his nose…it was cute and sexy and pressed all Kris's buttons. He cleared his throat self-consciously and gave his full effort to finishing making the tea.

"And you're a radio producer?" Shaunna said, still laughing.

"Yes, and it involves no chemicals or latex gloves, although if you saw the state of some of the engineers—honey!" He laid his hand dramatically on Shaunna's arm.

"Some of the actors are a bit suspect too," Shaunna said. The dog gave a woof as if joining in with the tormenting.

Red-faced but no longer caring that they were ganging up on him, Kris took over their tea but didn't join them. He didn't want to get in the way of them getting to know each other.

"May I use your loo?" Ade asked. "I've been bursting since dessert."

"Of course. Top of the stairs, first door on the left."

"Thanks." Ade dashed off.

Shaunna tilted her head, listening. As soon as the bathroom door closed, she whispered, "I love him. He's perfect for you."

"What does that mean?"

She shrugged. "He's sweet and intelligent and fun. And he adores you. And he adores Casper."

"And you."

"We do seem to have hit it off, don't we? We're going to have so much fun together if you can make this work."

"Hey!" Kris nudged her, feeling the weight of the judgement, which had been given in jest, but there was a truth to what she'd said. His insecurities had been a big part of why their marriage failed. Even now, after a successful date and Ade sticking around, he was still thinking *I hope I can be good enough*, not *I am good enough*. If he could find a way past that, then maybe he could make it work. He definitely wanted it to, a fact confirmed when Ade reappeared and floored him with a single, dazzling smile.

"I'm just going to pop upstairs myself," Shaunna said casually, as if Kris wouldn't know it was a ploy to give him and Ade a moment alone and an opportunity to figure out their sleeping arrangements. As she passed Ade in the doorway, she kissed his cheek and murmured, "Welcome aboard."

He watched her leave and then turned back to Kris. "Hello, you."

"Hey."

Ade held out his hands, and Kris took them.

"This is so…" Ade trailed off and shook his head. "I confess, I was a tiny bit worried it would be awkward, but it's not at all. Shaunna is amazing. Casper is an absolute sweetie. And this house…it's everything I thought it would be. I see now why you both stayed. Who'd willingly give up all this?" Ade looked around him in wonder as if he were in the ballroom of a grand country mansion rather than an ordinary kitchen in an ordinary semi-detached house.

Kris tugged gently on Ade's hands to bring him closer. "I know it's weird—"

"Not weird. Different. In a good way."

"OK," Kris conceded. "I just wanted to say thank you for being so accepting of our *different* living arrangements. It means a lot."

Ade moved closer still, their faces only inches apart. "Thank you for being so open with me. I'd tell you it doesn't matter what I think…"

"It does," Kris whispered, closing his eyes as Ade moved their hands out to the sides and reduced the space between them to zero. Ade's scent filled Kris's senses, already so familiar, their chests meeting as they breathed together, in and out, falling into a synchronised rhythm. Kris hardly dared move, afraid of ending what was surely a prelude to their first kiss, but if Ade was holding back because of where they were, then Kris needed to take the lead.

Eyes still closed, he swayed forward, his lips brushing against Ade's, feather-light but electric. Ade gave a tiny gasp, which Kris hoped was because he'd felt it too. Before Kris ruined the moment by asking, Ade freed his hands and slid them around the back of Kris's neck, drawing him into another kiss, firmer than the last. It zinged through every muscle, sparking myriad sensations and making his breath catch in his throat. Ade laughed against his lips.

"What you said in the taxi about giving me your bed for the night…"

"Hmm?"

"Would you consider sharing it with me?"

"Yes."

"Good."

"I only said I'd consider it—"

Ade cut off Kris's tormenting with another kiss, this time with lips parted, breath mingling. Their tongues touched and darted away, then touched again, no longer an intrusion but an invitation. Ade's hands slid down to rest in the small of Kris's back, and Kris mirrored Ade's pose, keeping the kiss going, slowly, lazily, no pressure to do anything more, although it was as arousing as it was comforting.

They could probably have kept going for hours, but the sound of footsteps on the stairs reminded them they were not alone, and they eased apart as the door opened. Shaunna didn't even look at them—Kris envisaged he was as flushed and plump-lipped as Ade. She scooted past, picked up her tea and scooted back again, calling, "Going to bed. Good night!"

"Oops," Ade mumbled and tried to move away, but Kris kept hold of him, watching over his shoulder. Shaunna peered over the banister on her way up the stairs and grinned at him. "Have fun."

A moment later, her bedroom door closed.

"Is she OK?" Ade asked.

Kris smiled. "She's fine. She's giving us some privacy."

"Probably for the best," Ade said, his words merging into a yawn. "Oh God. Sorry."

"Tired?"

"Shattered. It's been a long day."

"Tough one too," Kris reminded him.

"Yeah. Nice end to it, though." Ade smiled sleepily.

"Come on," Kris said, releasing him and taking his hand. "Let's get some sleep."

13: Checklist

Kris

"INEED TO WARN you," Ade said, unfolding the T-shirt and shorts Kris had offered as sleepwear and laying them out on the bed. "I have a couple of bruises on my arms from being…held a bit too tightly."

Midway through threading a pillow into a case, Kris lost his grip on it, and it plumped to the floor. He picked it up and gave it a shake. A really hard shake. "If you want me to leave while you change—"

"Oh, no! I just didn't want you to get a shock, that's all. I bruise easily, you see, and…well, they look a lot worse than they are, I promise."

Kris really hoped he never came face-to-face with Ade's ex, because right at that moment, if they'd been in the same room, Kris may well have got himself into hot water. He wasn't a violent man, far from it, but bullying, abuse, domestic violence—any exercise of power over someone who couldn't fight back—was an instant and devastating trigger for him. And here was this incredible person, attractive, funny, sweet, hurting and trying not to shock, because of a hideous scumbag of an ex-boyfriend. However angry Kris was, it wouldn't help Ade to know it.

As it was, Kris didn't get to see the bruises on Ade's arms, as he shoved his shirt off and pulled the T-shirt on in almost one motion, and it was a size too large for him, so it covered much of his arms. Not so the bruises around his neck. Kris turned away, to conceal his shock, but wasn't quick enough.

A shaky breath escaped Ade. "It's really ugly, I'm sorry."

"That's not why... I just..." Kris turned back and made sure Ade saw him looking at the bruises and not shying away. "I can't believe someone would do this to you."

Ade bristled. "Don't pity me, please. That makes me feel worse."

"It's not pity. I want to get in a taxi right now and hunt that bastard down."

"It's not your fight. It's mine."

Ade's eyes beseeched Kris to let it go, and he was trying, but it was hard with the purple bruises that clearly formed the impression of two hands around Ade's neck, symmetrical thumb prints below his Adam's apple. Suddenly the urge to hold Ade overwhelmed him, and Kris pulled him in tightly.

"Oh God, Ade. He could've killed you."

"Yes. He could, but he didn't," Ade said, or that was what it sounded like. His voice was muffled by Kris's shoulder. Ade laughed and jutted his chin against Kris's collarbone. "Could you let me go?"

"Sorry." Kris loosened his grip, but he didn't—couldn't—let go completely. He backstepped, steering Ade towards the bed. "Which side would you like?"

"I don't care."

Kris released him, finally, and stood back to give him the choice.

"It's your bed. Get in it and I'll follow."

Kris huffed in protest but moved to the left side of the bed. He paused again. Ade nodded to encourage him. Kris got into bed, and Ade climbed in next to him.

For a while, they lay on their backs, side by side, arms touching from shoulder to fingertip, the spark of arousal from earlier lost. Kris was desperate to hold Ade, but seeing his bruises had been a painful reminder of the importance of consent at every stage, and he'd already mis-stepped.

Ade slid his hand under Kris's and laced their fingers together. "Is that OK?"

"Yes."

"Are you going to turn out the light?"

"Soon." Letting go, Kris rolled onto his side and propped up on his elbow so he could look at Ade as he spoke. "I haven't done this in a long time either."

"Slept with the light on?"

"Spent the night with someone."

"You share a house with Shaunna."

Kris sighed in mock exasperation. "Bringing someone back... not that I've ever brought anyone back here, but you know what I mean."

Ade smiled up at him. "I do," he said, the smile becoming a frown. "I don't think I've ever spent the night with someone I wanted to."

Kris reached across and smoothed his fingers over Ade's cheek, trying to make sense of his mixed emotions—sadness that Ade had never experienced this before, elation at being someone he wanted to spend the night with... "I feel like we've done this forever. What I said earlier about new relationships and that you can't have the closeness without sex? It's the furthest thing from my mind right now. I mean, I'm not saying no to sex if it's something you want..."

"What's in your head?" Ade asked.

"What d'you mean?"

"When you think about us, now, what do you see?"

Kris lowered his eyes. "I don't know if I should tell you because it's kind of...lovey-dovey."

"Come on," Ade goaded. "Tell me."

"OK, well...I see birthday cards and breakfast in bed, watching fireworks together, opening Champagne and drinking Bucks Fizz on Christmas morning." Kris met Ade's gaze and found no ridicule there. Just the soft glow of the bedside lamp and maybe something more before Ade's eyelids began to droop.

Kris switched off the light and shuffled down under the duvet, taking care not to jostle the bed. Ade stirred anyway and nestled his cheek in Kris's hand.

"Mmm, this is nice," he murmured drowsily.

"Can I put my arm around you? Is that OK?"

"Uh-huh."

Kris rested his arm lightly on Ade's side. "Good night," he whispered, placing a soft kiss on his palm.

***

Ade

"GOOD MORNING."

Ade took a second to get his bearings before opening his eyes and smiling at the vision of a perfect start to the day. "Good morning."

"Sorry to wake you, but I wasn't sure what time you needed to leave."

"What time is it?" Ade asked.

"Just gone six."

"Are you working today?"

"This afternoon."

Ade rolled onto his side, bringing him closer to Kris, and snuggled in. It was so blissful. Comfy, cosy. Safe.

"Can we stay here a little longer?"

Kris kissed him on the forehead. "Of course."

*

"...It's almost nine."

Ade slid up into a sitting position and watched Kris sidestep along the wall to set a mug of coffee on the cabinet on Ade's side of the bed.

"How did you know?"

"That you were a coffee-in-the-morning person? You have it at work, plus your comment last night about it being too late for coffee implied you usually drink it rather than tea. Did I do bad?"

"Not at all. Thank you. You're very observant." Ade waited for Kris to move to the other side of the bed and then pulled back the covers in preparation for getting his phone to call work. He could go in over the weekend to catch up if need be, but for now, he wanted to stay in this idyllic escape, free from the stress of Fergus's constant harassment.

"What would you like for breakfast?" Kris asked. "Can you eat OK now?"

"I managed the meal last night."

"Kashmiri chicken curry for breakfast?"

Ade laughed. "Maybe not. Give me a minute to make this call and then we can discuss it."

"I'll go give you some privacy."

"No need. I'm only ringing work to tell them I won't be in today."

"OK." Kris picked up his coffee and ebook reader and settled back against the headboard.

The call started out well enough. Ade worked flexibly, and he frequently did more hours than he was contracted for, so his boss was fine with him taking the day off. It was what came next that threw him straight back into turmoil.

"Your mate from upstairs is sitting with me. I'll hand you over. See you tomorrow."

"Yeah, bye." This couldn't be good.

"Hi, Ade."

"Hey, Pip. What's up?"

"You-know-who turned up here this morning."

"What?"

"Yep. He was getting in the lift as I arrived. Apparently, he told the guard you forgot your lunch."

Ade was on his feet, too agitated to stay still.

"What time was that?" he asked but missed her response when he caught sight of his reflection. The colour had drained from his face and neck, and the bruises were dark as a thunderstorm sky. Nauseated, he turned away and tried to tune back in to what Pip was saying, but he'd heard enough to get the gist.

"I'm sorry, Ade. I didn't know how else to get rid of him."

"It's OK. I'll call him now. Thanks, Pip. Love you." Ade hung up and slumped down on the bed, staring at his phone screen. Not a single missed call or text, and *still* Fergus was getting what he wanted. What was the point in even trying to get away from him?

"Ade?"

He brought up Fergus's number, but his hands were shaking and he accidentally clicked the wrong button.

Block and report? Confirm/Cancel

Kris's face appeared in front of him. "Ade, what's happened?"

He clicked *Cancel* and locked his phone. "He went into work looking for me. Pip saw him charm his way past the security guard and intercepted before he reached the studio. She thought that's where I'd be. She told him I didn't want to see him, and he acted like she was lying and asked her to pass on a message."

"Which is?"

"He wants what's his and he loves me."

"He wants what's his? Has he got clothes at your place?"

"That and…he means me. He thinks I belong to him. And yes, I know it's insane, but he thinks because he financially supported me when I was an intern, he owns me."

Kris shrugged. "I financially supported Shaunna when Krissi was little. I don't own her."

"I'm not saying I agree with him. But that's how his mind works, and he has a point. I do owe him."

Kris drank his coffee and stayed quiet, but what he thought was patently clear.

"Plus, there is still quite a lot of his stuff in my apartment," Ade added.

"Does he have a key?"

"Not anymore. I'm going to have to go home." The thought of what he was going back to made him want to abandon the flat and everything in it, but damn it, he'd worked his backside off to keep it this long. He couldn't just walk away.

"Do you want me to come with you?" Kris asked.

"Thanks, but no. It'll make him worse, and I need to deal with it."

"So what will you do? Leave his things outside?"

"That's my plan." Ade opened the notes app on his phone and visualised his apartment, trying to recall everything that belonged to Fergus.

"What are you doing there?" Kris asked casually, though his expression was anything but.

"Making a list of Ferg's things."

"So that's his name."

"Yeah." Ade paused, surprised he hadn't mentioned him by name to Kris before now. He hadn't intentionally avoided doing so; despite Kris's remark about hunting Fergus down, he was a very gentle, albeit persistent man.

"Didn't you say you were together for ten years?"

"Yeah. Why?"

"No reason really..."

Ade gave Kris a pointed look.

"All right. I was thinking about all the stuff in this house. Other than our clothes, toiletries, jewellery and whatnot, none of it's mine *or* Shaunna's. It's *ours*."

"You were married."

"True. I'm not sure it matters, though, because if you're sharing a living space, don't the fixtures and fittings belong to you both?"

"Well, legally, I suppose it's all mine, as my name's on the mortgage, but there's no point fighting him when some of it's always been more his than mine."

"Like?" Kris pressed. No doubt he had Ade's best interests at heart, but it was stressing him out. He went back to his checklist, saying aloud each item as he added it.

"The TV. The stereo is fifty-fifty, but he can have it. What else in the living room? The PlayStation's mine...I think that's it. In the kitchen—"

"I'm sorry, but I don't understand this," Kris interrupted. "What do you mean, the TV's his? Did he buy it?"

"He chose it. I didn't really want one that big."

"So *you* bought it?"

"We bought it together."

"Then it's yours too."

"It's only a TV."

Kris pursed his lips, but Ade knew what he was thinking. *It's only a TV... It's only a stereo...* The rate he was going, there'd be nothing left.

With a great deal of care, Kris put down his cup and rounded the bed. "Shower," he mumbled as he left the room.

Heated towel rail Ade added miserably to the list because it was a compulsion. People commented all the time on how organised he was; none of them realised he couldn't stop. Except maybe Kris had.

At least when Kris returned from his shower, Ade had managed to set aside his phone and drink his coffee. He smiled and shrugged in defeat.

"You're right," he admitted. "But what can I do? If I don't give him what he wants, he'll keep coming back again and again."

Kris sat on the edge of the bed and took Ade's hand. "I'm sorry about the way I spoke to you before. I kind of lose my mind when it comes to people like him."

"I've noticed," Ade muttered with no venom at all. "And I know that even if I do give him all that stuff, he'll find other reasons to keep coming back. I just want him to leave me alone."

"If I can help you, tell me. I'll be there. I promise."

"Thank you." Ade looked up and smiled again, with a little more feeling. "It's not the best way to woo someone, is it?"

Kris leaned sideways and kissed his cheek. "I feel very wooed," he said playfully.

Ade rolled his eyes.

"I'm joking, Ade. Or kind of joking. I'd gladly spend the rest of the day in bed together, but not when you have this looming over you, unless you wanted to?" Kris shook his head, swallowed... turned pink. "What I mean is, I'm not rejecting you, but I'm trying not to put any pressure on you either. Does that make any sense at all? You know what? I'm just going to shut up. I don't—"

Ade kissed him, and that did shut him up but also put temptation in Ade's way, as Kris tasted delicious, of mint and cologne, and he was wearing only a towel.

Ade eased back from the kiss. "It makes perfect sense, but I'm not made of porcelain, and you don't need to protect me. In fact, I'd rather you didn't try so hard to do the right thing."

That wasn't true, as being cared for was quite a turn-on, and he loved that Kris paid such attention to how his actions might put Ade under duress. But he'd achieve nothing by delaying. He needed to go home and sort out his apartment, then face Fergus.

Face Fergus. Two words with the power to make him tremble until he thought he might shatter to pieces, but he was going to bloody well do it, even if it meant giving Fergus every last piece of furniture in the apartment. This was it. The end of the road. Do or die. *I hope it's do.*

14: Trouble Ahead

Ade

"Ade, Ade! I've been worried sick!"

"Sorry, Mary. I stayed at a friend's place last night."

"And a good thing it is too. He was here first thing this morning, hammering on the door and swearing loudly enough to wake the dead." Mary cupped her hand around her mouth and muttered conspiratorially, "Even old Benny heard him, and his hearing aids haven't worked since that time he washed them in Fairy Liquid. Anyway, Benny ordered him to leave or else he'd get the police and then threatened him with that starting pistol he keeps next to the bed—don't ask how I know that. It's very private."

If ever there was an invitation to ask, that was it, but Ade had no intention of encouraging her. The mental image of toothless Mary and whiskery old Benny getting it on was not one he wanted to explore.

"So," Mary continued, "Fergus told him to eff off or he'd call the effing police himself."

Ade laughed, despite how scared he was, but he had a new weapon of his own today: resolve. Whether it would be enough, he didn't know, but for the first time in as long as he could recall, he was thinking about the future, and it was Fergus-free. That future may or may not include Kris in the longer term; for now, he featured very prominently, as did Shaunna. New friends, a new beginning. Hope. All he had to do was put the past behind him and move on.

If only it were 'all'.

"Mary, can you do me a favour?"

"Of course, lovey."

Ade unlocked his front door, grabbed the notepad from the table in the hallway and copied a number from his phone. He ripped off the top page and gave it to his neighbour. "If anything happens to me, will you call this number?"

Mary pulled her glasses down from the top of her head and peered through them at what Ade had written. "Kris?"

"Yes. The friend…" Ade paused and rephrased. "He's my date from last night—I'll tell you all about it another time," he said when Mary clutched her emergency call button in delight. "But if it…if it gets bad, no-one will know to tell him."

"Oh, Ade. You're not planning on doing something silly, are you?"

"No!" However low Fergus had driven him over the years, he'd never thought that was his only way out.

"Promise me."

"I'm just going to tell him to leave me alone."

"How many times have you told him before?"

"And then let him come crawling back, I know. Not this time."

Mary nodded. "All right, I'll call this Kris if…" She scurried away without saying it, but Ade heard Kris's words from the night before. *He could've killed you.* Fergus was no murderer; he just got off on power and control. But when that red mist descended…

Ade fled inside his apartment, fumbling the key with shaking hands to lock the door behind him. He leaned back against it and took a minute to steady himself, as always on high alert, listening for signs of danger, but all was quiet.

Safe for now, he headed for the kitchen, thinking it would be the easiest place to start, and almost fell at the first hurdle. In his haste to meet Kris the previous day, he'd dumped the empty wine bottles on the side and ignored the pile of dishes in the sink. He could only assume Fergus had been juggling toast, as there were crumbs and smears of butter across every surface, and something plastic had melted onto the stove top—the rings from a four-pack of baked beans or beer, it didn't matter which. It was just one more mess to clean up.

The action was automatic, reaching for his phone to make a list of jobs, and he had the app open before he talked himself out of it and instead grabbed the egg slice and set to work on removing the molten plastic mess. It was stuck fast. Swapping the useless egg slice for the butter knife, he jabbed at the least stuck edge. The knife slipped and took a strip of enamel off the stove.

That was when the tears started, but Ade wasn't giving in yet. He'd leave the stove for later, deal with the things he could do.

Leave the wine bottles by the door to take out later. Check.

Wash the dishes. Check.

Wipe down the surfaces. Check.

He kept track in head—everyone did that, he was sure—and moved on to the living room, which wasn't too bad, since he'd removed all the dirty dishes and cleaned up the glass yesterday. He sat on the sofa and picked up the two halves of the TV remote, flipping them and sliding them against each other, but the lugs had snapped and they wouldn't stay together. He supposed it made no difference if Fergus was taking the TV anyway.

Leaning forward to put the remote on the table, he froze as a chill spread across his lower back. A literal chill.

"He's pissed on the sofa."

Ade leapt to his feet and stared at the dark circle on the seat cushion. It didn't matter whether Fergus had done it on purpose or not, and he'd probably just been so drunk he wet himself; after a night of soaking in, the smell would never come out. Something else ruined. He yanked each cushion from its cover, his disgust at the sensation of the heavy, damp fabric dissolving into tears.

How foolish to imagine he could simply cast Fergus out and move forward as if they'd never met. It wasn't just the physical reminders of piss stink and scratched cookers, scars and healed fractures. Even now, with so many people on the outskirts of his life prepared to go into battle for him, the years of anguish, of existing in constant fear of harm and humiliation formed an impossible barrier. He couldn't accept their help, but he couldn't do this on his own either. It was hopeless, futile. This was his lot.

Stuffing the cushion covers into the washing machine, he overfilled the detergent drawer and chose the hottest cycle, startling when water surged into the drum. He whipped his head around in panic even though he knew Fergus wasn't there. Or not in body. He was always in Ade's head, tearing to shreds everything he'd achieved, extinguishing every glimmer of hope, a noxious, bloated cloud suffocating everything that was good in his life.

Snot and tears itched his face as he whirled around the apartment like a dust devil, stirring up chaos. The patio chair was broken. There was a crack in the left pane of the French doors, a gouge in the frame. The more he tried to fix and clean and make it right, the weaker he became until he slumped, spineless and jelly-like, onto his bed.

How had he let Fergus do this to him? In high school, like Kris, Ade had been out and proud—a mouthy little shit, his sister used to call him, since the bullies he took on sought her out, expecting her to take him in hand. She'd stood up for him, of course, and a few years later, he'd been able to return the favour when the boyfriend she'd thought was The One had given her chlamydia and then had the audacity to ask Ade to talk her into giving him another chance. She almost did go back to him, even though their parents, Ade, her friends and colleagues all hated him. He was a pilot who worked for the same airline she had at the time, older, charismatic in a sleazy kind of way, and a terminal womaniser. Ade hadn't held back in telling her he was making a fool of her.

He'd been so naïve, arrogant really, thinking he'd never ever fall into the trap she had, but men like that pilot and Fergus were master manipulators, emotional con artists who hit you at your weakest, like a tick you didn't notice until they'd got a good firm grip and sucked half your life away. It was easy for others to say *just pluck it out*. That was what Ade had said before he was there, on the inside, losing himself to the ruggedly handsome Scotsman who'd offered his broad shoulders for Ade to cry on when his dad died and his family was so wracked with grief that no-one saw it until it was too late.

"How long do I have to put up with your stupid fucking self-indulgent whining. So your dad died. People die all the time. It's pathetic."

At the time, he'd convinced himself that Fergus was being cruel to be kind. Now he knew he was just being cruel, although ironically, it had got him through those first few months of bereavement, because he'd been so caught up in trying to figure out how *not* to make Fergus angry that missing his dad became secondary. By the time Ade started to question whether he really was to blame for the arguments, and that was all they were back then, the acute grief had dissipated, but he was too drained to fight.

His every waking moment was filled with monitoring what he said and did, trying not to rock the boat, and nothing he ever did was right. He was too noisy, disturbing Fergus's lie-in or early night or TV programme. He was creeping around because he was hiding something. He'd let himself go because he wasn't showering enough. He was having an affair because he was showering morning and night. It didn't matter what he did or didn't do, it was a reason for Fergus to attack him, verbally and then physically. Then came the grovelling. Fergus didn't mean it, he'd just lost his temper—he'd do anything for Ade, he loved him. Would he talk to a therapist about his anger? Yes, Fergus said, if you come with me. So Ade booked an appointment, briefly optimistic until Fergus lied through his teeth.

"I may have lashed out once or twice, but we talked it through, and we're OK about it now, aren't we, Adrian?"

Ade remembered nodding in agreement and silently vowing to go straight home and pack his stuff, stay at his mum's until Fergus got the message. That was eight years ago.

"Not me. Not my fault. Not my fault." Ade hit stop on the memory replay and unplugged his tablet. He couldn't do this without a checklist.

To go:
1. TV
2. stereo
3. DVDs (top two shelves)
4. …

Tablet in hand, he opened the wardrobe, the drawers and bedside table.

4. Clothes in left wardrobe
5. Shoes
6. Aftershave

He set down his tablet and examined the aftershave bottle, still full. He'd bought it for their first Christmas together, and it hadn't been cheap, but he'd thought it would suit Fergus. He couldn't recall what it smelled like now, but Fergus had hated it, or so he said. Ade popped the stopper out and sniffed. A wave of panic and nausea hit him and sent him into a cold sweat. He quickly shoved the stopper back in lest the genie fully escape and left the aftershave next to the wine bottles in the kitchen.

Back to the bedroom, he continued his inventory of the bedside table.

6. Aftershave
7. Books
8. Condoms

He flipped the box over in his hand. *Fruit-flavoured condoms. Since when?*

9. Get tested

A fury ripped through him, but somehow he stayed in control long enough to put his tablet down. So many of his things had been destroyed over the years that even when all hell was in uproar around him, he had the sense to stash his most valued possessions out of harm's way. Everything except himself because he was worth nothing. Less than nothing.

"No, no, no, no, no, no…" Why did his brain default to this? Because it was easier to be the useless, ugly creature that Fergus had turned him into? Easier not to break the habit? He didn't love Fergus anymore. He wanted him out of his head and his life. He wanted a life, goddammit.

He was a thirty-six-year-old man, apparently not unattractive, with a successful career, a beautiful sister, gorgeous nephew and niece, a lovely mum who never once judged, never once put him on a guilt trip. Kris's reaction to the bruises the night before had given him a flashback to the first time his mum saw them and the fear she tried to hide. But he'd seen it, felt it…was feeling it all over again.

He breathed deeply, in and out, one breath after another. What she must have been going through, like a parent whose child is dying and there's nothing that can be done to save them. Because he was dying, slowly being destroyed by a vicious, vindictive monster who didn't deserve to be that important. His mum was worth more than a million Fergus Campbells.

"And so am I."

Pulling the biggest suitcase off the top of the wardrobe, he took the clothes, shoes, books, the *fucking cheating-and-not-even-bothering-to-hide-the-fact* bastard's condoms and piled it all into the suitcase. Then he climbed onto the bed and knelt on the case, zipping it shut and tugging the two leather straps tight.

High on adrenaline and the release of years of repressed rage, Ade dragged the case to the floor and hauled it out into the hallway. Next, he unplugged the TV and stereo, dumped those in the hallway too, followed by the DVDs, the coffee maker, which was Ade's, but he didn't give a shit, Fergus's favourite mug, which, naturally, he'd bought himself, and any other stupid odds and ends left lying around and claiming ownership of Ade's space. Tie clips, cufflinks, pens, balled, dirty socks, half-eaten chocolate bars—it all went into a bag and out to the hallway.

Lastly, because he was feeling supremely brave or dangerously stupid and regardless, the gesture was overwhelmingly everything, he took the hideous couple portrait photo from where he'd hidden it behind the sofa, removed it from its frame and ripped it in half, straight down the middle. He forced the two halves through the shredder, emptied the resultant heap of paper into an empty shoe box, along with the token apologies—the promise ring, his half of a silver mizpah, the two ceramic bears holding up their lying 'I luv U' heart—

Not once had Fergus apologised for real, actually said the words *I'm sorry*.

—and the finishing touch: Ade took off his watch and bashed it hard against the corner of the table, shattering the screen and sending the little chrome hands into a timeless, satisfying tailspin. He whacked it a couple more times, just to be sure, laid the pieces of the completely destroyed watch on top of the rest of the meaningless trinkets and shredded remnants of their well-and-truly-dead relationship, and stuck the lid of the shoe box firmly shut, wrapping the tape around and around until there was only cardboard left on the roll. Taking a Sharpie, he wrote THE END on the top of the box, put it with everything else and took a step back to admire his efforts. This time they would *not* be in vain.

Next: go and make things right with his boss and Pip.

He didn't have to go very far. As Ade opened the door to leave the building, he almost ran straight into Pip, who immediately flung her arms around him.

"Thank God. I've been calling you for ages!"

"I was dealing with…something."

Pip stepped away and eyed him with concern. "Is he here?"

"No, but I'm going to call him and get him to come for his stuff."

"Ade—"

"I've packed it for him and left it in the hall."

"Ade, you know—"

"I'm done, Pip. I can't keep going through this."

Pip's expression remained unchanged.

"It's the last time, I swear. Are you free later?"

"Why?" she asked suspiciously. "Do you want me to chair yet another reconciliation?"

Ade delayed answering. For as much as this was his fight and he didn't want to embroil her in it, he thought he might need a witness.

"I'm doing this for real, Pip. It's over."

She sighed and kept shifting her eyes between him and the building, her expression doubtful, and who could blame her?

"What do you need me to do? Supervise and make sure he doesn't take anything he shouldn't?"

"No. I need you to supervise me. Make sure I don't fall for his bullshit again."

Pip nodded solemnly, and Ade hugged her.

"Thank you. For everything," he said sincerely.

"Don't," she croaked. "Or I'll cry." Too late.

Ade held her tightly, gulping back his own tears, but they were no longer tears of hopelessness or frustration. They were tears of relief and maybe a little bit of grief.

"You mustn't let him come back, Ade, you mustn't. I'm so scared one day he's going to…"

"I know, I know. Shh." He stroked her hair, snuffling his nose into it and inhaling a few strands. He snorted them out again, along with some snot. She poked him in the side, feebly indignant, and they both laughed and cried together for a little while longer before setting off, arm in arm, for the radio station.

"Where did you stay last night?" she asked, trying to pass off her nosiness as concern. Ade hummed secretively. Pip gasped. "Were you with him?"

"Who?" Ade asked innocently.

"That guy from Monday morning?"

"Maaaaybe."

"No way. What's his name? Is he an actor? What did you do? Did you get up to anything—"

"Kris, yes, went for a meal, and no."

"Oh." Pip looked dead ahead, her cherub cheeks colouring up. She peered sideways at Ade and grinned. He was pretty sure they had matching blushes. "Are you seeing him again?" she asked.

"Yes. I think so. I hope so." He really did. Pip squeezed his arm with hers until he squeaked.

"He seemed nice," she said.

"He is. And so's his wife."

Pip stopped walking and narrowed her eyes. "You're such a wind-up…"

His mouth twitched as he fought the smile.

"You're serious?" she said.

Ade nodded.

"He's married. To a woman? Ade!"

He burst into laughter. "It's not like that. Come on."

They moved off again, and Ade explained properly about Kris and Shaunna being separated, and Casper, and Kris's stepdaughter, and his shellfish allergy, and so on, chattering away the entire ten-minute walk to the studio. When they parted company at the fourth floor, Pip still didn't look fully convinced, but he promised he'd keep her posted on any developments and confirm the arrangements for later as soon as he'd spoken to Fergus. He was dreading it, but for the first time ever, he was confident he could see it through. A few hours from now, Fergus would be out of his life, for good.

15: Ginger

Kris

Kris kept checking his phone, hoping to see a missed call or a text message—anything to confirm that he was worrying over nothing. He'd tried to convince himself he was being paranoid, but the longer that passed without contact, the greater his anxiety that Ade had done something awful...or something awful had been done to him.

Rationally, there was no reason Ade would have called. He'd only left a few hours ago, and they hadn't known each other for much longer than that. Whatever was going on was really none of Kris's business.

But maybe he should have been clearer about wanting it to be his business. To him, this wasn't just another chance meeting through work, and if that was all it was to Ade, wouldn't last night have involved a little less sleep and cuddling and a lot more action?

So I'm being pessimistic...and ignoring the bigger picture. Or trying to, at least. It was far easier to pretend Ade was being ordinarily dismissive than the real reasons he wouldn't think to call—or couldn't call.

In an attempt at distraction, Kris took the dog for a long walk, but that still left an hour of sitting at home, going out of his mind with worry, and Shaunna was at work, so there was no voice of reason to reassure him that he was overthinking it, focusing only on what could go wrong instead of all that, so far, had gone right. Ade would be at work, that's all. And if his ex turned up there again, someone would call the police.

He'll be fine. But what if—

No. Mustn't think like that.

Kris could stand it no longer. He grabbed his coat and headed for the salon where Shaunna worked.

"Just send him a text," she suggested without looking away from the straighteners she was pulling through a woman's hair that was so over-bleached it crackled with the heat.

"The wrong person might see it."

"Wouldn't he keep his phone in his pocket or somewhere it can't be seen?"

"And then he opens the message and they ask who it's from—"

"Surely, he'd be able to sneak off to the loo to read a message?"

"I don't even know if he's at home or at work. He could even be in the hospital or—"

"Kris, stop it!" Shaunna's raised voice drew the attention of her boss, who had been sitting behind the counter, reading a magazine. Now she came over and took the straighteners from Shaunna and nodded towards the stockroom behind the salon, where they could talk in privacy.

Kris followed Shaunna through into the dimly lit room. It was vast, stacked with plastic bottles and smelled strongly of chemicals but with coconut overtones.

"How about this?" Shaunna suggested. "I'll call him, number withheld."

"I don't want to involve you in this."

"I already am involved, hun."

Kris wanted to tell her to leave it, but how could he, when every time he closed his eyes, all he could see was the bruising around Ade's neck?

"Give me your phone," Shaunna said.

"But—"

"Give me your phone or give me his number."

"I really don't think it's a—"

"I don't care what you think. Well, I do, but whatever. Hand over the phone or else."

She glared at him until he relented and handed over his phone, then, withholding the number, she called Ade. It went to voicemail. At the cue to leave a message, she said in a prim telephone voice, "This is Ms. Hennessy of the recently formed Ginger Appreciation Society, looking after the well-being of those possessed of red hair everywhere. We wondered if you'd be available to join us for our next meeting and would be most grateful if you could call at your earliest convenience, quoting reference Casper. Thanks so much. Bye now."

She hung up and passed the phone back to Kris, her serious expression completely at odds with the ludicrous cryptic message she'd left. At any other time, it would have made Kris laugh, but not this time. He blinked at her in bewilderment. She smiled and gave him a gentle hug. There was nothing she could say to dispel his anxiety, but at least Ade would know he was worried, and with any luck, he'd check in to confirm all was well.

"I need to go to work," Kris said, reluctantly stepping away. "How the hell am I supposed to do that?"

"You're a professional. You'll find a way."

"I might call in sick and go and find him." Kris realised the futility of the idea as he was saying it, because he couldn't imagine his actions being anything other than a hindrance, whatever situation Ade might be in. "Maybe I'll just go home and wait."

"You'll be able to get to him a lot quicker from work than here," Shaunna reasoned. It was true; the two radio stations were barely half a mile apart, and if Ade lived nearby, Kris could be there in a matter of minutes.

"OK. I'm going," he said. They returned to the salon and he gave Shaunna a swift parting hug. "Thank you."

"You're welcome. If you hear anything…" Shaunna called after him. He nodded his agreement and left for the train station.

***

Ade

Ade took out his phone and unlocked the screen for about the twentieth time in the past quarter of an hour, just to look at the missed call and voicemail notifications. He was alone in his office so could have listened to the message or called back without being overheard, but should he?

At least Fergus was a known quantity, not that Ade had any intention of backing down when he'd made it this far, but it was utter folly to go haring from one relationship straight into another. OK, technically he wasn't doing that, as he'd officially ended things with Fergus a year ago. Still, he should wait, give himself a few months properly on his own, doing what he wanted whenever he wanted, without having to think about someone else's needs like he'd been doing for the past eleven years. Shouldn't he?

The first time Fergus had left, Ade had missed him like crazy and hated himself for it. That was when he started to understand how it worked. Fergus had slapped him, and Ade had screamed at him to get out. It had been such a shock that it left him emotionally numb for days, and while his defences were down, Fergus had whittled away at him with promises he'd make it up to him and it would never happen again. He was devastated, or so he'd claimed. He didn't know what he was doing, Ade had made him angry and over what? He'd bought green apples and Fergus wanted red.

What Ade wished he'd done was ram one of the apples down Fergus's throat. What he actually did was apologise for his mistake and hold Fergus while he cried and begged for forgiveness. Then the mind games began, one minute calling Ade a cissy for acting like he'd been stabbed, not slapped, the next showering him with presents and more tears and promises. All lies.

Ten years of going around and around. Each time Ferg lashed out, the walls of the cycle grew taller, became more impenetrable, until Ade could no longer see a way out. So he'd ended the relationship, yet here he was, a year later, still clawing at those walls.

Then there was the wonderful safe cocoon of last night. Ade had no idea he was so tired, but it wasn't that surprising when he was constantly on edge, always self-monitoring, avoiding the dreaded 'R' in conversation with strangers, avoiding setting Ferg off when he was anywhere near or waiting for him to suddenly appear from nowhere with that glint in his eyes, the sneer—

Ade made a quick dash from his office to the toilet at the end of the corridor and retched, no vomiting, but it still burned his insides. It also gave him pause, for a moment crowding out the image of Ferg and the dread that came with it, displaced by a random, self-sabotaging thought.

And I love seafood.

He sluiced his mouth with tap water and gave his face a quick splash before returning to his office. It was true. Mussels and scallops were his all-time favourite things to eat, but if he and Kris had a future, there would be no more seafood medleys or prawn puris or butterfly king prawns and definitely no more mussels and scallops.

Was that really enough reason to turn his back on the chance of a new relationship, especially when it wasn't the reason at all?

Since he'd arrived at work, he'd done nothing but go over and over the last forty-eight hours and in the process convinced himself that Kris was no better than Fergus. And how had he achieved this rather impressive, all-in-one annihilation of what he suspected was the prelude to a wonderful, teenager-foolish, tumbling head-over-heels courtship? By focusing on the one and only thing Fergus and Kris had in common: cheating.

Of course, he didn't know for sure Fergus *had* cheated, because leaving the condoms where Ade would find them served more nefarious purposes, taunting him with the possibility while giving Fergus ammunition to throw back at Ade for snooping and not trusting him. Win-win—for Fergus, whether he'd cheated or not, and honestly, Ade didn't care if he had. Maybe he wasn't worth more, maybe he was, but it didn't matter, because Kris had admitted straight up. He'd had an affair—an affair he was ashamed of. And really, how stupid would it be to go from a relationship where he literally feared for his life to one with a cheat?

Before he tumbled any further down the rabbit hole of that thought, some form of self-preservation kicked in, and he picked up his phone. *I'll just text Kris and tell him I need some breathing space.* That was what he planned to do. What his subconscious decided on his behalf was to call his voicemail.

You have one new message.

His thumb hovered over the delete button, but he left it too late.

First new message.

This is Ms. Hennessy of the recently formed Ginger Appreciation Society...

16: Brave

Ade

ADE LET THE message play, smiling, and then laughing out loud at 'quoting reference Casper'. He saved the message and sat back in his chair, reconsidering his options.

He still didn't want to call Kris. True, he had an issue with the affair, but he was projecting, and it wasn't fair on either of them, particularly Kris. No, what he needed to do was clarify the situation, for his own peace of mind, and that meant talking to Shaunna, except he didn't have her phone number. But he did know what she looked like, and she was distinctive enough, with her long, wavy, so incredibly beautiful red hair, that he'd be able to recognise her profile pic, as long as it was of her and not an avatar, although that would probably still have long red hair.

Ignoring the voice calling him a paranoid snoop, Ade went online and searched the social networks, first for 'Kristian Johansson', which brought up the professional profiles he'd already seen. Next, he tried 'Kris Johansson', which did the trick, but his profile was locked down and Ade couldn't access Kris's list of friends, although he felt his heart pumping that little bit faster at the sight of Kris's profile photo. Not the cheesy fake smile on his pro shots, but the genuine article, radiating real happiness; Ade spent a moment studying it before he changed his search to 'Shauna Johansson'. After ten minutes of going forwards and backwards between the list and the profiles of the seemingly infinite number of Shauna Johanssons in this world, Ade paused to rethink his approach.

The only other information he had was that Kris and Shaunna's daughter was called Krissi, so he typed in 'Krissi Johansson' and was duly rewarded with a fully accessible profile of the stunning young woman from Kris's phone pics—there really was no mistaking the similarity to her mother in facial features.

By this point feeling like a stalker for real, although he'd come this far so he might as well continue, Ade delved into Krissi's friends list and scrolled down...a little more...and a little bit more...and there, finally, was her mum. Shaunna—with a double 'n'—Hennessy.

"Hennessy. Of course!" Ade resisted berating himself for being an idiot and not realising sooner. The treasure hunt over, he clicked on 'Send Message'.

> Hi Shaunna. I hope you don't mind me contacting
> you like this. Are you free to talk?

Before he had a chance to regret pressing 'send', the three dots appeared.

> Hi Ade – at work. Give me your number and I'll call
> you in 5.

He did that, and then he sat, repeatedly watching his phone screen darken and reactivating it, wishing they were doing this through text rather than talking, as there was no getting around the letter 'R', given the reason for making contact. Strangely, Ade was far less bothered by that than usual. Five minutes passed by, and then six; he was just at the point of convincing himself she wouldn't call when his screen lit up by itself: unknown number. He answered the call with a cautious, "Hello?"

"Ade?"

"Yes."

"Hiya. Are you OK?"

"Yes, thanks. Are you?"

"I'm fine, hun. Sorry about the voicemail. Kris was stressing, and he didn't want to cause more problems for you."

Ade laughed lightly. "Ginger Appreciation Society—I love it."

"We should totally start one, if there isn't one already."

"We totally should," Ade agreed. He hadn't planned out what he wanted to say, but Shaunna must've been able to tell he was preparing to say something, as she stayed quiet. After a fairly lengthy pause, he found his tongue. "Kris told me a bit about how you ended up separated."

"Right?"

Ade continued hesitantly, "And that he had an affair?"

"Ah. Well, it kind of wasn't an affair. I mean, I didn't know about it, but it wasn't really behind my back, and he was a bit bonkers at the time. To be quite honest, I think Jack took advantage of the fact that Kris wasn't able to think it through."

"He could've said no," Ade reasoned, fully aware he was playing devil's advocate. Saying no to Jack Malton was only marginally easier than saying no to Fergus Campbell. "And if you were still together, then doesn't that count as cheating?"

"Yes, but…not?" Shaunna paused, and Ade jumped in.

"I'm sorry. Kris told me you were separated when it happened—"

"But you wanted to check he was telling the truth," she guessed.

"Not at all. I mean, I do have trust issues…but he was the one who called it cheating."

"OK. Well…the thing is…hold on." Shaunna paused again, and Ade heard a door close. "Sorry. My boss is lovely, but she has bat ears, and this isn't mine to share. And before you ask, no, I shouldn't be telling you, but I saw you and Kris together last night—"

"It was very disrespectful," Ade said, ashamed.

"Kissing in my kitchen?" Shaunna laughed. "It's fine, hun, honestly, but I meant the chemistry between you, which is why I think you need to hear this. Kris would've got around to telling you himself eventually, and he'll probably go ballistic when he finds out I've jumped in first, but..."

"Forewarned is forearmed," Ade said.

"My mum used to say that, and she'd finish off with, 'Like Vishnu—wouldn't that be a godsend? Then I could do the dishes and plait your hair at the same time and never be late for work again!'"

Ade laughed. "That's brilliant! I think your mum and mine would've got on like a house on fire."

"Yeah. She was amazing. I miss her every day."

"Aww. I'd give you a hug right now if I could."

"Save it for me."

"Promise," Ade said. Shaunna was so easy to talk to and so gorgeous, any guy would be lucky to be with her. For those reasons and because it was taking her an awfully long time to tell him this thing, he knew that whatever had come between her and Kris had been a lot bigger and more devastating than a poorly judged bout of extramarital intimacy.

"OK," she said finally, "I'm just going to put it right out there. Kris was sexually abused by his great-uncle."

"Oh." The word was little more than an escaped breath that Ade had to fight to replenish. His chest ached and his stomach cramped as if invisible hands had invaded his windpipe, twisting and knotting his insides.

"So the affair..." Shaunna continued, possibly *not* oblivious to how the news had walloped Ade, "I'm pretty sure Jack went after Kris, knowing he'd keep the secret, because as far as the world is concerned, Jack's a happily married heterosexual man. He's a disgrace."

Shaunna didn't hide her anger, and Ade was waiting for it to descend on him too, but it didn't. In an instant, he'd plummeted from level-ten gut-wrenching shock into a calm peacefulness that settled over everything like a soft, warm blanket.

After a minute or two of Ade saying nothing, Shaunna asked, "Are you still there?"

"Yes. Sorry. I was thinking. Did Kris tell you what's going on with me?"

"He gave me the basics."

"That's all I gave him, really, but I could tell when I told him…" There'd been something.

"Kindred spirits," Shaunna said.

"Yeah. God, men are bastards."

"Not all of them. I know at least a couple of good ones. There probably isn't anything I can do, but if you need me at all…"

"Thanks, Shaunna. That means so much. Please can you tell Kris I'm OK and I'll call him later?"

"I'll ring him as soon as we're off the phone. I guess you know he's completely fallen for you."

"Has he?" Ade squeaked in surprise. Even though Kris had told him as much, hearing it from Shaunna added extra validation, despite her giggling at his reaction, which set him off giggling too. *Hysteria*, he decided. That, and a sense of wonder.

"And in case it escaped your notice, which wouldn't be surprising in the circumstances, I think we've hit it off pretty well too."

Ade smiled and nodded, not that she could see. "We have, haven't we? And I could happily chat to you all day, but I'd better let you get back to work."

"All right, hun. You've got my number now, so just call, OK?"

"Will do. Look after him for me?"

"Of course! And you take care of yourself."

"I'll try," Ade said and ended the call. "OK. Let's get this show on the road." His determination renewed, he brought up that number for what he hoped was the last time.

It rang out, once, twice—

"Fergus Campbell."

"Hey, it's Ade."

Fergus didn't respond.

"I'll be home at five. Come and get your stuff." Ade hung up, deleted Fergus's number from his favourites and dropped his phone onto the desk. His hands were shaking so much he had to grab the arms of his chair to still them.

He wasn't sure how long he sat there, playing out all the ways this evening could go wrong, before his phone beeped with a notification that he couldn't access because his fingers had gone numb. He was expecting a terse text message from Fergus, but there was nothing from him at all. Instead, there was a friend request from Shaunna, with a message—*whatever happens*—and a text message from Kris.

> Glad you're OK. I'm going to hang around at work,
> so I'm close by. x

Unworthy, said the voice in Ade's head, at the same time as the knock came, followed by Pip's cautiously smiling face peeking around the door. Ade growled in exasperation.

"I came to see if—"

"Yes. I'm fine," Ade snapped. "I just wish everyone would leave me alone!"

Pip shrugged. "You got it," she said and stepped back out, banging the door shut.

"Shit." Ade bolted from his chair and ran after her. "Pip, wait! I'm sorry. Please?"

She was already halfway to the lift, but she stopped and turned around. "You asked me to come!" Her quietly hissed words sounded a lot angrier than if she'd been yelling at the top of her voice. "I know you, Ade. You're frightened, and you have every right to be, but don't you dare push me away, not now, not after everything you've been through. *We've* been through."

She stood before him, looming vast and formidable, even though at five foot three her head only reached Ade's nose. He was stunned by her anger, but it was justified, and she was right. She'd been at his side through it all, witnessed Fergus systematically destroying him. Not once had she grumbled when Ade asked her to take him to hospital or to come and stay over because Fergus had left but he might come back. Through all of it, Pip had been there, and now Ade was telling her he didn't need her, but he did. He really did.

"I'm sorry," he said quietly.

"Whatever," Pip said. "Don't you think I want this to be over too?"

Ade nodded but kept his head bowed. "I didn't mean to shout at you. I'm trying to keep it together so I'm in right frame of mind to face him." Ade looked at his wrist. "Damn." No watch. "What time is it?"

"About ten past four. I've just finished and thought you might like to come across the road with me, top up your Dutch courage, but if you'd rather not have the company…"

"No. I mean, yes. I'd love your company. I don't even know why you put up with me." Ade's eyes filled with tears of gratitude.

"Oh no," Pip said. "Don't fall apart on me now. You have to be strong, Ade. Come on. We're getting out of here."

"OK." Ade nodded. "Yes, OK. But I'm thinking I should maybe give the Dutch courage a miss."

"Good," Pip said coolly. She was hurting and making sure he knew it. "Get your jacket," she instructed. "I'll wait here." She folded her arms.

Ade speed-walked back to his office, grabbed his coat and phone and returned to the lift. Pip must've called it already, as it arrived as he did. They stepped inside.

"Cauliflower cheese tomorrow," she said.

"Excellent. Save me some?"

"I might."

If I'm still alive to eat it?

They went to the pub across the street, bought non-alcoholic drinks and sat in a back corner, out of direct line of sight of the door yet still able to see who came and went in the mirror opposite the bar.

"You know what's really wound me up?" Ade said once they'd gossiped about inconsequential stuff and were both a little calmer. "I think he was seeing someone else, and it shouldn't matter, because we broke up ages ago."

"So why does it?" Pip asked.

"I've no idea. I don't want him. Like, if I was minted, I'd walk away right now, leave the apartment and everything in it so I never have to see him or listen to his *I love and miss you* bullshit again. Then he can bring back whomever he likes, can't he? Get down and dirty with his fruit-flavoured condoms in my bed because it won't be mine anymore."

"Yuck." Pip shuddered. "I bet he left them on purpose."

"Yeah, I thought that too, and I'm sick and tired of the games, Pip. I'm so, so done…"

"But…?"

"Why does it hurt so damn much?" Ade covered his eyes with his hand, disappointed with himself and ashamed for being so. "I'm such an idiot."

"No. Look at me."

Ade shook his head.

Pip reached up and moved his hand away, keeping hold of it, squeezing it. "Look at me, Ade."

He peered through his lashes.

"You're not an idiot. You're a wonderful, brave person, and you deserve better than Fergus fruity-knob Campbell. I don't think there's anyone on this Earth good enough you."

Ade snorted some very snotty laughter through his tears. "Ever my champion."

"You'd better believe it. Now, get that drink down you. You have an ex-boyfriend to dispatch."

17: Pip, Pip...

Ade

ADE WAS GLAD of Pip jollying him along. He was too worked up to think about what he needed to do, but with her arm hooked through his and the sound of her chatter to focus on, he kept going.

They reached the corner of his street, and Ade stopped. Fergus's car was parked right outside the main door, and he was sitting behind the wheel, banging his hands in time to the thud of his obnoxiously loud music. Pip gently tugged, and Ade stumbled forward.

"What shall I do?" she asked. He didn't know. "Wait in the living room?" He shook his head. His sofa was still full of Fergus's piss. "Then I'll go up and sit with Mary," she said. "If you're even slightly worried, you scream as loud as you can. OK?"

Ade nodded. "Yes. Scream."

"OK." Pip walked away from him, glancing back every couple of steps.

Ade drifted along, he wasn't sure how, closer and closer, his eyes locked on Fergus's outline, whilst Fergus pretended not to notice him until the very last second. The car door opened, and Ade quickened his pace. He kept walking, calling back over his shoulder, "It's all packed up and in the hallway."

He continued through the front entrance, up the stairs to his apartment, key now in shaking hand, trying to home in on the lock. Fergus's large, heavy palm landed on his arm, and he froze.

"Don't touch me."

"Adrian, come on. Does it have to be this way?"

Ade tried again to push the key in, but his nervousness had turned to pure fear—not of Fergus but that he wouldn't see this through.

"I love you, Adrian. And I know what you're going to say. I have a funny way of showing it. You're right. I've fucked up, big time. But if—"

The key finally slid into the lock. Ade turned it in relief and pushed the door open. His throat was seizing up, the tension in his muscles and the pain of the bruising like a clamp around his neck that turned his voice into a strangled stream of words.

"Just get your stuff and get the fuck out of my life."

He tried to step out of the way, but Fergus advanced on him, using his physical size to walk Ade backwards into his apartment.

"One more chance," Fergus said, the words themselves a plea, but the tone was a command. He expected Ade's obedience.

Ade stayed where he was, pinned against the wall with his foot positioned to stop the door from closing. "Get your things and leave."

Fergus shifted his weight onto his left hip and scratched his head in seeming puzzlement. He attempted a genial smile, but it only made him look more sinister and intimidating. There was no gentleness or humility behind that smile. No emotion whatsoever in his eyes.

"Remember when we went to see the therapist?" Fergus asked.

Ade didn't answer.

"Well, do you, or are you too stupid to remember anything without your little checklists?" Fergus looked around him and gave a mocking shrug. "Where's your tablet today, Adrian? Och, you haven't broken something else, have you? You clumsy boy." He took a step closer and trailed his fingertips lightly over Ade's cheek.

Ade's breath hissed out of his nostrils, hard and fast, but he fought the instinct to close his eyes and stared right back, unblinking, as he said again, slowly and clearly, "Get your things and leave."

"Is that what you want?" Fergus asked, his fingers and thumb now positioned over the yellowing bruises on Ade's jaw. He squeezed. Ade clenched his teeth tight so he didn't respond to the spike of pain that shot up into his skull. "Well, is it or not?"

Fergus clamped harder around Ade's chin. Unable to speak, he nodded slowly, forcing Fergus's hand up and down.

Fergus gave him a pitying smile. "If I go this time, it's for good, you know that?"

Ade elbowed Fergus's arm away. Immediately, his other hand rose and struck Ade's cheek.

Ade recoiled, but that slap seemed to ignite some vital light that had been too long extinguished.

"It ends as it began," he said resignedly, conclusively. It was a risk to challenge Fergus, he knew that well enough, but the resolve that had brought him into the bright new morning and then wavered with the passing of the hours had returned, as dazzling and invincible as the sun. For just outside the door, where Ade could see him but Fergus could not, was Kris.

Ade nodded towards the pile behind Fergus. "Everything out of my bedroom is in the suitcase—you can keep it—and the rest is in the bag and the shoe box."

Fergus spun on the spot and took in the curious collection of items. He turned back to Ade. "What would I want with your shitty stereo? It's about five years out of date."

"Take it or don't take it. I'm not bothered either way." That kind of talk would normally have ended with him being dragged by his hair to wherever Fergus decided suited him best.

But not this time. Fergus could feel the power being snatched away from him and was confused for real. He poked a finger at the shoe box. "What's in it?"

"Nothing important," Ade said dismissively. "Just the odds and bobs you left lying around my living room like you owned the place."

"We'll let the courts decide that one, shall we?"

"It's my apartment, Fergus. My name is on the deeds."

"And how did you pay the mortgage when you went whoring after your career in radio?"

"I'll send you a cheque." Ade took his phone from his pocket and checked the time, trying to appear nonchalant, hoping it would hurry Fergus along.

"Where's your watch?"

"It stopped working."

"When?"

"It's irrelevant. Could you hurry up, please? I have things to do."

Ade's masquerade of confidence was slipping, as Fergus now had the shoe box in his hands, and for one awful moment, it looked as if he was going to open it. The rest of Ade's potentially very short life was dependent on what happened next. But then Fergus put the box under his arm and picked up the suitcase. As a parting shot, he swung the suitcase into the TV, which fell, screen down, onto the floor.

In the doorway, he stopped and looked back, sneering at the TV and the pictures on the walls. "You can keep everything else. It's all worthless junk anyway." And on those words, Fergus Campbell finally left Ade's apartment and soon after left the building.

***

Kris

"You can come in," Ade called far too brightly as he picked up the TV and carried it through a doorway.

Kris stepped inside and slowly moved along the hall, watching Ade set down the TV, which appeared to be in one piece, and then flit about, flicking a speck of dust here, straightening a coaster there, examining book spines, plumping naked cushions…

"Ade."

…rubbing at a spot of something on the coffee table. "Would you like a drink. Cup of tea? I'll put the kettle on. We'll have to sit in the kitchen, I'm afraid."

Ade moved to walk past Kris, who knew better than to try to physically stop him and stepped aside.

"How do you have your tea? Weak? Strong? You have milk, don't you?"

Kris watched on silently as Ade lifted the kettle and flipped the lid open, turned the tap on…and fell apart. The kettle landed in the sink with an ear-ringing clunk, cold water sprayed everywhere, and Ade slid to the floor, his face broken and white.

Without a word, Kris turned off the tap and dropped to his knees beside Ade, utterly powerless, while Ade sobbed and gasped, his arms wrapped protectively around his head as if someone was raining down blows on him. Aware it might be the worst thing to do but desperate to do something, Kris gently rubbed Ade's back to comfort him and give him some connection to reality. Ade didn't react in any way, not even when Kris startled at a movement in his peripheral vision.

Not Fergus, thank God. It was the woman from the radio station cafeteria—presumably the 'Pip' who'd called Ade that morning—and she didn't seem at all shocked by what she was witnessing.

"I need…" Ade gulped.

Kris waited, then asked, "What do you need, Ade?"

He started to get up. "I need…" He wasn't sobbing now. He was wailing like a wounded animal.

Crying himself, Kris wrapped his arms around Ade, holding steady as Ade fell against him. He glanced up at Ade's friend, who was biting her fist, tears streaming down her cheeks, but her eyes, locked on Kris's, conveyed another emotion besides fear and distress. Jealousy.

I've taken her place. But what could he do? Ade was so out of it, he didn't even know she was there.

Pip turned away and, after a moment's nose blowing, turned back and stepped around them. "I'll put that kettle on," she said.

"No," Ade said thickly, pulling away from Kris to peer up at her through swollen red eyes. Snot hung from both nostrils, and his usually spiky hair was a dark, sodden fringe stuck to his forehead. "Pub."

"Pub," Pip repeated in blatant disbelief. "Are you serious?"

Ade sniffed and nodded.

Pip studied him a moment and put the kettle back on the side. "Better wash your face first."

Ade gargled a laugh and tried to stand again. He wobbled, and Kris caught him, eyes meeting. "Let me help," Kris offered and slowly rose to his feet, pulling Ade up with him.

"Bathroom," Ade said and staggered away.

Kris wiped his eyes on his sleeve and gave Pip a watery smile. "Hi, I'm Kris."

"I know," Pip responded dryly. She examined him suspiciously for a few seconds and then held out her hand. "Pip," she said. Kris shook the offered hand. "I suppose, as my GBF has a serious case of love at first sight, we'd best get to know each other, huh?"

"I hope the 'BF' is more important than the 'G'." Kris tried to say it lightly, but what he'd told Ade about being out at school and the bullying he had endured all came back to the same thing. He wasn't just out; he was outspoken, sometimes to an extreme. It mattered a great deal to him, though perhaps not as much as making a good first impression with Ade's friends. Pip still had him under scrutiny, and he started to fret. He redressed. "Sorry if I offended you. It's a bit of a sore point."

Pip nodded. "For me too." She gave him a friendly nudge. "I'm sure we'll get along just fine."

Kris carefully released a sigh as Ade came back into the kitchen, looking moderately more human now he'd washed his face. He'd stopped crying, although the occasional gulp still escaped.

"Have you done the introductions?" he asked them both.

"Introductions and mutual causing of offence," Pip said with a playful wink in Kris's direction.

"Oh good," Ade said. "I'm glad you're not standing on ceremony. I'm all out of tenterhooks."

"Do you really want to go to the pub?" Pip asked. "If you do, then that's absolutely what we'll do, but…"

But Ade didn't look fit to go anywhere.

"I just need to get out of here," he said.

"OK. Fine."

"You know," Kris started carefully, "we could always go back to our place."

"Your marital home?" Pip's disapproval was clear.

"Yeah," Kris confirmed. "It *was* our marital home. Now we're just some kind of weird and wonderful housemates. Plus—" Kris turned to Ade "—I hear there's a Ginger Appreciation Society meeting tonight." That raised a sweet, genuine smile from Ade.

"I like your thinking. What do you say, Pip? I'll drive there if you drive back."

Pip hummed, and she did seem to give it serious consideration, but in the end she shook her head. "You'll probably want to stay there tonight, and I'm on earlies again tomorrow. No, you go and wind down. We can catch up over a coffee at the weekend."

"Are you sure?"

"I'm sure."

Ade gave her a long, sniffly hug. "I love you."

"Love you too," she said, reaching up on tiptoes so she could kiss his cheek. She did the same with Kris. "Look after my boy."

"You have my word."

She locked eyes with him again, an unspoken understanding passing between them to put aside their rivalry and do all they could to help Ade through the coming months. He'd shown today how incredibly strong and determined he was; kicking Fergus out was massive, maybe the bravest thing he'd ever do, but it was only a step along the road, and a relationship like that carried a heavy toll.

After Pip left, Ade gathered a few things so he could stay overnight at Kris and Shaunna's place. "That's it now," he said, zipping his toothbrush and paste into a washbag. "No more excuses about his shit still being here. No reason for him to contact me again."

"Would it be wrong to tell you I'm proud of you?" Kris asked.

"Not for you." Ade winked mischievously but quickly became serious. "I can't look back, Kris. I can't afford for him to trip me up again. One way or another, it will kill me." He sighed shakily, then straightened his shoulders and nodded resolutely. "My turn to shine."

"You're already the brightest star in my universe," Kris said, only half joking.

Ade groaned. "Come on. I want to introduce you to someone before we go."

"Who?"

Ade didn't answer and instead steered Kris out of the apartment, to the next one along. The door opened as Ade went to knock on it.

"Oh, Jesus!" The older woman clutched her chest and took a step back. "Ade! Are you all right? We didn't know what to do for the best. We couldn't hear a thing, and then there was a terrible bang, and we were about to call the police, but then we saw Fergus leaving and this young man hanging around. Are you all right?"

"Yes, Mary, thank you," Ade said, once she stopped for breath. "This is Kris."

"Kris? The one who—oh." Mary's mouth stayed in an 'O' as she stared at him. He had a vision of a penny being fed into that 'O' and ricocheting its way through her insides, like a machine in an amusement arcade, until it finally dropped. "Your new man?" she asked Ade, still eyeing Kris up.

"We'll see, Mary. Anyway, the other reason I've popped round is to let you know I'll be away for a few days. I don't think he'll come back, but if he does, you've got my number and Kris's. Is that OK?"

"Sure it is, Ade." A loud beep sounded from within Mary's apartment. "That's my tea cooked," she said. "It's lovely to meet you, Kris. You take care, Ade."

"You too, Mary."

She shuffled backwards, giving them a little wave as the door closed in their faces, followed by a male voice within asking very loudly who she was talking to.

"I knew it," Ade muttered. "That Benny is a bad influence."

"Benny?" Kris queried.

"He lives downstairs. He and Mary are having…relations."

"Ah." Kris nodded slowly, totally bemused and feeling quite weary. It had been a very stressful day and he was running on his last reserves; God only knew how Ade was still standing.

As if he had read Kris's mind, Ade asked, "Can you drive?"

"I can. I don't have a car, though. I've never needed one."

"How would you feel about driving us to your place? My insurance will cover you, and I feel like shit."

"Yeah, of course," Kris agreed without hesitation. Ade moved away to go back to the apartment, and Kris caught his hand, pulling him close and giving him a soft, undemanding kiss. "You don't look like shit."

"I bet I do."

"No." Kris kissed him again to reassure him, aware that this was the first of many times to come when Ade would berate himself, but it wouldn't be hard to tell him how handsome he was, or how intelligent, witty, desirable and loveable, because it was the truth.

*

They were at almost the halfway point when the car started playing up. At first, it was only a slight judder as they took off from traffic lights. Next, the engine started to click and clatter, then the clicking and clattering was joined by a whirring. Kris pulled over, and Ade called his roadside recovery service.

"I don't understand," he said. "I check everything once a week—oil, tyre pressures, brake fluid—everything. It's never missed a service, and it's just had an oil change. This shouldn't be happening."

An hour later, the mechanic arrived and quickly diagnosed the problem. "Your oil pump's had it, mate. Your engine's taken a right battering."

With the MG on the back of the tow truck, Ade and Kris climbed into the cab, next to the mechanic. Kris couldn't help thinking it was something of an anticlimax, not that he was up for any more excitement today, but it should have been a chauffeur-driven Rolls Royce or the E-Type Jaguar Ade loved so much, taking him to a big party where the Champagne flowed to celebrate what he had achieved.

No, a breakdown truck being driven by an oily mechanic was nothing like the glorious exit Kris would have liked for Ade, but it was a move in the right direction.

18: Whatever Happens

Ade

BACK AT KRIS and Shaunna's place, the homely calm lulled Ade into a semi-catatonic state, and it was only when Kris freed his hand so he could go to the bathroom that Ade realised he'd been sitting on the Johanssons' very comfortable sofa for so long his cup of tea was stone cold. He watched Kris leave, the blank space filling with the image of that sneer, his throat constricting as if Fergus's hand was still around it. He'd thought Fergus was going to kill him, and in that moment, he almost hadn't cared.

"...today, hun?"

"Hmm?" Ade blinked out of his trance and looked over at Shaunna, who was curled up in the armchair, her gaze on the TV, but she was watching him too. "Sorry. What did you say?"

"Have you eaten today?"

"I...I honestly don't know."

"Is there anything you don't like?"

"I'm not hungry."

"That wasn't what I asked." She flipped her legs down and pushed her feet into her slippers.

"Don't go to any trouble on my—"

"Oh no you don't," she said, shaking her head. "I'm an old hand at this. Kris told you about his mental health, didn't he?"

Ade nodded. "You looked after him. But you're not my wife."

"And I did the same for my dad after my mum died, and my mate Adele after every relationship break-up because—"

"I don't want to be a burden."

"*Because* it's what I do, hun. I know you don't want to eat, but it's important, so, what do you like?"

Ade shrugged. He wasn't winning this one. "I'll eat pretty much anything."

"OK. I'll go and make dinner." Shaunna stood and picked up his undrunk tea. "Are you finished with this?" She was halfway to the door before he registered the question.

"Yeah. Sorry."

"Actually…" She backtracked and took his hand. "Come and help me."

Too tired to fight and quite sure he'd lose anyway, Ade let her pull him up from the sofa and lead him through to the kitchen. She released him, and he stuttered to a stop. Shaunna sighed fondly.

"See? You've run out of fuel." She pointed to a dining chair. "Sit."

Ade sat, his gaze falling to the pine kitchen table. With its multitude of scrapes and worn dark knots, it had clearly been in service for many years. He traced his finger around a faded circular scorch, along an ancient groove. The table seemed to have a warmth all of its own. *What a story you could tell, full of happy family life, Sunday roasts, homework, chats with friends—*

Ade's view was suddenly interrupted as potatoes, a peeler and a pan were set down on a sheet of newspaper in front of him.

"Peel," Shaunna instructed.

Ade picked up a potato and started peeling.

"What do you do for fun?" she asked.

"Fun?" Ade was bamboozled by the question.

"Let me rephrase that. What did you used to do before *It* stole all your fun?"

"Ah." Ade attempted a smile. He appreciated her candour. "I went to warehouse raves a lot when I was younger, but I prefer nightclubs these days—places with live performances."

"Strip clubs?" Shaunna teased.

"No." Ade's smile broadened. "Although I've seen some marvellous sights."

Shaunna went comically wide-eyed, her mouth forming a delighted *ooh*, then she laughed. "I bet," she said. "You can tell me *all* about them later. Do you like chicken?"

"Who doesn't?"

She took a bag out of the freezer. "How are you getting on there?" Like a teacher checking a pupil's work, she peered over Ade's shoulder on her way to the microwave. "Good job."

Ade chuckled. "Thank you."

"It helps, I find," she said, pausing to set three chicken fillets on defrost. "Having things to do. Like, when Krissi was giving us hell a couple of years ago, I just kept going, you know? And we'd have guests round, and they'd say, 'Oh, you're coping really well,' when I was actually just keeping my head occupied with baking, cleaning, gardening or whatever. I mean, there are worse ways of getting through, right?"

"Right," Ade said. He'd done the same himself—filled every void with activity to crowd out the pain—and it worked pretty well in the short term. Not so much when the problem never went away.

"So what kind of live performances do you like?" Shaunna cut in before he drifted off again. She had a knack for that.

"Any, really," he said. "Musical theatre and stage plays are my faves, but I enjoy dance too. How about you?"

"I'm not into dance the way you mean, but I love going out dancing and live music. We used to go to a lot of gigs—not sure why we don't anymore, actually. We've been to all sorts. Big stadium concerts, little shows in pubs. And it doesn't matter which it is, guaranteed someone always asks Kris for his autograph."

"How do they know who he is?"

"What do you mean?"

"With him being on radio."

"Oh! No, I meant because of him looking like Morten Harket."

Ade did a quick mental comparison. He couldn't see it, but he wasn't going to say so. "I suppose he does a bit."

"He was the spitting image of him till last year…" Shaunna became quiet, her expression shifting with her thoughts—trouble, sadness, fear. She sighed. "Kris has always been very slim, but for a while, he completely stopped eating. He lost so much weight, it was frightening. I don't know if it was the depression or the medication doing it, but it was like something was stopping the signals between his brain and the rest of his body, which I suppose is how antidepressants work. Anyway, I discovered if I stuck food in front of him, I could get him to eat. One. Forkful. At. A. Time."

"Wow."

"Yeah." She laughed. "So you're 'I'm not hungry' is a mere trifle to me."

"Actually, I quite like trifle," Ade said with a grin as the kitchen door opened and Kris came back in.

"What needs doing?" he asked, keeping his face averted from both Ade and Shaunna.

"Broccoli, maybe?" she suggested, watching with a worried frown as he passed her to reach the vegetable rack. As he turned back, he fleetingly met Ade's gaze, his bloodshot eyes giving away precisely what he'd been doing in the bathroom.

"Here you go." Ade handed Shaunna the pan, now full of peeled potatoes, and rounded the table. Grabbing Kris by the arm, he tugged gently. "Hey. Come here."

Kris shook his head and tried to carry on even though he'd dissolved into tears again.

"No," Ade said, tugging hard on Kris's arm until he spun around. "I will *not* be the cause of this."

Kris resisted a few seconds longer but then buried his face in Ade's shoulder. "I'm sorry." His voice juddered as he clung to Ade.

"Why are you sorry?"

Kris shrugged. "Because."

"Because?"

"What you went through, and I can't change any of it."

"Well, no, of course you can't."

"I'm supposed to stay strong for you, not the other way around."

"I don't think there are any rules for these kinds of messed-up situations, but this isn't you being weak. This is you caring and hurting because I am, and let me tell you, I already care too much about you to see you hurting like this because of me. Or because of him."

Kris sniffled. "You're incredible, do you know that?"

"Why, thank you," Ade said lightly.

"It makes me lo—" Kris swayed backwards and released his grip on Ade. He looked horrified by what he'd almost said, and if it was what Ade thought…

"Too fast," Kris muttered, backing off completely. "I invited you here because it's a safe space, somewhere to rest up, not so I could hit on you. We've only known each other three days. My mouth just ran away from me—"

"It's OK," Ade interjected gently, pulling Kris close again. He couldn't decide if his heart was going at a million miles a minute or he was picking up on both their heartbeats and rested his hand on Kris's chest as he looked him in the eyes. "It is fast, that's very true."

"That doesn't make it wrong," Shaunna said from across the kitchen.

Kris held Ade's gaze, the sparkle returning despite the pink puffiness that made his irises seem an even cooler blue than usual.

"She's a feeder," he said, trying to rally. "Did she tell you?" Shaunna tutted. "This potato-peeling gig she's got you on? It's part of her ploy to feed you up and turn you into a fatty like me."

"Ha!" Ade slipped his hand around Kris's side and ran a finger over his ribs. "What fat is that?"

Kris jerked at the touch.

"Oh, so you're ticklish, are you?"

"Nooo," Kris claimed, even though he was jolting about all over the place.

"He's *so* ticklish," Shaunna said.

Ade laughed but stopped his low-level torture and took over trimming and steaming broccoli, leaving Kris to mash the potatoes, while Shaunna concocted the creamiest, most delicious garlic chicken ever. The banter continued as they ate together, with a little help from Casper, who begged shamelessly, despite—Kris was quick to assure Ade—never being rewarded for such naughtiness in the normal scheme of things.

This was *far* from the normal scheme of things, yet it felt right and familiar. So they'd only known each other three days, only had one date, only shared a bed for convenience. Ade was emotionally wrecked, and Kris wasn't faring much better, but the longer Ade spent in the welcoming warmth of this well-loved kitchen and the company of two of the sweetest people he'd ever known—and Casper, of course—the stronger he became.

Friends of my own, whatever happens.

It was only the start, he knew. He had a lot more work to do before he could, finally, declare his life Fergus-free.

19: Splinters

Ade

As SOON AS they'd eaten, Kris took the dog for a walk. He was honest about needing a little time to himself and said he felt safe taking it, knowing Ade was in Shaunna's capable hands. Ade wasn't sure how he felt about that—relieved in one sense, as it meant he didn't have to monitor or censor his behaviour. It was a luxury he had long been without.

Fergus has gone. He's gone. For good.

Of course, they'd done this before, but it did feel different this time. He had reclaimed his apartment. He hadn't blocked Fergus's number because ignoring him—should he ever call again—was more powerful, though riskier. Tomorrow, he'd find a specialist garage to get the car fixed and head home because, as grateful as he was for Kris and Shaunna's support, this was *their* house, *their* life, and he was an outsider to their intimacy, the connection that only came from years of living, breathing, being each other's existence.

Just like Fergus and I had. It could've been different. It could've worked, if you—

"Here, look at this, Ade," Shaunna said, once again scragging him by the scruff and hoisting him out in the nick of time. Ade followed her signed instruction to sit at the table, where she spun a laptop to face him.

"What's this? Oh! Wow! I see what you mean." He leaned in and looked more closely at the two images displayed side by side. The one on the left was Kris, perhaps in his mid-twenties;

the one on the right was Morten Harket, at the peak of *a-ha*'s chart success. The likeness was astonishing.

"Yep. So," Shaunna tapped the screen, "I think it's the highlights that make Kris look different now, plus Morten's quite the hunk these days."

"Is he?"

"Hell, yes! Definitely been hitting the gym."

"You like 'em beefy?"

"Do I ever!" Shaunna grinned.

Ade laughed. "It's amazing, isn't it? The difference between the ideal in your head and who you end up with?"

"It is. Although I always thought Kris was attractive, even before I knew he was interested in girls, but it wasn't about his looks. It was…well, nothing specific and then everything all at once—the way you slowly fall for someone without realising it."

"Yes, I know what you mean. It usually takes me a while to work out how I feel, or how I think I feel, at least." Ade's mind drifted again, back to the early days with Fergus—the flirting, the overly romantic gestures, the *insistence* that Ade join him for dinner or a movie or whatever. But insistence wasn't romantic, and rejection was not something Fergus accepted well, because that was how he saw it. The gifts stopped, other than when Ferg had been so awful he recognised it for himself, and then he'd come crawling back, simpering and loaded up with wine and chocolates and teddy bears.

"You OK there?" Shaunna asked.

Ade nodded. "I will be. Thank you."

Shaunna squeezed his hand. "You're welcome."

"And are you OK with…" Ade didn't finish, but she got it.

"Absolutely. I'm just glad he chose someone I like!"

Ade gave her a nod that was both thanks and confirmation that the affection was two-way. "How about you?" he asked. "Found yourself a beefy hunk?"

"Er, no." Shaunna got up and switched on the kettle.

Oops. "Sorry. That was very forward of me."

Shaunna gave him a quick smile, but he'd obviously put her on the spot and she didn't want to share. He made a very clear shift of attention back to the photos.

"Morten is good-looking, but his eyes don't have that sparkle. And his chin is quite square—Morten's, I mean. Kris has more of a heart-shaped face. Not overtly masculine, yet manly at the same time."

"Uh-huh?"

It took a few seconds for Ade to realise she was watching him, utterly transfixed by the photo of Kris. He blushed and started to laugh. Shaunna joined in. "I think that makes us even," she said.

"I suppose. I do think Kris is right, though—about it being too much too soon. I was only thinking on Sunday that I needed some time away. I haven't had a holiday in years because of... everything. It was too expensive, and trying to figure out who would pay for what—well, there's no point in causing arguments unnecessarily. But then Monday morning, I meet Kris and now I'm here, and...we don't even know each other."

"There's no rush, hun."

"It's just that Fer—" Ade rubbed his hands over his face, freezing when he inadvertently brushed the tender spots. "I feel under pressure," he said from behind his hands.

"From Kris?"

He didn't answer, but it wasn't Kris putting pressure on him. It came from within, that long-conditioned instinct he had for picking up on what was left unsaid, even before it was consciously thought. If Ade stayed one step ahead of Fergus, he was safe, or safer.

"Kris won't push you into doing anything you don't want to," Shaunna assured him.

He didn't respond, until she touched his arm, only lightly, but he hadn't expected it, and he jumped. She immediately moved her hand away.

"Ade, I'm so sorry. I can't even begin to understand how you're feeling, but I do know Kris, and in all honesty, I think it will be you doing the pushing. He's not exactly forthcoming."

"With sex?"

"With anything. He's very talkative and not afraid to show his emotions, but the deeper stuff takes a bit of digging to reach—including the sex."

Ade uncovered his face. "It's a bit surreal, us talking like this. Don't get me wrong. It's wonderful, but…"

"Well, you know, Kris is very high maintenance, which is why I'm so glad to have you on board." Shaunna gave him a wink.

Ade managed a brief chuckle in response, but joking aside, it continued to bother him. "I'm sorry to go on, but it is definitely over between you, isn't it? I'm not into husband stealing." He rolled his eyes. "Listen to me, talking like I have oodles of experience. I've had three boyfriends—four if I count Maurice—we exchanged a very fast flash of willies behind the school hall when we were nine."

Shaunna burst into laughter. "Oh God. I remember doing that with a boy in third year of juniors. I can't even remember his name, but he started it, and once I'd seen his willy, I told him I couldn't show him because I had an awful disease and he'd catch it if he saw it."

"That's genius. I wish I'd thought of it."

"Though it was a one-off. In high school, there was no stopping me."

"Did you have lots of boyfriends?"

"Not boyfriends, no. Only Kris, really."

"And Krissi's dad?"

"Biological father," Shaunna corrected. "Kris is Krissi's dad. But it was a one-night thing. Not even that much. Kris reckoned we were only in the room about ten minutes."

"Kris was there?"

"Yep. It was a house party. They were always like that, weren't they? Loads of cheap cider, everyone completely off their face, and then the heavy petting begins. Except I had to take it to the next level. A few times." Shaunna grimaced. "A lot of times."

"Oh!" Ade said, surprised, yet not. Whatever else Fergus was, their sex life had been good. It was how he'd weaselled his way into the apartment the previous Sunday, knowing Ade would relent for a romp between the bedsheets, and Ade hated that he'd agreed to it, prostituting every other aspect of his self for that one small pleasure.

Fergus believed that if they were still having sex, all was well. It was less dangerous—and ultimately paid off—to allow him to keep that delusion. And the sex was incredible, perhaps because it always carried an element of risk. It was rough, loud, energetic— some of what Mary overheard had nothing to do with fighting. It left scratches, bite marks, red hand prints, bruises sometimes, but not the ones on his face and neck. Those came after. *Or was it before?* Ade couldn't remember now. Maybe he'd lost consciousness or repressed the memory. Either was a possibility. He'd done both too many times to count.

He'd often wondered if it was just a boundaries thing—that Ferg thought rough in the bedroom extended to the rest of their life together. That was the biggest difference between them: Ade could separate the sex from everything else; Ferg couldn't, and maybe it was wrong to mislead him. Maybe Ade had no-one to blame but himself, because hadn't he used Fergus, if he was completely honest? He couldn't even say he'd tried talking to him about it. What was the point when Ferg had no concept of the problem?

Ade's thoughts had pulled him so deep into introspection that he only knew Shaunna had spoken to him because she had that look of someone waiting for an answer.

"Sorry. What did you say?"

"Do you want to share?"

Ade wrinkled his nose. "I was thinking about sex with…*It*. We did OK with that bit. It was everything else that was wrong. Maybe I should've told him back at the start."

"Told him what?"

"That I wasn't happy with the way things were. How would he know otherwise?"

"Of course he'd have known. You don't hurt the person you supposedly love. Not on purpose."

"He might not have realised he was doing it."

"Ade, hun." Shaunna took his hand and held it in both of hers. "It wasn't up to you to tell him that he was hurting you. He knew what he was doing. This, now, the things you're saying? It all goes back to him manipulating you to think that he'd done nothing wrong and it was your fault. I know you've probably heard it all before, but he's a scumbag, and you deserve better. Really deserve so much better."

Ade nodded. Yes, he'd heard it all before, but hearing and believing were not the same.

"Am I good enough for Kris?"

The thought escaped aloud, and now he felt foolish, but Shaunna didn't let it pass. She tightened her hold on his hand.

"Right now, you need to focus on your own worth, not whether you're worthy in someone else's eyes. But I will answer your question. Yes, you are good enough for Kris. You're right for each other, and I truly believe you could have a brilliant future together, but it won't be easy. You'll both have to be so patient and forgiving. You've both been hurt horrifically by people you loved and trusted, and the scars will fade, but they might never go away completely.

"And you must, *must* communicate. That's the most important part. Talk about how he makes you feel, get him to tell you how he feels. He's not good at that, and I've not been great at it either. That's probably what finished our marriage—ignoring the splinters. Believe me, they're much easier to remove *before* they burrow deep under your skin and poison everything."

20: Heart-to-Heart

Kris

As Kris closed the front door, the conversation in the kitchen stopped. He unhooked Casper's lead and let the dog go ahead of him while he took off his coat.

"Hiya, hun. Good walk?" Shauna called breezily.

"A wet one," he replied, matching her tone. He'd caught the tail end of what she'd said, which more or less matched what he'd told Ade and hopefully had waylaid his fears that Kris was being unfaithful. Or maybe those fears were all in his own mind.

"Oh my god, dog, look at my floor!" Shaunna dashed past Kris and up the stairs.

"I'll mop it in a minute," he said, following the trail of muddy paw prints all along the hall and across the kitchen, to where Casper was rubbing himself dry on Ade's legs.

"What a soggy doggy...whoa!" Laughing, Ade clung to the edge of the table, in minor danger of being knocked off his seat. "I miss this."

"I told you, you can have him," Kris said and got the mop out, but Casper was re-muddying the floor quicker than he could clean it, so he set the mop aside and went to take the towel Shaunna had brought down to dry the dog. She snatched it out of his reach and shooed him away. Now he didn't know what to do. Ade seemed calm, and Shaunna was no different than usual, yet Kris felt like a stranger in his own kitchen.

"I'll make a nightcap," he suggested and managed to take one step towards the kettle before Ade hooked his belt loop and used it to pull him closer, lips pursed in invitation. Kris accepted, the

149

raindrops trickling down his nose onto Ade's upturned face so that he shivered and smiled into their kiss.

"I have a better idea," Ade murmured.

"What's that?"

A towel came down over both of their heads, plunging them into semi-darkness. The dog flopped noisily into his bed; Shaunna's footsteps retreated; the stairs creaked.

"Going for a bath," she called. The bathroom door closed loudly a moment later.

"Did we chase her away again?" Ade whispered.

"I think so," Kris whispered back. "Want me to stop?"

"Nuh-uh." Ade reached a hand up inside the towel and pulled Kris's head down until their lips were pressed hard together, sliding against each other. The contrast of cool damp and soft warm was exquisite.

Slowly, without breaking contact, Ade rose to his feet and flung the towel aside. It left his hair standing on end, and Kris reached up to smooth it, bringing his palm to a rest on Ade's cheek. Ade's muscles tensed beneath his fingers, and he tried to move his hand away, but Ade grabbed his wrist to stop him.

"It's OK," he murmured. "Carry on."

Taking him at his word, Kris combed his fingers through Ade's hair as the kiss continued, the soft bristles of Ade's stubble creating a wonderful tingling burn on Kris's chin. They pulled back, nibbled lips with lips, clashed teeth, their laughter soon lost to the reconnection, tongue against tongue, slowing, slowing, a sigh, content, but needing more.

"Can we go to bed soon?" Ade asked.

Kris raised his eyebrows. "I guess you're not talking about sleep?"

"Well, we can do that too, but it isn't foremost in my mind. Would you rather wait?"

Kris was as aroused as Ade was, but as second dates went, today had to be the worst.

"Are we ready for that? Are you sure—"

"I want you," Ade breathed, lifting his lips to meet Kris's again. "I don't want to wait."

"OK," Kris agreed, still reluctant, but Ade seemed certain, and it wasn't as if Kris didn't want it too. Right now, he wanted it more than anything.

"I'm almost tempted to call Fergus and gloat," Ade said, taking Kris's hand and leading him from the kitchen. Kris couldn't tell if he was joking or not so said nothing. "Almost," Ade added, turning back with a grin that faded instantly when he saw Kris's face. "I'm not actually going to call him."

"I know."

"Then what's wrong?"

"Nothing. It's just..." Kris glanced around, giving himself thinking time, and spotted Ade's bag at the bottom of the stairs. "Are you taking this up with you?"

"There's nothing I need until morning. Is it in the way?"

"No..."

Ade started up the stairs but came back down when Kris didn't move. "What's the matter?"

Kris attempted to speak twice before it came out, all in one stream. "Have you got condoms with you?" He wasn't sure they'd need them—they hadn't discussed such things yet—but it was the first thing that came to him.

Ade backtracked and picked up his bag. Kris smiled wanly.

"Come on," Ade said, getting behind him and pushing him up the stairs. "You must be gagging for it."

"Hey! It's not been that long."

"How long?"

"Er..." Kris really didn't want to answer that question. It could, potentially, make a liar out of him.

"A year?" Ade guessed. Kris shook his head. "More or less?"

"Less."

"Six months."

"Less."

"Three months."

"Less."

"Two?"

"Still less." Kris reached the top of the stairs and floundered again.

"With Shaunna?"

Kris nodded swiftly.

"Do we need to discuss this?" Ade nudged him forward.

"I guess." Kris opened his bedroom door and made a grand gesture with his arm to welcome Ade, officially, because it was different than the previous night. This marked the beginning of their relationship for real.

Ade sat on the end of the bed and patted the space next to him. Kris sat too. Ade took his hand and looked him in the eye.

"One question, and I want the truth. OK?"

"OK."

"Is it over with you and Shaunna?"

"Haven't we already—"

"Hold on, hear me out. You've both told me it's over, and I believe you mean it. You're telling me what you think is the truth. You said you're monogamous…"

"Yes."

"Yet you slept together in the last month."

"We did, but it was only one time, spur of the moment. There was a reunion, we'd had too much to drink, and we were both feeling…you know." Kris shrugged. "Horny and lonely."

"Did you use a condom?"

"Yes, for contraception. It's not like either of us has slept with anyone else. Not since Jack."

"It's just that 'we had too much to drink' and happening to have condoms lying around, which, incidentally, come in packs of at least three, doesn't sound very spur of the moment."

"OK. I see where you're coming from," Kris said diplomatically. He could explain, if Ade gave him a chance.

"No, you don't, because…" In a blink, Ade went from accusing to contrite. He let go of Kris's hand and ducked his head. "I'm sorry. It's absolutely none of my business."

"Yeah, it is." Kris took back Ade's hand. "You need to know you can trust me, I get that, and I should've explained instead of going on about condoms. Believe it or not, I was trying to pluck up the courage for this conversation. Well, not this one exactly, but we should talk about how fast we want to take things, what we like and don't like…"

"Consent," Ade said.

"Yeah."

"OK. We should definitely do that. I forget sometimes how these things are supposed to work. Can I ask, though…and this isn't an accusation…"

"Go on."

"The other two condoms?"

"There's a box of about a hundred in Shaunna's room, but I didn't want to ask her. Not because there's anything between us, or there is, as you've seen, but I promise it's just friendship. We always use condoms—I mean *used to use*. They're what's left over, probably expired by now." The more Kris said, the bigger the hole he was digging. Ade gave him a reassuring smile.

"You don't have to explain. I'm just being silly. If you're saying it won't happen again…"

"That depends," Kris teased, attempting to change the dynamic.

"Does it now?" Ade challenged flirtatiously. "On what, exactly?"

Kris turned and pushed Ade backwards onto the bed. "On whether you're planning to interrogate me all night." He paused to check Ade was OK, which his smile suggested he was, and then gently pinned him down by his arms.

"I'm sure you'll find a way to shut me…mmm…"

Kris kissed him, slowly and deeply, savouring the smell of Ade's cologne mixed with the sweet-tea scent of his breath.

He was nervous and hoping his uncertainty didn't show in his actions, because he wanted this. He wanted to make love to this beautiful man, but he wasn't used to taking the lead. He trailed his lips away from Ade's, over the crest of his chin, and stopped, his attention drawn and held by the bruising. It was healing, yellow, red, purple, still horrific.

"Don't look," Ade said.

"I can't help it. I wish I could kiss them all away."

"You're welcome to try."

Kris glanced up to see if Ade meant it and received another smile of reassurance. He pressed his mouth to Ade's Adam's apple, keeping his lips soft as he carefully kissed each and every bruise.

"I didn't bring any lube," Ade murmured, cupping Kris's buttocks and writhing against him.

"We can use massage oil."

"Not oil."

"It's not actually oil. It's gel." Kris unfastened the top button of Ade's shirt. "May I?"

"You may."

Kris began working his way down.

"Water-based gel?" Ade asked.

"Yep. It's very slippery."

"Slippery is good. What do you like?"

Only two buttons to go, Kris froze. More bruises, some the size of bottle tops clustered along Ade's ribs, one the size of a fist circling his nipple, and scars.

"Talk to me," Ade said.

"I…can't."

"Tell me how you feel."

"Sad."

"About me?"

Kris nodded.

"Don't be. I need you to overwrite, not highlight."

It took some internal arguing to convince himself, but Kris continued, pulling open the final button and peeling Ade's shirt back, his doubts quickly dissipating at the sight of the trail of dark-red hair running downwards from Ade's belly button and under the waistband of his pants.

The rest of their clothes came off in something of a frenzy, fears set aside in the bid to feel skin on skin. Ade pushed Kris onto his back, peppering his still-chilly torso with hot kisses, the differences in body temperature elevating every sensation. Kris rolled, taking Ade with him, and was on top once more, but it was becoming too much, and he quickly pulled away.

"Major short fuse," he admitted. He leaned across and collected the massage gel from the bedside table. "We don't have to...use condoms."

"We do," Ade said resignedly. "I think he was seeing someone else."

"No, I mean, we can carry on doing what we were doing."

"Oh, I see." Ade turned onto his side and kissed Kris's hip. "What would you like to do?" He took the bottle and tipped some of the gel onto Kris's palm.

"Make love to you in whatever way you want."

"I want you inside me."

That was all Kris needed, a direction to follow.

Ade scooted down the bed, retrieved a condom from his bag and scooted up the bed again. "OK. I'm ready."

Rubbing his palms together to warm the gel, Kris knelt beside him and smoothed his hands over Ade's lower body, covering him in a slick, clear film, a sensual exploration, each touch eliciting a shudder.

"And you terrorised me for being ticklish," Kris teased.

"I'm not ticklish, I'm just...super turned on right now." Ade sat up, delivering a kiss so messy that they laughed through the fumble of getting the condom out of the packet and on to Kris.

"I've never done this before," Kris admitted. "Not with a guy."

"It's kind of new to me too," Ade said but once more took the lead by lying on his side and beckoning for Kris to lie behind him. Kris did so, and immediately Ade pulled him closer, aligning their bodies.

"OK?" Kris asked.

"Perfect." Ade turned his head, holding Kris's gaze as he guided Kris's hand downwards. "It feels like we've done this before. It's... familiar. Comfortable."

"Yeah."

"How's your short fuse?"

"Longer than it was." Kris rocked his hips slightly and grinned. Ade laughed.

They stayed like that for a while, getting used to the probing contact and intimacy. As they began to move together, they watched each other, taking their cues from facial expressions, and they talked, or mostly Ade talked. Whether it was intentionally to reassure Kris, he didn't know, but it had that effect, easing his anxiety that he might accidentally hurt Ade and giving him the confidence to go a little faster, a little harder.

"Oh God, yes," Ade cried out, then clamped his hand over his mouth, and they both froze like teenagers sneaking a bit of nookie, but wherever Shaunna was, they couldn't hear her, so hopefully, she couldn't hear them either because Kris was close to the point of no return and Ade was already there.

That irrepressible motion took over, accompanied by Ade's moans, muffled by his hand, while his wide eyes urged Kris on. He wanted to stay there forever, in this crescendo to climax, tingling all over from the pressure, the closeness, the heat of the friction and the desire, all of his nerve endings awakened at once in a perfect moment, a voluntary connection of souls, hearts, bodies. Ade's muscles tensed, and Kris felt it in every part of him until his awareness was nothing outside of succumbing, first one then the other, to this gift of release and of trust.

21: Time

Kris

"MORNING!" KRIS WALKED straight past Shaunna, dressed for work, to the back door to let Casper out. Shaunna grunted and added more water to the kettle, frowning at Kris because he would usually either be walking the dog by now or have left for the studio. He smiled and gave her a wide berth. She was much more human once she'd had her first cup of tea. Until then, it was best not to get too close or too chatty.

"Sleep well?" she asked.

"I did. You?"

"Yes, thank you."

After twenty years, he was well used to the forced politeness. There were times he'd wondered how he and Krissi had made it out of the house alive, especially when Krissi was in her teens and seemed to think taking her mother on before school was a good idea. Other than that, she hadn't been too much trouble as a teenager, but like any dad, he missed the little girl who'd depended on him for everything.

Glancing around the kitchen, he could still see ten-year-old Krissi on the day they'd picked up the keys, opening all the cupboards and telling them exactly where everything should go. She'd mostly got her own way too. Now she'd left home, and her bedroom was Kris's, but despite having replaced all her furniture with his own, every night it had felt like he was sleeping in the spare room—proverbially, as they didn't have one—waiting for the dust to settle on an argument. Every night until last night.

"What're you doing?" Shaunna asked.

Kris shrugged. "Thinking about when we moved in here."

"OK." She narrowed her eyes, rightly suspicious that he was only telling her half the story. "Why?"

"I don't know. I've only just woken up."

"Really? Kris Johansson, always up with the lark, thinks he can waylay his long-suffering estranged wife with 'I've only just woken up'?"

"It's true. Ade's still out for the count. I'm not sure whether I should disturb him or let him sleep."

"Presumably, you're staying off today?"

"There was nothing on the schedule, and I want to be here when the mechanic calls."

"Ah, yeah. Good point. So what *were* you thinking about?"

"Hmm?" Kris chose that moment to refill the dog's water bowl and make his breakfast—anything to avoid cross-examination.

Shaunna huffed. "Fine. You don't want to talk about it."

"I don't know, honestly. I can't put it into words, but it feels… different."

"With Ade, you mean?"

"Everything. Ade, the house, you. I think I…not *love* him, but…"

"You care a lot about him?" Shaunna suggested.

"That's what I'd say about the old ladies and dogs we see regularly in the park. Wishy-washy."

"So you do love him."

"After four days?"

"Face facts, hun. You fell for him the minute you clapped eyes on him."

"I so did not!"

"You so did! 'Oh, I had such an *amazing* time at the studio today. The producer was this really hot, sexy—'"

"I said nothing of the sort!"

"Your face said it for you. Ooh, you're blushing!" Shaunna grinned, breaking with her traditional morning moodiness to torment him. Kris scowled, and she laughed. His scowl broke.

"Yeah, OK. Maybe I did fall for him straight away. But love is a big word."

"Four letters. Not so big."

"You know what I mean."

"And *you* know what I mean. Sometimes you have to go with the flow. So it's only been a few days. So what?"

"I'm nearly forty."

"That means you can't do the whole head-over-heels thing?"

"It's not that simple, is it? Not with..." Kris shifted his eyes upwards. She'd know he meant Ade and his situation.

"Nor for you," she said.

He shrugged noncommittally. He was gregarious and fun-loving and made friends easily, but deep, interpersonal relationships made him anxious, and with Ade, it was far from straightforward.

"Did you meet his ex?" Shaunna asked.

"Not meet, no. I watched him leave Ade's place." The image of Fergus, an intimidating, vile bully, right up in Ade's face, was stuck in Kris's mind, only leaving to swap places with the full Technicolor surround-sound replay of Ade's wailing as he cowered on his kitchen floor. Regardless of the fact Fergus would've made mincemeat of him, Kris would've intervened if he'd believed for even a second it would help. But he'd made that mistake before, when George had trouble with a violent boyfriend at uni, and while George said he was grateful for the support, he was angry, too, because he felt like a victim, dependent on other people to fight his battles.

Kris suspected Ade would have felt the same if he or Pip or anyone else had stepped in. Ade needed to be the one to stand up to Fergus, and he had, but Kris was afraid it was far from over.

Shaunna hugged him and kissed his cheek. "See you later."

He must've been lost in his thoughts a while, as she'd finished her tea and rinsed her cup. "Have a good day," he called after her as she went through to the hall to put on her coat.

"You too. I've got my phone if you need me."

"What d'you think I should do about Ade?"

"Let him sleep, I guess. Bye!"

***

Ade

THE LIGHT IN the room wasn't right. Ade could tell, even with his eyes closed. It was coming from the wrong direction, and it was too bright. It wouldn't be the first time he'd crashed out upside-down on top of the duvet, and he did feel kind of hungover. Then a dog barked, and Ade fully came to, opening one eye to observe his surroundings and catching sight of the clock.

"Eight-thirty—shit!" He rolled over and grappled for his phone, panicking as it rang out, trying to come up with a plausible reason—that wasn't the real one—to offer his boss. If he'd checked his messages first, he'd have already known it wasn't necessary, as Pip had stuck her oar in. Accordingly, Ade had food poisoning.

"Take as long as you need," his boss said. "You lost last year's annual leave. I doubt you'll take this year's if you don't do it now, so let's assume a fortnight."

And that was the end of the discussion.

Ade flopped back into the pillows and sighed. Something about his boss's tone suggested he knew more than he'd let on, to the point that he might as well have said, *Sure. Take as long as you need. You lost your mind eleven years ago. Now you've found it again, why don't the two of you take a couple of weeks to get reacquainted?*

Because that was the truth of the matter, Ade was beginning to realise. The people close to him had known all along, hadn't for a second believed his lies about why he was limping or couldn't stand the pain of clicking the computer mouse, why he didn't go on nights out, why he was often so desperate that he couldn't stop the tears. He could see it now, clear as bloody day, and he didn't know whether to be angry with them or send them thank-you cards for being there, in the background, ready to catch him when he fell.

"So..." He pulled himself up the bed and looked around the room, tinted sepia by the autumn daylight shining through the pale-yellow curtains. He'd been too stressed the previous morning to pay proper attention, but today he was feeling... better? Safer, certainly, and resolute.

I wonder if Julia's up for a house guest for a few days... He hadn't seen his sister in months, either because Fergus was around or because he'd been and gone but left his mark. But for once, Ade could tell Julia truthfully that it was the last time. So that was a plan; he'd drive up to Julia's...

"The car..." Ade groaned and banged his head back, a self-harm habit that failed, as Kris's headboard was soft, plush velvet, not iron bars. He had no idea why the MG had broken down, but he'd need to deal with that first, and then go back to the apartment to collect a few things. He didn't think Fergus would be hanging around, but he'd never understood how Ferg's mind worked and wasn't sure Ferg knew either, so it was entirely possible he'd turn up. He might even be there right now, banging on the door, or he'd broken the door down and changed the locks. Then what?

I'll call Mary, get her to scope the place out. No, car first. Or should I check with Julia before I make plans?

Too many things to organise, too much that could go wrong.

"You don't need a checklist," Ade told himself yet unlocked his phone and began making one anyway.

1. MG

As well cared for as it was, the car was older than him. Had it finally reached the end of its serviceable life? He couldn't even handle the thought of watching it being loaded onto a truck, off to the scrapyard, another death to grieve. *Come on, Ade. Keep it in perspective. It's just a car.* Except it wasn't 'just' a car, and his emotions were getting the better of him again, but right at the point where he completely fell apart for something like the fiftieth time in less than a week, the bedroom door opened, and Kris backed into the room.

"Casper!" he shouted as the dog tore past and leap right into the middle of the bed, planting a huge, slobbery, licky kiss on Ade's cheek.

"Morning, Caspy," Ade greeted, accepting the unconditional, very wet and boisterous affection he'd been afforded. Meltdown temporarily averted.

22: Murder

Kris

KRIS SET DOWN the tray of tea, coffee and toast and clicked his fingers at Casper. "Come on, move it." The dog didn't take a blind bit of notice.

"I don't mind if you don't," Ade said, laughing at the dog, who was wearing a groove into the duvet with his nose. Ade glanced up and met Kris's gaze. "Good morning."

"Good morning." Kris leaned in to deliver a kiss of his own. "How do you look and smell so good when you've just woken up?"

"Oh, I really don't." Ade ducked his head bashfully and tickled Casper's ears. "Nobody looks or smells good first thing in the morning, do they, Caspy?" He glanced up at Kris again. "Why didn't you wake me?"

"I didn't want to disturb you. You were in such a deep sleep." Ade had been tossing and turning most of the night and had checked his phone several times. Kris had kept his eyes shut so Ade wouldn't feel bad about disturbing him, but he decided to come clean. "I'm sorry. It wasn't my decision to make, but I know you had a rough night."

"It's fine," Ade assured him with a smile. "I hope I didn't keep you awake."

"Not at all. I pretty much went straight back to sleep. How are you feeling this morning?"

"OK-ish, I think. I called my boss to let him know I wouldn't be in, but Pip beat me to it. He told me to take some time off."

"That's probably a wise move."

"I guess," Ade agreed vaguely. "To be honest, I don't really care about work right now, which isn't me at all."

"It's not surprising, though."

"No, I know. I can hardly remember the recording on Monday—I don't want to think about what state I left it in. I've been so focused on getting rid of Fergus and..." Ade trailed off.

"Us?" Kris asked, hoping it wasn't, not the way Ade was talking about it.

"Yes, mostly for good reasons. Work's always been my go-to, you know? Keeps my head busy when everything gets too much. This..."

"Is too much?"

"No, but I've been in survival mode for so long that it's a bit of a shock to the system, sending Ferg packing, being with you—it hasn't really sunk in yet. So I was thinking...I might go and stay at my sister's for a while."

"OK," Kris said. He hadn't meant to sound ambivalent. "You can stay here as long as you like, but if it'll be better for you at your sister's..."

"I think so. I can't really..." Ade closed his eyes and swallowed hard. "I can't face going back to the apartment yet, and I love being with you. I really do. I just..."

"Need some time?" Kris finished for him.

Ade nodded. "You don't mind, do you? I'm not saying we cool it or anything like that."

"Whatever you want is OK by me." It wasn't Kris's decision, nor would it be fair to admit how much he wanted Ade to stay. The prospect of saying goodbye already had him in knots, but he couldn't ignore the possibility that the speed and intensity of his feelings were down to witnessing Ade stand up to Fergus. Trauma was not a good basis for a relationship, as he knew far too well. The right thing for them both was that Ade took the time he needed to process and heal, even if in the end he decided he didn't want this.

Kris hadn't realised he'd been staring at Ade for so long that his uneasiness at sharing his decision had morphed into cheeky curiosity.

"See? Told you I don't look good first thing," he joked.

"Have you looked in a mirror lately?" Perching on the side of the bed, Kris traced the contour of the freckle patch on Ade's nose. "These rock my world," he said.

Ade captured the roaming fingertip and kissed it. "I wasn't fishing for compliments, by the way."

Kris smiled. "You're the most handsome man in this room."

"Second-most, surely," Ade said.

"After Casper?"

Ade laughed. "However did you guess?"

"Just a hunch. The toast's going cold." Kris got up again and opened the curtains a few inches, throwing a shaft of surprisingly strong sunlight across the duvet. "I brought up the jam and marmalade, as I wasn't sure which you'd want or if you'd want anything at all."

Ade shrugged and picked up a piece of toast. "I'm easy." Frowning, he considered both the jam and marmalade jars before taking the lid off the marmalade and dipping the knife into it. "Do you always work so hard to get it right?" he asked.

"What d'you mean?"

Ade indicated the tray. "Breakfast with options, checking that I'm doing what's right for me…making love."

Kris's insides squirmed. "Was it awful?"

Ade smiled and shook his head. "No, babe. It wasn't. It was beautiful and satisfying, and I felt cherished and safe, which is exactly what I needed last night."

Kris still didn't get the point Ade was making. "I'm trying to avoid putting you in a situation where you end up doing something you don't want to."

"I know, and I would tell you if that was the case, because I can, safely, with you. It's not the same as with Fergus."

"You deserve to be happy."

"As do you. When—" Ade's eyes widened, giving away that he'd almost said something he hadn't meant to, but he covered up quickly. "I also want to get it right, which is why I'm going to my sister's, but only if you're OK with it. I worry that we're both rushing headlong into this before we're ready, or before I am, at least. I want to make sure we give it our best shot, and right now, I don't know that I can do that."

"Makes sense," Kris said, still curious about what Ade *hadn't* said.

"And I think we should both spend some time practising being a little less concerned about everyone else and being more attentive to our own needs."

Kris couldn't help grinning at that. "To borrow a phrase from my daughter, bossy much?"

Ade laughed. "You know it!"

"Will you be checking in with Shaunna to make sure I'm sticking to the programme?"

"Do I need to?" Ade affected a stern expression, then ruined it by taking a huge bite of toast and chewing in an exaggerated fashion, which was when Kris registered what Ade had said earlier.

"You called me babe."

"I did, didn't I?"

"I like it."

"Then we should keep it." Ade leaned forward and kissed Kris on the cheek, then swiped the spot with his thumb. "Marmalade looks good on you."

Kris laughed. "How's the toast?"

"Cold."

"You don't have to eat it."

"You didn't have to make it."

"True, but just because I did, doesn't mean—"

Ade took another huge bite, once again chewing laboriously, while Kris fought the urge to offer to make some fresh toast, if only to prove to Ade he didn't always pander to everyone else, although he'd do it in a heartbeat if Ade asked him to.

"And rubbery." Ade kept chewing. And smirking. He swallowed. "Not a good word for me, that."

"What?"

"Rubbery."

"Oh." Kris nodded sympathetically, which set Ade off snorting with laughter. Unfortunately—or not for the dog—he wasn't attending to his toast, and Casper whipped it out of his hand.

"Hey, I was eating that!" Ade protested through his giggles. "Sort of." He winked at Kris. "Should we let him eat the rest?"

"No!" Kris grabbed a piece of toast from the plate and tore a bite from it. "Mmm," he nodded, "very rubbery," and had to swallow it in a hurry so he didn't spit it out when he caught Ade's giggles. Casper saw his opportunity and dived for the tray, but Ade was quicker and lifted it out of the dog's reach. Kris took it from him and set it on top of the chest of drawers. When he turned back, Ade was serious again.

"I definitely want to give us a go," he said.

Kris nodded. "Me too."

"It's going to take time for us both to lose the habit of our previous relationships."

"Yeah."

"Promise me you'll try to be patient with me. If I tell you I miss Ferg, don't take it to heart. It's just so hard to leave it behind when there's a big part of me thinks that's all I'm worth. I still love him... well, no, I don't. I love who he was, or who I thought he was. But I want him out of my life."

"OK," Kris said. Ade looked as if he was waiting for the 'but'. "OK," Kris repeated.

"You believe me?"

"Why wouldn't I believe you?"

"Because..." Ade shrugged. "Because *I'm* struggling to believe me. I've gone back so many times, deluding myself that we could fix it if we tried hard enough—did I tell you we talked about starting a family?"

"I don't think so." Kris would've remembered if he had.

"It was when we first got together, then it came up again after…" Ade fell silent and absently reached for Casper, who wasn't anywhere near as dozy as Kris made out and settled beside Ade, his muzzle resting on Ade's knee, a perfect emotional support dog.

Ade had retreated deep into his thoughts and didn't respond when Kris said, "Popping to the bathroom," which he'd needed to do since he'd come upstairs with the tea and toast. He returned a couple of minutes later to find Ade and the dog exactly as he'd left them and got no more than a grumble from Casper when he squeezed onto the narrow strip of bed beside them.

"Are you OK there?" he asked.

Ade hummed ambiguously.

"What are you thinking about?"

"Children, and how glad I am we didn't have any."

"Do you still want them?"

"Yes," Ade answered without hesitation. "I'd love to be a dad. I'm not sure I'd be very good at it."

"I'm not sure any of us are any good at it. You just kind of muddle through."

"Do you want more children?"

Kris could also have answered 'yes' without thinking or qualifying, but he was mindful of what Ade had said about him trying too hard. "If the circumstances were right, yes, but it wouldn't be the end of the world if it didn't happen."

"Same," Ade said. "I'm cool with just being an uncle." He turned his head to meet Kris's gaze. "Does Krissi know about us?"

"Not yet, unless Shaunna's told her."

"Will she be OK with you dating?"

"Will she be OK? She'll be unbearably overjoyed. The first thing she said when we told her we'd separated was, 'Have you got a boyfriend yet?'"

"Was she asking you or Shaunna?"

"Oh! Well…she was looking at me, but now you say it, I don't know." At least he hadn't jumped down her throat when she'd asked.

"I'm guessing she's always known you're bi?"

"Yeah. It's totally ordinary to her."

"How it should be," Ade mused. "Ferg has three kids with his ex-wife, and he's not a bad dad for the most part. They used to come and stay with us when they were little. Then they started asking questions, and the visits became less and less frequent and eventually stopped altogether. I asked him if it was because he was ashamed of me." Ade laughed without humour. "He said no. He just didn't need the hassle of explaining why Daddy's clothes were in Uncle Adrian's bedroom."

"He's in the closet," Kris said.

Ade nodded. "Before his mum died, he'd only ever had relationships with women. He said if she'd known he was gay, it would've killed her. All he cared about was that she'd got to be a grandma. I think that was why he was fine with the idea of us having kids, but my sperm count's too low, and he had a vasectomy years ago. Just as well, really."

"What about adoption or fostering?"

"He wouldn't even consider it. After all, he already had kids."

"You could always do it on your own," Kris reasoned.

Ade took a breath as if to say something but released it in a sigh and gave Kris a watery smile instead. "I don't plan on doing anything on my own, but thank you for saying it." He reached over the dog and took Kris's hand, interlocking their fingers. "Do you know, you're the only person who hasn't lectured me?"

"Other than giving you a hard time yesterday morning…"

"You encouraged me to question my actions. You didn't tell me what to do."

Kris shrugged. "Only you can make those decisions. It doesn't matter what anyone else thinks. But I will say this. You are the most incredible, strong man I've ever met. I'm excited for the day you can see that for yourself, even if you also decide you're too good for me, which you are."

Ade drew breath again, but Kris shook his head and turned, sitting cross-legged, so he was fully facing Ade, albeit with Casper between them. He reached across and brushed his fingers down Ade's arm. "I'll promise to be patient if you will. There's a lot of stuff in my head that I need to tell you about, but let's deal with one thing at a time. Is that OK?"

"Yes," Ade agreed. Casper groaned like an old man and rolled onto his back, legs sticking straight up in the air, like a flipped furry occasional table. It instantly lightened the mood.

After that, they finished their lukewarm tea and took turns to visit the shower, Kris first, a kiss passing between them like a relay baton as Ade went to take his turn. Typically, Ade's phone started ringing the second he closed the bathroom door. Kris checked the screen: it was a local number, which meant it was the garage calling about his car. It stopped and then rang a second time. Kris answered it.

"Ade Simmons' phone. He can't speak right now, but I can take a message for him."

"Good morning. It's McCoy's garage. The recovery service brought Mr. Simmons' car in to us last night. We need to have a chat with him about how he wants to proceed, as it's not an easy fix, I'm afraid. Can you ask him to give us a call?"

"Will do."

Kris ended the call. "Damn." The dog flipped the right way up and belly-crawled down the bed, nudging Kris's hand for fuss. Kris sighed. "He'll be devastated, Caspy."

***

Ade

"BEEN RACING ALONG the beach?" the mechanic asked from under the bonnet of the car he was working on—*not* the MG.

"You've got to be kidding!" Ade said. There was no way he'd take it anywhere off-road.

"In that case, someone's tampered with your oil. There's sand in it, and it's worked its way through your engine. It's probably a write-off, mate. Sorry." The mechanic put down his wrench and rubbed his hands on an oily rag. "The boss said he could give the MG specialist a call, see if he can get hold of a re-con. There's not many about, but it's worth a try…"

Ade was no longer listening. He was furious. As if Fergus hadn't done enough damage already, now he'd destroyed his most treasured possession. Not flash—*an out-of-date heap of scrap*, as he'd told Ade often enough—but a trusty friend and an irreplaceable memento. Fergus was nothing short of a murderer. However, Ade was still here. He would live to fight another day, and he wouldn't be wasting any more time or energy on defending or justifying his shit of an ex-boyfriend.

Fergus's latest attack might not have been a physical strike, but it was no less brutal, and it made Ade more determined than ever that it ended here, curtain down, no encore. Fergus Campbell was history.

23: Mum Knows Best

Ade

JULIA'S HOUSE WAS, like most family homes, a bipolar residence. The evenings were vibrant and loud, with Ade's nephew and niece yelling and squealing and running up and down the stairs, two low-carriage basset hounds yapping and attempting hot pursuit, while Julia and Russ hollered at the four of them to 'pack it in' or 'pipe down' or 'get in your bed, *now*!' and tried to catch a little R-and-R in front of the TV before turning in for some much-needed rejuvenation...only to do it all over again tomorrow. Then there were the daytimes, when everyone was out and the warm glow of family turned to a foggy, off-white blankness, leaving Ade with too much time to dwell and ruminate and generally do his mental well-being no favours.

On the plus side, Fergus hadn't tried to call. In fact, nobody had called. Kris and Pip had both said they'd wait for Ade to call them so he had a chance to rest, and he'd pretty much crashed out for the first forty-eight hours. Truthfully, it had been years since he'd felt safe enough to properly sleep, but acknowledging how long he'd allowed Fergus to hurt and control him reminded him how pathetic he was...no, how pathetic *he had been*, so he was trying not to consciously think about it.

His subconscious, however, had different ideas—panic attacks, nightmares, flashbacks...he felt like some kind of nut job, sitting up half the night, reading trashy novels to fill the hours, and then napping half the day away in front of the TV. He couldn't face going out, but being alone was turning him morose. He was missing his job, missing Pip, missing Kris, and much to his shame, he was missing Fergus. He kept reminding himself: breaking the habit was the hard part, and he mustn't give in to the craving. What he needed was a new routine, or any routine at all, so he could get back to normal ASAP and stop malingering like some kind of unemployed lodger.

Come the following Saturday, Julia had clearly had enough and took charge, insisting Ade accompanied her for the weekly grocery shop. He went along with it purely out of guilt for being such an atrocious house guest, and he was glad he did, as they spent the entire day cruising the Trafford Centre, buying clothes and eating lunch and doing very little in the way of grocery shopping, just like they'd always done before *It* stole his fun.

The next morning, feeling a little less the worse for wear than he had, Ade joined Julia's brood for their usual Sunday ritual of a family walk and a full English breakfast. It was the first meal Ade had felt like eating, but Julia killed his appetite in one fell swoop when she informed him he was going to church with them, and it wasn't optional.

He tried not to freak out, telling himself *it's only communion.* Julia wasn't to know Fergus had forced him to go too, which had to have been some kind of self-flagellation, given the reason Ade had stopped going in his teens was that he'd realised his sexual 'preferences' went against the Church's teaching. Or maybe Ferg thought an hour or two of praying for forgiveness gave him a free pass for the rest of the week.

For the sake of peace, and because he didn't want to be alone with Ferg squatting in his head, Ade went to church, and it turned out to be OK. Maybe more than OK, as the vicar had a rainbow pinned to her sweater—no stuffy robes—and made a point of letting Ade know he was always welcome in her church.

"I swear I didn't tell her anything about you," Julia assured him frantically as soon as they were outside.

Ade hooked his arm through hers. "Gaydar strikes again," he said, and they laughed and reminisced his coming out to their parents, which began when a Year 9 boy approached Ade in his first week of high school to invite him to the pupil LGBTQ group, led to Ade panicking that he would be accidentally outed at parents' evening and concluded with him bravely deciding to get in there first. He could still recall every single second of that Wednesday night, standing in the kitchen, Julia sniggering because every time Ade began speaking, their mum interrupted to tell him it didn't matter if he wasn't doing well in maths or science or English or *every other subject on the curriculum* until Ade just blurted, "I'm gay!" That had shut them both up, leaving Ade waiting for the other shoe to drop, but then his mum said, "I thought you might be," and hugged him and that was that. His dad took a little longer to accept it, perhaps because he wasn't around day-to-day, but it made no difference to their relationship or their shared love of classic cars.

Julia had been right, though, he had to concede. Going to church had been good for him, but it also underscored how much the world had moved on while he hadn't been looking. It wasn't that he was totally out of touch with reality—working in radio guaranteed he'd be up to date on current affairs—but all the small, important things, like his sister's career change for instance, had passed him by. He needed to do better. But first, he needed to get better.

The rest of Sunday was of the typical working-family variety— roast dinner, ironing, homework, preparing for the week ahead. And then it was Monday, and Ade was on his own again. He had a lie-in, took the dogs for a walk, checked his email, ignored the phone...

Mum kept calling, and he couldn't avoid her forever. In the evenings, Julia fielded for him, reassuring their mum that he was fine and in the bath or on the loo or already in bed. When she called during the day, Ade let it go to voicemail, listening back to the increasingly weary request that he call when he could and then sending a message to say he was OK but busy. All lies.

By Wednesday, despite his best efforts, he'd slipped right back to where he'd been a week ago. He needed a shower and a shave, but it hardly seemed worth the effort. Still, he decided that when his mum called today, he would answer. Except she didn't call. She turned up in a taxi and let herself in, and the first he knew about it was when she said his name. He leapt from the sofa, palm to his chest.

"Mum! You frightened the life out of me."

Her eyebrows rose, unimpressed, but as she gave him a once-over, her expression softened, no judgement, only warmth and love. She opened her arms, and he readily went into them.

"I'm sorry, Mum. I'm so sorry," he said over and again, incapable of articulating any of the million things he was sorry for.

"Shh. It's all right, sweetheart. Mum's here now."

Incredible how that childhood truth still held. From grazed knees to broken hearts, his mum had fixed everything, protected him from mean big sisters, the bully next door, even his dad, who had been a decent, laid-back sort of bloke but hadn't always been supportive of Ade's choice to study 'arty-farty subjects'. His mum soon set him right. But as fierce as she was, she had a heart condition, and Ade's fear that the stress would kill her was real, which was why he'd put off seeing her. That and his shame for remaining in a situation any sensible person would've ditched at the first opportunity.

She held him for a long time, while he sobbed and sniffed, on the one hand wishing he could stop crying, on the other knowing the second he did she'd start asking questions. He was almost right: she sent him off to make coffee first.

Ade returned with the two mugs and sat in the chair, both to keep his distance and for the change of scenery. He'd spent far too much time curled up on that sofa.

"Has he gone, love?" his mum asked. Ade nodded.

"Yes. For good." The tears welled again, and he picked at a stray thread in an attempt to thwart them. It was holding a button on his pyjama top and fell off into his hand. His mum laughed, her laughter quickly turning to tears, which set Ade off again. He moved back to the sofa, his arms around her now.

"Thank God," she said. "I'm proud of you."

"Why? You told me, and I didn't listen. After Dad—"

"It doesn't matter now." She turned and tilted her head back to look at him as she smoothed his messy but hopefully not greasy hair. It hadn't seen product in days and badly needed cutting. "I'd say no harm done, but…I can't stand thinking of all he's put you through."

Ade shrugged glibly. "I'll heal." It was better she didn't know the finer details, but there was no getting out of telling her about the MG. Just gearing up to saying the words had him cowering in anticipation of violent repercussions, but of course, there were none. She didn't even raise her voice, though she was clearly upset.

"I'm sorry," he said uselessly.

"As am I, sweetheart. I know how much that car means to you. But in the end, it's just a thing, and you still have all the lovely memories with your dad, so you can let it go."

*

Fergus chose that afternoon to break the non-contact. He called Ade's mobile phone; Ade hung up. He called again; Ade hung up again. After a short delay, Julia's house phone rang. Ade met his mother's steely gaze.

"Did you tell him you were here?" she asked.

Ade shook his head. "No, but he knows I came here last time."

"Right," she said. "If he calls again, I'll deal with him."

And call he did.

"Adrian wants nothing to do with you."

"He's a grown man. Surely, he can make up his own mind."

"Is there something wrong with your hearing?"

"Look, I don't want to fall out with you, Rita, so if you wouldn't mind just—"

"Right. You listen to me, Fergus. If you come anywhere near my son again, I will go to the police and tell them exactly what you've done. Do you understand?" She hung up before Fergus had a chance to answer.

Ade covered his face with his hands, his breathing amplified by the cocoon of his palms.

"All right, sweetheart?" his mum asked.

He gave a quick nod. Yes, he would be, in time.

***

Kris

KRIS'S USUAL FEAR of forgetting his lines kicked in just as he hit the call button, but he'd needed to rehearse so he didn't say the wrong thing. He and Ade had chatted online briefly, in text form, and there had been a couple of missed calls from a Manchester landline that Kris assumed were from Ade, but he hadn't called him back. He'd asked for time, and Kris had tried to give him that, but it was almost two weeks since he'd gone to stay with his sister, and Kris was starting to worry that Ade had changed his mind about giving their relationship a go.

The call rang out a few times, but Kris held on with fingers crossed.

"Hello, you!" Ade answered warmly.

"Hey." It was such a relief to hear his voice. "I'm not disturbing you, am I?"

"Not at all. I've just got out of the shower, and before that my mum popped round to see me. It was really hard but good."

"Is that the first time you've seen her since..." Kris stalled at *since you kicked Fergus out.*

"Since I came to Julia's," Ade finished for him. "Yes. He called while she was here, actually."

"He?" Kris hated pressing the point, but he wanted to be sure they were talking about the same person.

"He. The ex. I decided I'm not even going to refer to him by name anymore. In fact, I'm considering just going with *It*."

"OK." Having seen Ade pinned to the wall by 'It', Kris was struggling to find the funny side to what he supposed was a little gallows humour on Ade's part. "What've you been up to?"

"Not much. Slouching around in my PJs, watching daytime telly, sleeping…and sleeping. I can't seem to get enough." Almost as if to emphasise the point, Ade broke off into a yawn. "Ooh, sorry. I promise you're not boring me."

Kris did manage to chuckle at that. "It's fine. Shaunna's the same. After her mum died, she was asleep more than she was awake."

"Well, you know," Ade said airily, "being a redhead is *dreadfully* exhausting."

"So I'm told."

They both laughed and then fell quiet. Kris took a breath, ready to make his invitation, but Ade jumped in first.

"I was thinking I might come over and see you at the weekend, if that's OK with you?"

"Yeah, I'd really like that. In fact, I was about to ask if you'd consider coming to a party with me on Saturday."

"What kind of party?"

"My friends, Dan and Adele?"

"The ones with the fancy garden?"

"That's them. They're getting engaged. And if you think their garden's fancy, wait until you see Dan's mum's house—where the party's being held. It's one of those grandiose Victorian mini mansions, but it should be a fun night."

"Is it a big party?"

"Fairly." Kris had prepared himself for disappointment, understanding that it might be too much for Ade to face, but he was still secretly willing him to say yes. "If you'd rather not—"

"No. I'd love to."

"Are you sure?"

"Yes."

"OK." Kris sighed in relief.

"Did you think I'd say no?"

"I hoped you wouldn't."

Two weeks apart, forty miles or so between them, yet the connection was still there, that undeniable, irresistible attraction. Kris had missed Ade like crazy but didn't want to put pressure on him by admitting it, so he stayed quiet and simply appreciated knowing Ade was on the other end of the line.

"So will you get the train?" he asked eventually, at the same time as Ade said, "I'll either get the train…"

Kris waited for the 'or', but nothing else came his way. "Ade?"

"Still here. Just…the car. I had to tell my mum what happened, and I'm so mad about it. But anyway, I'll figure out the train times and let you know."

"I wish I could fix it," Kris said.

"You in greasy overalls, pulling an engine apart? *That* I'd love to see!"

Kris laughed. "Never happening!"

"Shame." Ade was laughing too. "I can't wait to see you."

"Me neither. Can I meet you at the station? Is that OK?"

"That's perfect," Ade said.

24: Connections

Kris

IT WAS TOO early for Casper's evening patrol of the neighbour-
hood, too late and too wet for playing Frisbee in the park.
In need of something to occupy his mind, Kris took him anyway,
but the dog must've been picking up on his mood and was
reluctant to leave his side. After no more than half a dozen half-
hearted throws and fetches, Kris put him back on his lead and
continued onwards to the salon to meet Shaunna from work.

"What's the matter?" she asked the second she saw him.

Kris shrugged. "Ade's coming to the party."

"That's good. Isn't it?"

"Yeah," Kris said glumly.

"Weirdo." Shaunna hooked her arm through his and they
fell in step, taking a slow stroll homeward, or as slow a stroll as
Casper would permit. "So why the long face?" she asked.

"Don't know."

Twice more, she tried to start a conversation, but Kris genuinely
had no idea why he was feeling so miserable. Ade had seemed in
good spirits, and he was the one who'd suggested coming over at
the weekend. There was no reason for Kris to worry he'd pushed
Ade into anything, yet he couldn't shake it off.

They arrived back at the house, and Shaunna went upstairs
to shower, leaving Kris with instructions to make cups of tea
and get ready to explain himself. Tea made, he sat at the table
and awaited her return, using the time to think through how
he was feeling, hoping that once he put it into words it would
make more sense.

"Oh dear."

He glanced behind him to where she was standing in the kitchen doorway, arms folded, watching him.

"I didn't hear you come down."

"Hmm." She came over and sat, still watching him as she picked up her tea and took a sip. "Ahhhh. That's better."

"Tough day?"

"No tougher than usual, although Hayley went to the wholesaler's, so I've been in the stockroom all afternoon." She took another sip of tea and relaxed back in her chair, waiting patiently for him to talk to her. Another sip...

"It hurts," he said, but that was all he'd come up with.

Shaunna peered at him over the rim of her cup.

He shook his head, utterly confused. The feelings were so intense he didn't know how to deal with them. He was missing Ade like they'd been together for years. It was too soon to need someone so much, and it was frightening. He put down his cup and pressed his palms together, trying to centre his thoughts.

"Are you praying?" Shaunna asked.

"No, but I'd give it a shot if it meant not feeling like this."

"Like what?"

"I'm not sure."

Shaunna narrowed her eyes at him. "Why?" she asked.

"Why what?"

"Well, even for you, it's a bit soon to be worrying about how you'd cope with the break-up."

There was mischief in her gaze, but she'd hit the nail on the head. "You know me too well."

"It's been a long time, hun."

Kris picked up his tea, watching the surface of the liquid shimmer under the lights. "Ade needs someone emotionally stable, with no baggage. Not me."

"No?"

"You think I'm wrong?"

"I think Ade knows his own mind."

Kris opened his mouth to contradict her but stopped and instead considered her words. She was right, but she wasn't just talking about Ade. She was talking about herself and their marriage. Kris had worked hard and saved up to buy them a family home so that she could concentrate on being a mum, but he'd never asked her if that was what she'd wanted or expected. After they separated, she said she understood he had done it with the right intentions, but they should've discussed it first, communicated what they both wanted from the relationship. If they had…well, who was to say whether it would have saved their marriage, but learning to communicate had at least saved their friendship. In fact, it was stronger than ever.

Kris didn't want to lose that. He loved living there, and he loved Shaunna, which was a significant part of why he was struggling so much with falling for Ade. The two of them—Shaunna and Ade—had got along brilliantly, but it was…unconventional. He couldn't see how it was sustainable in the long run. Added to that, what Kris had been through with his uncle meant he felt Ade's pain so strongly it could have been his own. He hadn't been close to his abuser, had trusted and respected him purely because he was an elder, but to suffer at the hands of someone you'd fallen in love with… Thinking about it was unbearable.

Kris had heeded Ade's warning. He *would* miss Fergus, and that was fine. But what if Fergus asked him for another chance? Would he go back again? There were so many unknowns beyond Kris's control, and his instincts were pulling in two directions: back away while he still could or hang on tight and ride out the storm.

Shaunna reached across the table and took his hands in hers. "Carpe diem."

Kris couldn't help smiling at her movie-night reference. *Dead Poets Society* was one of their all-time favourite films. If she was preparing to mop the kitchen floor? *Carpe diem*. If she was about the head out to work in the rain? Up went the umbrella and *carpe diem.* He glanced up from his tea, to find her smiling right back at him.

"Take the chance," she said. "That's all."

"I feel like I'm going crazy."

"You've always been crazy. This is just the first chance you've ever had to really express yourself."

"I don't want to drive off the cliff, Louise. What if—"

"What-if, nothing, Thelma. Do or do not. There is no try."

At that, Kris rolled his eyes. "If I agree, will it stop you quoting Hollywood wisdom at me?"

She grinned and raised her eyebrows. "Perhaps this is the mysterious Mr. Right you have been waiting your whole life to meet."

Kris laughed. "Riffing still counts."

Shaunna got up and made her way to his side of the table, putting her arms around him in a motherly hug. He snuggled against her, and she planted a kiss on the top of his head. "Hearts will never be practical until they can be made unbreakable. But I still think you should have one."

***

Ade

As THE TRAIN pulled into the station, Ade's stomach lurched in anticipation, and in his eagerness to open the door, he pushed at the button before it illuminated to indicate it was no longer locked. Not once had it occurred to him that Kris would stand him up, and rightly so, because he could see him on the other side of the barrier, peering over the heads of others, scouring the passengers moving along the platform. They made eye contact, and Ade waved, quickening his pace, his heart fluttering with excitement. And it was excitement, rather than dread. He made it through the ticket barrier, and they embraced. Kris kissed his cheek, sending a little spark chasing through him.

"Hi," Ade greeted breathlessly.

"Hi," Kris replied, offering to take Ade's bag, but he waved the offer away.

"I've missed you."

Kris had a huge smile on his face.

"What?" Ade asked.

"I'm glad you said that, because I've missed you too."

Ade took Kris's hand, and they set off towards taxi rank. "I'm a bit nervous about this party."

"Because of meeting my friends?"

"Maybe a little. More because I'm not used to going out." As soon as he said it, he wished he hadn't, as Kris flinched. "Hey." He squeezed Kris's hand. "I'm made of sterner stuff than you think."

"I know."

"Have you been thinking about it a lot?"

"Trying not to. But since you told me…or maybe even before that, because I kind of knew from the get-go, I can't get it out of my head."

"And you're struggling to process it," Ade said.

Kris nodded.

"That's understandable. It's not normal, is it?"

"It's selfish. This is about you, not me."

"Yes, well, I don't want to talk about it. So…"

"Right, OK." Kris nodded and obediently changed the subject. "How was Julia? Did you have fun?"

"Oh, she was wonderful, and yes, I did. Thank you for asking."

"You're most welcome," Kris said theatrically.

Ade laughed. "Seriously, it was so nice to spend time with her, and the kids have grown up so much! It's amazing—you only have to miss out for a few months and they turn from babies to toddlers, to preschoolers, and before you know it, they're starting high school. I can barely get my head around the fact that Emmett's almost a teenager. Was it like that for you with Krissi?"

"Yep. Baby one minute, at school the next, then suddenly she's a grown-up with her own apartment."

Ade gave Kris's hand another reassuring squeeze. "I can't wait to meet her. I bet she's a credit to both of you. And I don't think they notice how much time has passed, you know? Emmett's convinced I was there for his birthday last year, but my wrist was splinted, so I know for a fact I wasn't. I told him the truth, too, because he was asking awkward questions, and there seemed little point lying, especially after *the ex* called me again, but I felt ashamed." So much for not wanting to talk about it. At times, he wondered if that was all he was, the sum of what Fergus had made him. He bit down on his bottom lip, quite hard, banishing the thought. "Anyway, I promised Emmett I'd make it up to him. He loves the theatre too, so we're going to catch a couple of shows together."

"Any excuse," Kris teased.

Ade laughed. "Quite right."

"Emmett's an unusual name."

"It is. Julia and Russ are total *Back To The Future* nuts. Like, for instance, when I told them about the MG, Jules said, 'At least it wasn't a DeLorean.' They had one as their wedding car."

"That's fun!"

"It was a great day, if not a bit geeky. Their wedding cake was on a hoverboard, and of course, *the ex* had to point out it wasn't real, like we didn't all know that. He made such a fool of himself that day, but at least he had the decency to pass out in the hotel lobby and not ruin it for anyone else." He was doing it again. *Back to the future, Ade. Take the hint.* "So, Julia and Russ have been together fifteen years. Emmett's thirteen next month, and Jenny's just turned nine."

"Oh, right." Kris looked bamboozled but didn't comment on Ade's flitty chatter, so he carried on once they were in the taxi.

"I've sorted out what I'm doing with the car, by the way. The specialist that the mechanic brought in is a partner in a British cars museum, and they'd been looking for a BGT for their collection. They'll replace the engine and keep the car in the old RAF hangar they lease down in Suffolk. I can visit any time, he said, and take it out for a spin."

"That's great news."

"It is! Did I mention they also have a BRG E-Type?" Ade waggled his eyebrows.

Kris laughed. "No?"

"Oh, yes. I'd much rather take that out."

For the rest of the journey, Ade stayed quiet, conscious he'd hardly let Kris speak and trying to calm his nerves. He really didn't want to talk about Fergus, but he kind of wanted Kris to ask what had happened when Fergus had called so he could share how proud he was of his mum for doing exactly what she'd said she would. Now all he had to do was back up his statement with a brief court appearance, and Fergus would be on a permanent restraining order.

They arrived back at the house, but before Ade even had a chance to reach for his wallet, Kris had paid the taxi fare.

"In that case, I'm buying the drinks at the party," Ade said.

"It's a free bar."

"Boo." Ade followed Kris to the front door. "Dinner's on me at some point then—what's up?" Kris was still rummaging in his pocket.

"Think I've lost my key again."

"Again?"

"Yep. I'm on about my twenty-fifth by now." He tried the other pocket. "I have a suggestion."

"Hmm?"

"We could go down for a weekend sometime."

"Go where?"

"To the classic car museum."

"You'd come with me?"

"I'd love to."

"Wow. OK." Ade was taken aback.

"There're some gorgeous old hotels in Suffolk. If we hired a car, we could..." Kris trailed off and frowned. "What's wrong?"

"Nothing." Ade's expression morphed into a wide grin, and Kris's gaze immediately went to the gap in his teeth. Ade blushed. "That's the source of all my twubbles," he said, exaggerating his rhotacism.

"It's the source of your allure," Kris said, his voice low and sultry.

"Oh, really?" Ade blinked flirtatiously. Kris laughed and spun him in for a kiss.

"Yes, really. I like it," he said, lips lingering on Ade's. "I feel it needs further exploration."

"I might let you if we ever get inside."

Kris held up the key. "Found it."

"Well, what are you waiting for? Get that door open. We have things to do!"

25: Brief

Kris

IT WAS MID-AFTERNOON, and Shaunna was still at work, so they had the place to themselves, give or take a Labrador retriever. Casper couldn't have been more pleased to see Ade and knocked him flat on the kitchen floor, alternating between snuffling him affectionately and sniffing him all over, no manners whatsoever.

"He knows I cheated on him," Ade said when Casper finally bounded away and he was able to get up from the floor. He brushed himself down and accepted Kris's offer of a damp paper towel to wipe his face. "He's a lot less spitty than basset hounds, let me tell you."

Kris grimaced. He loved having a dog and didn't care about the hair or the wet-dog smell Shaunna spent a small fortune on candles and incense to disguise, but dogs with droopy jowls, all that slobber…he shuddered just thinking about it. Ade saw it and laughed.

"No spitty dogs." He wrote in the air, finishing off with a tick. "Duly noted."

That sounded a lot like future plans to Kris, and it kicked a few more of those *what-ifs* into the wings, though he was still anxious about their weekend together and sensed Ade was too. This was the first time they'd been alone somewhere private, and while they'd both made it clear outside that they were of the same mind in wanting some intimacy, everything seemed much more real and important than it had before Ade went to stay with his sister.

"I was thinking," Ade began but got no further, as Casper was back with his Frisbee. He trotted straight past Kris and dropped it at Ade's feet. "OK. Never mind. Is there something you want, Caspy?" He looked over at Kris and shrugged. "W-A-L-K-I-E-S?"

"We don't have to—"

Ade silenced him with a look. "There's nothing we *have* to do, but it would be remiss of me to refuse an invitation to accompany such handsome gentlemen for a promenade."

"There won't be much promenading, but OK," Kris accepted and followed Ade and Casper back to the front door. He couldn't help thinking the dog looked decidedly smug as the three of them set off for the park, where the Frisbee fetching commenced in earnest.

"He's really good at this," Ade remarked, circling his shoulder after having launched the disc for about the tenth time. "Did it take a lot of training for him to learn?"

"None whatsoever," Kris admitted ruefully. "I'm pretty sure it's instinctive, a case of 'does exactly what it says on the label'."

"Have you had him since he was a puppy?"

"Nope, although he was only young when we adopted him. He's a failed Search and Rescue dog...I say failed, but he was channelling Lassie when we were Wales. Our friend's six-year-old son went missing, and Casper found him."

"Oh no! That's horrifying! Was he OK?"

"He'd fallen and broken a couple of bones in his foot, but he was alive and well."

"Thank God!" Casper brought the Frisbee back and Ade threw his arms around him, fussing and praising him for being such a clever boy—*a hero.*

"You realise you'll never get a moment's peace now?" Kris joked.

"I don't care." Ade launched the Frisbee again. "He deserves all the accolades!"

The fact they hadn't talked about any of this before really pressed home how short a time they'd known each other. There again, they'd had bigger concerns than Casper's heritage, so it was perhaps a positive sign that their relationship was settling into something more normal, less fraught.

When they returned from walking the dog, Ade went straight upstairs to deposit his bag, he said, but several minutes on, he was still up there. Kris had a good idea why, too, but as much as he wanted to follow him, he needed Ade to initiate so he'd know he wasn't pushing him into anything.

Several more minutes passed before Ade called downstairs, "Where should I put my clothes?"

"In the drawers next to the window," Kris called back.

"Come and show me."

Kris looked up at him from the bottom of the stairs. "There is only one set of drawers next to the window."

Ade shrugged. "But still...I'd like you to show me."

"OK." Kris made his way up, sighing for effect. He arrived at the top, stepping into Ade's space because there was nowhere else he could go. Ade stood his ground and captured Kris's gaze.

"I think I know which drawers you mean, but I may need some assistance with the bed."

"Is that so?" Kris's voice wobbled as Ade caught hold of him by his shirt front and pulled him closer.

"That's so," Ade murmured, huffing warm breath over Kris's lips before nipping lightly at the bottom one. "You play hard to get so wonderfully well."

"Thanks. I'm a professional," Kris said with a shaky laugh.

"A professional player?" Ade tugged on his shirt, using it to lead him to the bedroom.

"Not a player." Kris stumbled along, mesmerised by the hazel-green eyes staring into his, the feathery sensation of his shirt being unbuttoned. He felt his belt slide out of its buckle and swallowed hard. He'd never been seduced before, or not this gentle undressing, and it was an incredible turn-on.

Ade took a step back so he could remove his sweater and stood, topless and smiling at Kris's appreciative visual appraisal. Even with the bruises, Ade had been a beautiful man, but now they'd disappeared and the scars were starting to fade, he was confident, no longer trying to hide his body. Kris could've looked at him all day, but Ade stepped closer again, overriding the desire to look with the urge to touch when their bare chests made contact.

"Oh God," Ade groaned. "That feels good." He eased Kris's shirt off his shoulders and ran his palms up his back, stretching up as he cupped Kris's head, bringing their mouths together in a hot-breathed kiss. Kris gave in instantly, the proverbial putty in Ade's hands...and lips, which nibbled a trail down his chin, over his Adam's apple and continued downwards as Ade dropped to his knees. Kris's entire body erupted in goosebumps.

"I need you," Ade murmured against Kris's belly. "In so many ways I can't prioritise. Are you cold? Do you want to get under the duvet?"

Kris shook his head. "Keep going."

"Talking or kissing?" Ade peered up at him, his cheeks and lips a debauched deep pink.

"Both."

"I need to get these off you for starters," Ade said, unzipping Kris's jeans and pulling them down over his hips. He paused and looked up again. Kris knew he should nod to let Ade know what he was doing was fine, but he was caught up in the moment and delayed too long.

"OK." Ade rose to his feet. "*We* need to work on communicating when we're less compromised by—"

Without warning, Kris put his hands on Ade's cheeks and drew him in for another deep kiss, probing with his tongue and then dragging it back over the gap in Ade's teeth. Did it count as a fetish? He wasn't sure, but he didn't waste time dwelling on it. With Ade's hot palms pressed to his boxer-clad buttocks and his jeans around his thighs, he was teetering on the line between succumbing to a vague but haunting flashback and giving in fully to whatever Ade wanted to do to him.

Ade withdrew and reached for his bag, from which he took condoms and lube. "I'm prepared this time," he said and set them on the bedside table, then sat on the edge of the bed to remove his shoes. "Like a Boy Scout," he added and glanced up at Kris, who was standing exactly as Ade had left him. "Is something wrong?"

"I, er…" He pulled his jeans back up but didn't fasten them. Ade slumped in disappointment. It would feel like rejection to him, and that was the last thing Kris wanted—for either of them—but he wasn't sure he could go through with sex right now. "Have you ever heard of erotic massage?" he asked.

"No, but I imagine the clue's in the name."

He edged past Ade to reach his bedside table, where the massage oil was…somewhere. He found it and turned back. "Oh!" He swallowed at the sight before him.

"I'm going to feel terribly naked if you don't strip off soon."

"Not terribly naked. Beautifully naked," Kris said, gazing open-mouthed. He was beyond being able to undress himself, but that seemed to suit Ade just fine, and he guided Kris down onto the bed, pushing gently on his chest until he was lying on his back, kisses landing all over his belly.

"Lift," Ade commanded.

Kris did as he was told, breathing steadily as Ade shuffled down the bed, taking Kris's jeans and boxers with him.

"Tell me more about this erotic massage." He kissed a trail back up again and settled on his side next to Kris, smoothing his hand over Kris's chest…and downwards. "Isn't that what we did last time?"

Kris captured Ade's hand and kept hold of it as he turned to face him. "Well, it was definitely erotic," he said with a smile. "But it was foreplay, leading up to sex."

"And this wouldn't be?"

"We might end up in the same place, but it's about the massage, exploring each other's body."

"OK. I think I get it. Would you like to go first? Show me how it's done."

Ade rolled onto his back and put his arms behind his head, offering himself up. Kris stayed right where he was.

"Problem?" Ade asked.

Kris shook his head. "I don't actually know how it's done."

"I thought, as you'd suggested it, you must've done it before."

Kris shook his head again.

"Is it something you made up?"

"No. George—" Kris screwed his eyes shut and clamped his teeth together. *Will I ever learn?* "I'll get the oil," he said, turning away and swinging his legs off the bed to sit.

"Babe?"

The mattress shifted as Ade crawled across to sit beside him.

"Look at me."

Kris glanced sideways, making fleeting eye contact.

"It's OK, you know. Everyone has a past."

"It's not that."

"Then what?"

"I betrayed a confidence."

"George's?"

Kris nodded.

"Well, you didn't tell me anything. I mean, I can glean from what you've said that the erotic massage idea came from him, and I promise it won't go any further."

"I know. I trust you. Completely, which is…" Kris picked up the bottle of massage oil and shook it, not realising the lid wasn't shut properly. It flipped open, spilling oil over his hands and thighs. "Shit."

"You know what this means?" Ade asked, shifting again so that he was kneeling behind Kris.

"What's that?" The words merged into a gasp as Ade leaned forward, sliding his palms over Kris's shoulders, chest, belly, down to his thighs, then back up again, spreading the oil as he went.

"We can't waste all this oil, so we'll have to make it up as we go along." Ade kneaded Kris's shoulders. "You may need to relax a bit."

"I'm trying," Kris said, but he was so tense, the gentle pressure was uncomfortable and not in the least erotic. "I'd rather massage you."

"You can…soon." Ade kissed Kris's neck as he worked his way down his arms.

"And find all the places that feel good for you."

"This is more of your 'making it right for everyone but Kris syndrome', isn't it?"

"Maybe. But is that so bad?"

"What you want matters too."

"I really want to get to know your body. We could be in the throes of passion and I touch you somewhere or say something that reminds…that takes your mind off what we're doing."

"Same's true for you," Ade pointed out. "Now, tell me how this feels." He slid his hands around Kris's sides, spanning his stomach and applying just enough pressure with his fingertips to keep it on the right side of tickling.

"It feels OK," Kris said.

"OK?" Ade repeated. "We can do so much better than that. Give me that oil."

Kris handed over the bottle.

Ade squeezed a good amount into his hands, some of it spilling over and trickling down onto Kris's belly. "What were you going to say about trusting me completely?"

"That it's freaking me out."

"Oh."

"Only a little," Kris quickly qualified. "I've known George and Shaunna for nearly thirty years, and there's things I've never told them, yet I've only known you three weeks—" Kris stopped there, since the rest would've taken him into talking about 'the ex' territory, and it was a no-fly zone.

"Go on," Ade said.

"That's all."

"No. It's not."

Without thinking, Kris rubbed his eyes, covering his face in oil, which didn't contain menthol or lemon or anything else that would've stung, but it wasn't pleasant. For a few seconds, Ade made not a sound, then a snort escaped next to Kris's ear and Ade burst into full-on laughter. He circled his arms around Kris and kissed his cheek, over-acting a 'slip' from there to his lips. That raised a laugh from Kris too.

"That's better," Ade said. Climbing off the bed, he plucked a handful of tissues from the box on the chest of drawers and knelt in front of Kris to wipe the oil from his face, dabbing at a spot here and there. "Talk to me."

"You don't want to talk about it."

"Ah, it's about *the ex.*"

"Yeah."

"Sorry. I didn't mean to silence you."

"It's OK."

"It's not. Tell me."

Kris was still reluctant to say more, but maybe it was better out in the open. It certainly couldn't be any worse than churning his fears around in his head. "Thinking about what he did to you...I don't know how to deal with it. It hurts too much, and you need someone strong who's going to support you. I'm not strong, Ade. I want to be, for you, but I'm also terrified that he'll ask you to give him another chance, because I'd lose you, and—"

"OK," Ade interrupted. "Can I jump in for a moment?"

Kris stared at the floor, embarrassed he'd let his mouth run riot again. "Sorry."

"Don't be, but I need you to listen to me. Can you do that?"

Kris nodded, but Ade was waiting for a proper answer from him. He looked up and said, "Yes."

"No doubt, you're going to dismiss this as me telling you what you want to hear, but I promise you, there is *no way on Earth* I would give Fergus another chance. Do you want to know why? Because I don't want to lose you either."

Kris didn't respond. He believed Ade, but the words hung like lights beyond a curtain he couldn't push aside. What use was he to Ade when he couldn't even handle his own issues?

"Hey." Ade shook Kris's hands. "You're all tense again."

"Am I?"

"You are. Do you want a hug?"

Kris gave a swift nod and once again let Ade take charge as he lay down and pulled Kris to him, locking him in a firm yet gentle hold. "You know, a lot of this pain you're feeling is empathetic. You're too good at putting yourself in my shoes." Ade kissed him on the forehead. "That's probably why you picked up on it from the beginning, the same way I picked up on it with you...even before Shaunna told me about your uncle."

"Did she?" Kris's voice barely sounded, but he was too preoccupied with his thoughts to repeat himself.

"Yes, but only to stop my paranoia. I got caught on the idea of you being a cheat, and she told me so I'd understand how Jack made a move on you when you were vulnerable. She didn't go into any details."

"It was a long time ago."

"But it's still fresh in your head?"

Kris nodded against Ade's chest.

"That doesn't mean you're not strong." Ade lifted Kris's face so that they were nose-to-nose. "And anyway, I don't want a protector. I want someone who respects me and cares how I feel. Is that you?"

Kris attempted a smile. "I think so."

"Good." Ade touched his lips to Kris's—not quite a kiss. "I think so too."

Kris reciprocated the brush of lips, lingering so that it became a kiss, allowing Ade to roll him onto his back. He closed his eyes, listening to the squeeze of the bottle, the brushing together of palms to distribute the oil, then focused on the sensation of Ade's fingers tracing the line of his jaw, down his neck, to his chest, brushing over his nipples, continuing down for a few seconds before returning to his nipples.

"That's better," Ade murmured, sending a buzz through Kris's sternum. At last, his body was responding to the touch in the right way, so he oiled his hands too, and they massaged each other, following their instincts, exploring with fingers, lips and tongues, pausing to tell each other places that elicited good feelings or bad, working together to begin the healing process. It would, of course, take more than one very short massage session, which ultimately proved to be a little too erotic and left them both in an oily, slightly tearful but satisfied mess.

26: Atrium Antics

Ade

KRIS HADN'T BEEN exaggerating when he called the party venue a 'mini mansion'. The three of them—Ade, Kris and Shaunna—were on foot, and to reach the house they had to crunch their way up a lengthy, though thankfully well-lit gravel drive that widened out at the top to accommodate an illuminated round stone pond with a tiered fountain at its centre, foregrounding the magnificent Victorian redbrick property.

Ade leaned in to Kris and stage-whispered, "You didn't say you had rich friends."

"They're not. Dan runs a small haulage business with his brother, and they're doing OK. All of this—" Kris indicated the house and the expensive cars parked outside "—is down to their mum's fourth husband."

Shaunna nodded conspiratorially. "He's a gangster."

Ade gasped.

Kris scoffed. "He is not!"

"He is! Ask Adele."

"Oh, because she's such a reliable source of information."

"God!" Shaunna stretched the word to two syllables and affected a teenage huff. "You're such a bitch."

Ade couldn't stop laughing at their faked argument, which carried them right up to the massive front door. Shaunna pushed the big, shiny brass button, and from somewhere inside they heard tubular bells chime a loud *ding-dong*.

"What if they hate me?" Ade said, although it was really a thought escaping aloud.

"They won't," Shaunna assured him. "They're nice people with excellent taste in friends."

"Other than Jess," Kris muttered.

Ade's mouth dropped open. He looked to Shaunna to see what she thought. She weighed it up and shrugged.

"He's got a point."

The door was solid wood, so they had no idea if anyone was coming to let them in, but they'd been standing there long enough for a couple more cars to pull up and unload.

"And Ellie can be quite mean," Kris added.

Ade's eyebrows rose in alarm.

"Would 'nice' be the right word for Josh, even?" Kris rested his index finger on his chin in a thoughtful pose. Shaunna shoved him in the side, and he grinned.

"Don't listen to any of it. He's winding you up," she told Ade.

He wasn't convinced, but then Kris smiled and winked at him, and he realised the whole performance had been to put him at ease. Kris and Shaunna were good people; there was no reason for him to believe their friends weren't good people too. Regardless, he planned on sticking close to Kris and Shaunna for the duration.

By the time the door opened, there were another eight guests waiting behind them, none of whom Kris or Shaunna knew. They shared a polite 'hello' and all trooped inside together, or rather, they stepped through the door and then drifted forward, gazing in wonder at the sight that greeted them.

"Well, you're not the only one who doesn't know anybody," Shaunna said to Ade out of the side of her mouth.

He hardly heard her, totally bowled over by the grandeur of the enormous atrium in which they now stood. There were easily fifty people present, but the place was so big that they were scattered, with yards of chequered floor space in between, like the pieces of a vibrant chess game.

Wide twin staircases with ornate ironwork banisters ran up either side to the first floor, connected by a balcony extending right across the atrium and currently cluttered with professional light and sound equipment. Moving-head lights swept across the expanse, reflecting off the gleaming black-and-white marble floor before chasing up the white marble walls and into the dome above, within which hung the biggest chandelier Ade had ever seen.

"Wow! This is beautiful!"

"Yeah, it is," Shaunna agreed. "We've only been here once, haven't we?" She nudged Kris.

"Hmm?"

"I said we've only been here once."

"Oh, yeah. Looks a bit different now."

Shaunna gestured to the staircases. "Those rails were stripped back to bare metal, and the treads were untreated wood. I ended up with a huge splinter in my foot."

"Ouch," Ade said with a grimace.

"And there's a pool house at the back, which is…well, have you seen the conservatory at Kew Gardens?"

"Only on TV."

"It was like an apocalyptic version of that."

"Right." Ade was having trouble visualising it.

"Basically, it's a big greenhouse with a swimming pool in it," Kris said. "Except when we came here, it was a pool of green sludge."

"Nice."

"Dan and Andy's mum and stepdad were away for the weekend, and—"

"And we were promised a pool party," Shaunna interrupted.

Ade nodded, highly entertained by their tag-team storytelling.

"They'd only just bought the place then, and Dan and Andy had volunteered to clean out the pool," Shauna explained. "Either they were being overly optimistic about how quickly they thought they could get it done or—"

"They scammed us," Kris finished for her.

"Whatever, we spent the entire weekend clearing a foot of gunk with shovels and a wheelbarrow, then hosing down the tiles. They're gorgeous—blue mosaic, like something from Ancient Greece."

"Now you can see them," Kris said.

"There's that," Shaunna agreed. "It was a fun weekend, though, even if the pool was nowhere near ready for water by the end of it and I was stiff as a board for days."

"They won us over with food and alcohol," Kris added.

"An excellent strategy," Ade said, coveting their experience a little. Perhaps now he was rid of *It*, he might be able to do things like that himself instead of enjoying them vicariously.

"What d'you reckon then?" The question came from behind, and the three of them turned to see who'd spoken.

Ade watched Kris and the stranger greet each other with the kind of hug granted only to family and very close friends. Or ex-boyfriends, maybe? Ade really hoped this wasn't George because the guy was gorgeous—tall, with olive skin, deep-brown eyes, brown-black hair and muscles to die for. He felt himself swooning and tugged at Shaunna's sleeve, which was enough of a prompt for her to grant the introduction Kris had failed to.

"Ade, this is Dan."

Kris and Dan released each other, and Dan extended an arm. Ade did the same, expecting a finger-crunching handshake, but it was nothing like that at all. Dan squeezed his hand and dazzled him with a charming smile.

"Good to meet you, Ade."

"You too. Congratulations on your engagement."

"Cheers." Dan briefly glanced around him. "Adele's here, somewhere." He turned back to his friends and shrugged. "Ah, well. She'll turn up."

"The place is looking great," Kris said.

"Yeah. Andy's been hard at it since we got back from Wales."

"He's staying here at the moment, isn't he?" Shaunna asked.

"That's right. And *she's* gonna be here tonight, so, er…"

Shaunna gave Dan a nod of reassurance. "Don't worry. I'm on it."

"Thanks." Dan hugged her and kissed her cheek. "Nice perfume," he complimented.

"Nice aftershave," Shaunna replied with a flirtatious smile.

Dan gave her a cheeky wink in return. "Right. The bar's in there." He indicated the room on his left. "And the buffet's in there." He pointed over to his right. "I'd best see if I can find my fiancée. Glad you could make it."

Kris gave him a disbelieving look.

"Well, I know you've been busy with work and…things…"

"As if we were going to miss this!"

"Yeah, all right. I'll catch you in a bit."

With that, Dan headed off into the crowd, which had grown in size while they'd been chatting, forcing them to slowly edge forward to accommodate more guests arriving. Someone turned the music up, and all of a sudden it felt like a real party. Shaunna shifted from one foot to the other, leaning on Ade. He glanced down at her feet and up again, offering a sympathetic smile.

"I knew I should've warn flat shoes," she grumbled.

"The price of glamour, eh?"

"Hmm." She lifted one foot off the floor and rubbed her instep, losing her balance and staggering against Kris. "Ouch. Sorry."

"Why don't you two go find somewhere out of the way, and I'll get the drinks?" he suggested.

"Good thinking."

"OK. Red wine and…G and T, Ade?"

"Perfect," Ade confirmed.

Kris headed off to the bar, and Shaunna and Ade made a beeline for a free spot near the back of the atrium. It was lucky it was a big room; it would have been unbearably warm otherwise, with this much body heat. Shaunna leaned her back against the cool marble wall and bent a knee so she could rest one foot on it.

"Why don't you just take them off?" Ade said.

"Because Adele will be wearing six-inch heels, and I'll look like a frumpy shortarse."

Ade laughed. "No way could you ever be frumpy. You're always so gorgeous."

Shaunna smiled. "Thank you. You're pretty fabulous yourself, but you'll see what I mean. Adele is stunning, and the dress she bought for tonight is out of this world. It's pale lemon in colour, and the bodice has no back whatsoever. I'd love to be able to wear stuff like that."

"Why can't you?"

"Boobs. Adele's are fake, and I swear they defy gravity. Maybe they're helium implants." Shaunna switched feet, leaning on Ade for support. "See over there?" She subtly pointed. "That's Jess."

"OK?" Ade sensed there was a bit of gossip coming his way. Shaunna cupped her hand around his ear. "She ditched us all for a fling with an ex-boyfriend, who then ripped her off. The woman she's with is her personal assistant, as none of us want anything to do with her."

"Yet she still turned up this evening?"

"Yep. I think Andy asked Dan and Adele to invite her."

"He's Dan's brother?"

"That's right. He and Jess were...together-ish. Friends with benefits."

"Right." Ade was trying to commit all the details to memory. "And is Andy here tonight?"

"He will be. He organised it."

"Wow! Great job!"

"Yeah," Shaunna agreed absently, glancing around the room. A woman waved at her, and she waved back. "That's Ellie," she said. "The one who got married last month."

"The group honeymoon." Ade grinned impishly.

Shaunna laughed. "It wasn't anything like that...mostly." She cleared her throat and continued her surveillance.

Ade leaned forward and peered into her face. "Ooh! You are most definitely giving me the low-down on that!"

Shaunna smiled edgily, and Ade instantly let it go. However well they were getting along and however curious he was, he wouldn't pry. He turned to see if Kris was on his way back, hoping it would get them both out of a tight spot, and instead came face-to-face with an attractive, blonde-haired woman. From the description Shaunna had given earlier, this *had* to be Adele.

"Hiya," she said brightly. She gave Shaunna a big hug.

"Hiya, hun. You look beautiful!"

"Thank you." Adele stepped back and pirouetted, her full skirt swirling around her and showing off her matching high-heeled sandals—an easy six inches. "So do you," she said. "And your hair smells gorgeous." Adele lifted a few locks of Shaunna's hair and sniffed. Shaunna rolled her eyes, feigning boredom.

"This is Ade," she said, gesturing to him. "And this is Adele."

"Hi," Adele said. She and Ade shared a quick hug and cheek kiss, and then Adele was off again. "See you later."

Shaunna watched her totter away and switched feet. "Well, that was short and sweet. She obviously doesn't have any juicy news to share this evening."

"Or she didn't want share in front of me," Ade suggested. "She's only just met me, after all."

"That wouldn't usually stop her."

"Does she know about me and Kris?"

Before Shaunna had the chance to answer, they were joined by another woman—Ellie, Ade thought, and thank goodness she wasn't as dressed to the nines as Adele, although her floor-length smoky-grey evening dress was lovely and flowed around her like mercury as she, too, gave Shaunna a hug and kiss.

"Hey. Wow! I love that dress," Ellie said.

"Thanks. I love yours too."

"Is it new?"

"Yep. I bought it a few weeks ago for *someone's* wedding, but then they sent out the order that no-one was to wear blue."

"Ah." Ellie grinned guiltily. "Sorry about that."

"Not to worry. I got to buy another dress. And shoes." Shaunna glanced down at her feet and frowned. "Maybe that wasn't such a good thing." She looked up again, nodding at the glass of orange juice in Ellie's hand. "On call?"

"Yep. Only till midnight, though."

Shaunna explained for Ade's benefit, "Ellie's a GP."

"Oh, right," he said, nodding and trying not to let his bewilderment show. It was far too much to take in.

"Well, I'd best go congratulate the happy couple," Ellie said. "Lovely to meet you, Ade."

"And you." He watched her wander off towards the bar room, wondering how she knew his name when they hadn't been introduced. He turned back to Shaunna. She was smiling at him.

"What?" he asked.

"I'm glad you came tonight, that's all. And in answer to your question about whether Adele knows, no-one's been told about you and Kris officially, but they'll have figured it out."

"Are you saying I look gay?" Ade asked with a pout.

Shaunna burst out laughing. "That's so not what I meant. I asked Adele if she'd mind Kris bringing a plus-one that wasn't me, and she'll have spread it all round our friendship group. But now you come to mention it..."

Ade pretended to be outraged for a moment longer, but he couldn't keep it up. He was flamboyant, and most straight people assumed that that, coupled with working in the performing arts, meant he *had* to be gay. LGBTQ people were a little more discerning with their assumptions, but it was rare he didn't ping their gaydar. He could hardly criticise when he could see those qualities in himself and had likewise recognised them in Kris...which also meant he was almost certain he had correctly identified the guy on his way over to them now, giving him about three seconds to prepare for the introductions.

27: New

Ade

"Hi, Shaunna."

"Hi, George. How are you?"

"I'm..." George grinned. "Great."

"I bet!" Shaunna laughed and gave him a hug. "George. This is Ade. He and Kris are together."

"Oh, OK." George smiled at Ade, who was still processing 'are together' but managed to smile back. "It's good to meet you."

"And you," Ade said, shaking George's hand. He seemed a nice guy, not dashingly handsome in the way Dan was, more of a rough diamond, but it was difficult meeting exes, and first boyfriends were no ordinary exes, either. Those inaugural relationships broke hearts irreparably, and from what Kris had said, it had been a difficult break-up.

Of course, Shaunna was also Kris's ex, though it didn't feel like it to Ade. The longer he spent in their house, the more he'd come to realise they weren't *ex*-anything. True, there was nothing romantic or sexual going on between them, but they were still together in every other sense, and Ade was unexpectedly fine with that.

"Where's Josh?" Shaunna asked, and Ade realised he was still shaking George's hand. He released it and blushed, no clue how long he'd been lost in thought, other than it was long enough to amuse George, who turned away and pointed across the atrium to a man standing, arms folded, against the adjacent wall.

He was a similar height and build to Ade, perhaps a little slimmer, with dark-blonde hair that covered his eyes until he shook it back and looked over, briefly meeting Ade's gaze before shifting his attention to George. While Kris and Shaunna had mentioned Josh's name, neither of them had told Ade that he and George were a couple, but there were probably satellites going haywire from the charge zipping between them. No, George was definitely not someone Ade need worry about.

Dan stepped in front of Josh, interrupting the current, and the two men moved off towards the bar room, reminding Ade that Kris had been 'getting drinks' for ages. He'd no doubt got caught up chatting to one of his and Shaunna's many, many friends.

"So, Ade," George said. "Have you been together long?"

"Oh, er…" *A fortnight and a half? Twenty-one days?* There was no work-around without it sounding convoluted. "Three weeks," he confirmed quickly.

"Ahh! That's what he's been up to."

Ade nodded, even though he and Kris hadn't spoken or seen each other for two of those weeks. Sadly, he suspected Kris had spent them in a very bad place.

"How did you meet? Online?"

"At work. He was in a play I produced, and we hit it off."

"Cool." George smiled. He wasn't expressive in the way Kris was, but Ade could tell he was genuinely pleased for them.

"Have you seen who's over there?" Shaunna asked, nodding across the room to the woman she'd earlier identified as Jess.

"Where?" George turned to look. Jess and the woman with her were dancing on the spot, seemingly oblivious to everything else going on around them. "She looks happy enough," he said.

"I didn't think she'd come, did you?"

"She told Josh she and Andy had sorted stuff out, so it probably would've been worse if she'd stayed away."

"Maybe."

"And I do kind of feel sorry for her," George said.

"Hmm." Shaunna clearly didn't. "Anyway, we're not here to bitch. We're here to have fun." With that, she dropped in height by three inches and kicked her shoes away. "That's quite enough being glamorous for one evening."

Ade looked her up and down. "Nope. Still fabulous, honey."

"You do look beautiful," George agreed. "That dress is the perfect complement to your hair."

"Oh, enough with the hair already. He's a ginger too, you know." She tilted her head in Ade's direction.

George squinted at him. "Oh, yeah. So you are. I hadn't noticed."

"I wonder why that is?" Shaunna teased.

George turned pink. "I'm gonna leave you to it," he said, giving a final nod to Ade. "Good luck."

Ade laughed. "Thanks." Message received, loud and clear. Being with Kris wasn't going to be easy, but he wanted it enough to make it work. He watched George retreat across the atrium, to where the other guy—Josh—was standing once again.

"They've only been together since the summer," Shaunna said.

"Really?"

"Yep, but they've been in love since high school."

"That explains it."

"The sparks?"

"Yeah." Josh leaned in and said something in George's ear, then glanced past him, making eye contact with Ade. Ade raised his hand in acknowledgement. Josh gave him a quick smile and returned his attention to George. "How did it take them so long?"

"God knows."

They were fascinating to watch. Josh was subtly trying to draw George closer, but George was resisting. Even though they weren't touching, it was so intimate that Ade felt he was intruding, so he shifted his gaze to a guy carrying a tray of flutes of Champagne.

"Maybe we should just grab a glass from him," he suggested, watching him weave his way through the crowd towards them. "Oh, hello there!" Ade grinned. "I'm guessing that's Dan's brother?"

Shaunna nodded. "That's Mike."

"I thought you called him Andy earlier."

"There's three of them. Mike's the eldest, then Andy, then Dan."

Ade continued to appraise the glorious Adonis as he headed over. Like his younger brother, Mike was tall and dark, though not as ripped as Dan but muscular nonetheless, his tight T-shirt showing off his pecs and abs to full effect. He paused for Ade to take a couple of glasses of Champagne, gave him a nod and was on his way once more.

"And is Andy a fittie too?" Ade asked Shaunna.

"Hmm?" She wasn't listening, her eyes trained on a spot on the balcony. "Be right back," she said and off she went, across the atrium and up the right staircase, leaving Ade with both drinks. She reappeared on the balcony a few seconds later.

"I guess that's a yes," Ade muttered. The guy she was standing next to could have been Dan's twin, the differences between them largely superficial—longer hair, an earring, a more casual stance—and he was hot as hell. He leaned on the banister rail, and as the lights passed over him, his gaze shifted from the room below to Shaunna. There was history there, for sure, and once again Ade sensed that same intimate connection he'd felt between George and Josh.

Perhaps it was down to them all being friends for such a long time. Whatever the cause, Ade stopped watching, downed both glasses of Champagne, and went off in search of Kris—or that was his intention, but he only moved a couple of feet before Krissi grabbed him and pulled him into the centre of the floor to dance. They'd met the previous evening for the first time and instantly hit it off.

"Have they abandoned you?" she asked breathlessly.

"Looks like it." He took her lead and got into the groove, quite sure the music was going up a few decibels with every song. It was an eclectic mix too, spanning about forty years of pop and rock with a few hardcore dance tracks thrown in.

The current track faded out, and Ade and Krissi paused to catch their breath.

"Woo! I love a good dance, don't you?" she said. "Are you having fun?"

"I am! Are you here on your own?"

"No. My friend Jay's about somewhere. The lights are giving him a headache, or so he says. More like he's just being miserable and boring as usual." The next track properly kicked in, and Krissi groaned. "God, I heard enough of this growing up to last the rest of my days." It was *a*-ha—'Take On Me'.

"Don't you like them?"

"They're all right, I suppose. My mother's a Morten fan girl. She's obsessed. I reckon that's why she fell for Kris."

Ade laughed, thinking Krissi might well be on to something. But for all of her complaining, it didn't stop her from grabbing Ade's hand, and they sang and danced their way through to the end of the song, at which point Ade felt a tug on his arm. Kris had finally made it back with the drinks.

"Sorry," he said sheepishly. "I got sidetracked."

"Don't worry. Is everything OK?"

"Yeah." Kris looked doubtful. Ade mouthed *see you later* at Krissi, and he and Kris moved to the side of the atrium, where they'd been standing before, although they'd lost their spot, and Shaunna's shoes were gone.

"Shall we get some air?" Ade suggested.

28: Uncle

Kris

KRIS LED ADE away from the crowded atrium and down the deserted passageway towards the conservatory. It was too dark to pick out the décor, pictures on the walls appearing as indiscernible black rectangles. A closed door on their left opened as they passed, providing a glimpse of deep-green tiles and an ornate porcelain hand basin and toilet with brass fixtures. They exchanged polite nods with the person who exited and continued onwards, stepping into the shaft of tungsten-tinged light coming from the open door to their right.

"Wow!" Ade slowed, taking in the vast kitchen. An empty shell last time Kris had been there, it was now fully refurbished in the Victorian style. An enormous scrubbed-oak table took up the centre of the room, with a solid oak worktop around the perimeter, providing a warm contrast with the polished steel cookware and enormous shiny black-and-chrome range. It was a stunning kitchen, mixing modern and traditional, in keeping with the house, as was true of the atrium, the bathroom they had just passed and the conservatory they now entered.

"This place is incredible!" Ade said, gazing around him in awe.

"Yeah. It looks a million times better than the last time I saw it." Despite his fractured frame of mind, Kris was as impressed as Ade by the transformation. "You couldn't even see out of the windows—well, the ones that were still in one piece."

Ade lifted a corner of the pool cover to peer underneath. "Imagine the work that went into laying those tiles." He dropped the cover back into place and caught up with Kris. "Did you know the Victorians built these as a conspicuous display of their wealth?"

"I didn't."

"Sometimes they used them for growing fruit, vegetables and herbs for the kitchen, but they existed primarily for the purposes of entertainment and showing off."

"Your knowledge is amazing."

"It's really not. I did a stint on *Gardeners' Question Time* during my internship. Which means I can also tell you that those palm trees or whatever they are will thrive as long as there's good ventilation."

With the pool covered, the smell of chlorine was present but not overpowering and mingled with the warm earthy scent of the tropical plants in large pots along the glass side walls. Kris and Ade edged past those and the loungers, eventually making it out of the doors to the garden beyond.

Kris put his arms around Ade, pulling him close. "I'm sorry I left you on your own. Are you OK?"

"A little overwhelmed, but yes. I'm fine. You're not, though, are you?"

"I'm all right."

"Babe?"

"I just don't like it when someone else has all the limelight." Kris smiled to make it clear he was joking.

"Naturally! You're used to being the star of the show," Ade said, playing along briefly before asking, "But that's not the whole story, is it? What else is going on?"

"Why would there be anything else?" Kris tried to withdraw from their embrace, but Ade kept hold of him.

"Have I upset you?"

Kris shook his head. "Of course not."

"Is it about Dan?"

Kris hid his face against Ade's shoulder. Whether it was a lucky guess or he'd picked up on Kris's unease earlier, Ade had got it in one.

"Is that where you were? Talking to Dan?"

"No," Kris mumbled. "His mum."

"OK." Ade kissed Kris's cheek and kept his head turned, speaking so quietly it was little more than a rumble in his chest. "If you don't want to tell me more, I understand, but you've got me second-guessing, so I'll ask one more question, and if you can answer it for my benefit…"

Kris straightened up so he could look Ade in the eye. "I'm not in love with Dan," he said.

"Phew!" Ade laughed, but admitted, "I did wonder. You're very close to him."

"Yeah. We've known each other since we were kids. His mum was my childminder." That was how he'd become caught up in conversation with her—she'd just found out she was Krissi's grandmother, and to say she was in shock was putting it mildly. By the time he escaped, he felt as if he'd been through a military interrogation, interspersed with pearls of misplaced but well-meant wisdom about being true to himself and gratitude for 'the wonderful thing he'd done', standing by Shaunna and her daughter all these years.

Dan's mum, like most people, saw the world in shades of straight and gay, and her son's engagement party was not the place to challenge her, even if Kris had felt up to doing so, but she was right in one respect. The abuse was as much a part of who he was as his sexuality, and until he told Ade the full story, he wasn't being true to either of them.

"It wasn't just me." The admission rushed from him in a barely intelligible stream. He didn't dare look at Ade for fear of seeing judgement, revulsion, pity. Moments passed, thick and heavy in the silence, as Kris tried to get the rest of it out, but the words rattled around inside like forgotten lines from a script he'd never rehearsed because he'd never wanted to play this part.

"It was Dan too, wasn't it?" Ade said eventually.

Kris nodded. The silence resumed. Ade reached out and gently lifted Kris's face until he had to look at him.

"I'm here and I'm listening."

"I don't…" Kris sighed, his breath stuttering with his shivering.

"You don't want to tell me?"

"No, I do. I don't know how."

"I can understand that."

"You managed to tell me about the ex."

"Not really. I gave you the basics and let the bruises and drama do the talking."

Kris didn't have that option. His bruises were deep beneath the surface, and the drama…well, it was nothing compared to how Ade had suffered.

"He never even touched us."

"He still hurt you."

Kris heard the words, could still hear the music from the party, could feel the cold bite of frost forming around them, but he was straddling two worlds now, the thrum of the bass beat falling in time with the thump of heavy feet on the ladder up to the treehouse.

"He just watched, told us what to do, told us we liked it, that this was what little men did. You don't want to get aroused by it, but you do. It's over quicker if you can just make it happen, and you're waiting to hear it, that grunt that tells you it's finished.

"And you think, *I'll never get in this situation again*, but there's nothing you can do when he's the one who's supposed to be keeping you safe. We tried to stay away from the treehouse. We asked if we could go to Dan's house after school, but there were no other grown-ups to look after us. My dad said maybe, when we got to high school, they'd think about it. So we played outside and talked about how we couldn't wait to go to high school, pretending what we were feeling was excitement for that instead of it being a countdown to when it was over."

Kris closed his eyes, but it only made the image stronger. Sometimes it consumed him completely and he was back there, inhabiting the memory, missing the football every time Dan kicked it to him, neither of them acknowledging it, just talking about learning new subjects with new teachers. Now, with Ade's arms around him and the quiet hums to confirm he was listening, Kris was watching his younger self from a distance, saw the resignation settle on his and Dan's faces as the sky darkened and the trees began to sway. He held out his hand, palm up, behind Ade's back. The rain was in his head too.

"We got away with it for ages," he said. "Keeping out of his way. But then there was this massive storm and we had no choice. We were drenched in seconds, and we thought Uncle Anders was in his room, so we'd be OK sheltering in the treehouse. But he was in there already. It stank of his sweat—he'd been gardening, and his hands were covered in soil, the trowel was on the floor next to him, his boots..."

Sweat and shit and hot damp wood, drip-drip-drip through the hole in the corner, heavy feet, a voice—

"Dan?"

"Mike came to pick Dan up, and he caught us. Literally dragged Dan from the treehouse. He was crying. And Anders... he just smiled, said, 'What a shame,' and left me there. I wanted to stay there forever, but Mum and Dad came home from work and made me come inside. Mike had told his mum, and all hell broke loose. They wanted to know why we hadn't told a grown-up, but how can you? How do you even begin to say the words when you don't know what they are?

"Uncle Anders went back to Sweden. I don't know what happened to him after that. Don't care. Maybe he's dead. Nobody talks about him or what happened. I don't remember much after that, like the whole summer holiday was deleted from my head. The only other thing I remember was being at Dan's, and Mum and Dad came to pick me up, both of them together, which they never did, and we were sent up to Dan and Andy's room to play. I went to a different primary school to them—a private one— and I was supposed to stay there for high school. I'd pretty much begged my parents to let me go to school with Dan, but they didn't like the British education system.

"After a while, they called us downstairs. My mum and Dan's mum had been crying, and my dad explained that his cousin Eric, who lived with us, was sick and needed to go to a special hospital, so they'd decided I could go to school with Dan after all. I couldn't work out what Eric being sick had to do with me being allowed to change schools, and I didn't ask. I was just glad they'd changed their minds. I get it now, obviously.

"When we got home, there was a private ambulance outside, and they were trying to get Eric out of the house, but he's albino and it was a sunny day. His room was so dark and cold because the light hurt his eyes, and he burnt even in the winter. He was all wrapped up in a blanket, and a nurse had to guide him, like he was a little old blind man. He was only nineteen. They took him away in the ambulance, and it was over. That's what they said. It was over, and everyone tried to act like everything was normal again.

"When George and I started going out with each other…that was the first time I went back in the treehouse, and I had to make out like it was OK being in there, but I could still see Anders, sitting with his back to the wall and his hands in his pockets, playing with himself. I never told George. He was nervous enough about getting caught without me adding to it. He still doesn't know. The only person I've ever told is Shaunna…"

Kris stopped talking and took a step away from Ade, but Ade caught his hands and kept hold. He smiled sadly. "And now me."

"I'm sorry."

"I know you are, because I was too when I told Pip, but it doesn't feel the same for other people as it does for us. Or so she tells me. I bet she's enjoying the break from me, though."

"Have you spoken to her since…"

"*That Afternoon*? No, but we've been texting. She's going to come round tomorrow, help me sort out the apartment, catch up on all the news and gossip. Then I think I'll have a long soak in the bath and an early night so I'm bright and fresh on Monday morning."

"Back to normal," Kris said.

"Minus the violent ex-boyfriend," Ade added with an almost playful wink. "You realise, of course, this *is* our normal."

"More baggage than Paris Hilton." Kris nodded in agreement. He still felt raw and exposed, but dwelling on it didn't help any more than sweeping it all into the back of an ambulance and slamming the doors on it, and he was absolutely freezing. Even so, he needed a bit longer before he went back inside. "Thank you for listening. I didn't mean to go on like that, especially at a party. I should've waited—"

"Shhh. I'm glad you were able to tell me. Now I understand why you're struggling this evening. Or at any other time, really. Because it's not just your own pain you're feeling. It's Dan's and Eric's too. That's probably why it's so important to you that everyone around you is OK. Have you ever talked to Dan about it?"

"No. It's not like we pretend it never happened, but his coping strategies are…different from mine, shall we say."

"He starts fights," Ade said, adding in response to Kris's astonishment, "Not a shot in the dark. These days, I have a finely tuned violence detector."

"He's not a violent man as a general rule, but when he loses his temper, he goes up like a barrel of gunpowder."

"Right. Don't wind Dan up. Check," Ade said.

"Or his brothers." Kris released one of Ade's hands and turned, moving off slowly, back towards the conservatory doors. "And don't get caught in the middle of one of their fights."

"I'll keep it in mind."

"Not that I think they'll come to blows tonight."

"No, but forearmed is forewarned." Ade grinned. "Like Vishnu."

Kris laughed. "Shaunna's mum used to say that."

"Yes. I'm afraid I shamelessly stole it."

"I think she'd approve."

They returned to the atrium, where the party was still swinging, although the music wasn't quite as loud as it had been before. Kris grabbed George, who was on his way back from the bar.

"Ade, this is George."

"Hi, George. Again!"

"Hi, Ade," George said with a grin.

"Oh. You've already done all that." Kris sagged.

"We can do it all again, though," Ade suggested. He held out his hand for George to shake, both of them playing along for Kris's sake. "You didn't tell me what you do for a living, George."

"Ah, well, I've just started work on a farm, actually. An educational farm, with lots of miniature animals—Shetland ponies, pygmy goats—I'm only part-time till spring, but it gets busy then with lambing and school visits, the boss says, so hopefully, he'll make me full-time. And you're a radio producer?"

"I am," Ade confirmed. "Drama and documentaries. Mostly drama." He tilted his head in Kris's direction.

"I hear you," George said.

"If you two gang up on me, I will be…outraged!" Kris declared over-dramatically, appreciating that he'd put the other two men in a potentially awkward situation and they were giving their fullest efforts to stopping it from becoming so. He looked around, searching for Shaunna in the hope of having someone there to stop him further dropping himself in it, quickly locating her on the opposite side of the atrium, talking to Jess. Shaunna saw him, excused herself from her conversation and headed over.

"Hey," she said, giving him a once-over, followed by a small smile that confirmed she knew he'd told Ade. "I'm going for a drink. Anyone else want one?" The question was intended to give him a get-out, but he didn't take it.

"I'll come with you," Ade volunteered and hooked his arm through hers. Kris watched until they were out of earshot and turned back to George.

"So what do you think? Honest answer."

George shrugged. "He seems nice."

"Nice?"

"Right for you."

"That's what Shaunna said."

"Well, then."

"Is that all I'm getting?"

"What d'you want me to say? I like him."

Kris sighed loudly.

George grinned. "He's got the measure of you already, and he's not gonna take any of your melodramatic crap."

"I am not melodramatic!" Kris protested. George was still grinning. "I'm not!"

"If you say so."

Kris was about to complain further but contained it, as it only would only serve to prove George's point. "But you do like him?"

"Yeah. He's kinda…cute." George's attention had wandered, no need to check why.

"Not as cute as Josh," Kris remarked.

"I didn't say that."

"But you thought it."

George gave him a sheepish smile. He was blushing.

Kris hugged him. "I'm so happy for you, George."

"I know. You told me weeks ago."

"OK. I'm *still* happy for you. And you're definitely OK with me and Ade?"

"Yep. You know what they say—first time for everything."

"Us agreeing on something, you mean?"

"Well, yeah, that," George said, "and us both having boyfriends at the same time."

"We've done that once before," Kris reasoned.

George tutted. "OK, wise guy. Boyfriends that aren't each other."

Now Kris grinned. "You said the B-word, in public. Twice."

"I did, didn't I? Guess we're both finally getting it right."

Ade and Shaunna were on their way back with the drinks, and the sight of Ade laughing and chattering away made Kris's heart pump faster. "Yeah," he said, his voice quivering from the effect Ade was having—*always* had—on him. "I guess we are."

29: Out

Ade

A DE ONLY NEEDED a quick shower and had promised to be back at the pub within the hour. Kris was meeting him there—the first time Ade would be accompanied by his boyfriend to a work do.

My boyfriend.

What an extraordinary feeling, not to mention going on a night out with people *he* knew. On reflection, that was probably what had made him most anxious about attending Dan and Adele's engagement party. He'd been to after-show parties, birthdays, weddings, funerals—the whole array of social functions—as someone else's partner, since they were Fergus's friends, colleagues, family. Never Ade's.

But the party hadn't been like that. He'd met all of Kris's friends, and they were lovely. Two weeks on, Ade was settled back into his apartment and starting to enjoy life again. Tonight, Kris was staying over; tomorrow, they'd take the train to his place and stay there. It was uncomplicated, safe, and very liberating.

As Ade speed-walked home, he tallied how many nights out he'd missed during the past eleven years—colleagues he'd never had the opportunity to wish well, Christmas parties that kept the station in gossip for months while he listened on, no idea how much of it was true and nothing to contribute. Because that was the thing with abusive relationships; the physical side was tough to endure, but the psychological part was what really beat him down. Being isolated from his friends, having to tell lies and make excuses for why he could never be a part of the social whirl—

he needed to remind himself of that, in those moments when the what-if reared its ugly head. What if he'd let Fergus come back? The honest answer: he'd have been stuck in that same rut, and he'd have lost Kris.

He cleared the stairs in twos, the sound of Mary's TV audible in the hallway outside their apartments—a sure sign that Benny was keeping her company for the evening. They were an unlikely couple, what with Mary's hearing being as keen as it was and her intolerance of noise of any sort, and Benny's loud insistence that his hearing aids were working perfectly well.

Once inside, Ade set the shower running and went to his bedroom, grabbing the closest shirt and pair of trousers from his wardrobe and laying them out on the bed. As he turned to leave, he glimpsed something that stopped him in his tracks. On the bedside table, where he had left it weeks ago, was his tablet, fully charged and switched off. He hadn't made a single checklist since he came home from Julia's. He hadn't needed to. And that felt good. *Really* good.

Back to the bathroom, grinning like an idiot, Ade showered quickly, ran a razor over his already smooth chin and slapped on cologne, still hissing with the sting as he returned to his room and pulled on boxers and socks. He picked up the shirt and slid one arm into a sleeve, but then stopped and shook his arm free, leaving the shirt where it landed. He opened the wardrobe again and eyed the grim selection—greys, blues, blacks—all the crappy dull clothes Fergus had considered acceptable, and that was about the best he'd get out of him. He was never 'handsome' or 'alluring' to Fergus; just acceptable.

Ade about-turned and dropped to his knees, reaching under the bed for the storage bag he'd stashed there long ago. It was the sort that vacuum-sealed, so the contents were no doubt horrifically creased, but it wouldn't take long to iron a shirt, and it was worth it. Tonight, he would be stepping out as himself, not Fergus's shadow.

Unzipping the bag, he watched in wonder as the contents expanded, almost as if they were living, breathing things. He knew exactly which shirt he wanted for his rebirth and lifted away one garment after another, each triggering happy associations long forgotten, until there it was. He shook it loose and studied it for a moment then clutched it to his chest, overwhelmed by how much he'd missed it. It wasn't until he had the iron in his hand that he realised he was crying.

Of course, the shirt was terribly outdated, but that didn't matter. This was the one he had worn for five minutes, at most, on the night he'd been told he looked like a clown and nobody would ever take him seriously or find him attractive if he dressed like that. In the years that had passed since, he'd believed Fergus's cruel words, and even in those rare moments when his mind attempted a coup, he'd never had the confidence to test that assertion.

But tonight he could handle it. He would wear the shirt, and if people mocked, he'd just laugh it off, maybe even explain to them why he was wearing something old enough to have come from a vintage boutique. It might clash dreadfully with whatever Kris was wearing, but so what? He was celebrating with his friends— and his boyfriend—on a work night out. It was the best feeling in the world.

With the shirt ironed and given a quick spruce with fabric freshener, Ade returned to his bedroom to finish getting ready, using the tips of his fingers to scoop up a little of his new styling wax—Shaunna's recommendation—envisaging that it would be in his favour to keep his hair as goo-free as possible for the private afterparty.

While he hated to compare, it was hard not to when the differences between Fergus and Kris were so stark. Where Fergus was brutal, Kris was gentle. Other than his temper, Fergus was robotically rational, whereas Kris was over-emotional. But the one that really stood out was the physical contact. Outside of sex, intimidation and violence, Fergus had touched Ade so rarely he could recall every single occasion. Kris, by contrast, was constantly seeking out a hand to hold or stroking Ade's arm or playing with his hair. *A fully paid-up associate of the Ginger Appreciation Society.* Ade laughed at his reflection. He felt great, and his self-confidence had grown enough for him to like the person laughing back at him. He was ready for a good night out.

Without further ado, he collected his phone, wallet and keys and headed out to the hall to put on his coat. There was a knock at the door.

"Hold on a sec," Ade called, pausing to fasten his coat. Mary didn't miss a trick, and it was kind of sweet, although it could be a bit of a pain when he was in a rush, as she did like a chat. With any luck, she'd see he was on his way out and leave whatever it was she wanted to tell him until the morning. Ade opened the door, breath drawn, words at the ready.

"Hello, Adrian."

For a few seconds, Ade stopped breathing entirely as he stared in horror and disbelief at the man standing before him, an arm raised, hand casually resting on the doorframe, widening his posture, staking his claim.

"You aren't heading out, are you? I hoped we could talk."

The question, as always, was phrased to lead Ade to give the required answer. *Not happening.* "What are you doing here?"

"I told you. We should talk, but in private."

Ade shook his head, no.

"Adrian, come on. There's too much past for us to simply walk away."

Ade started to close the door. Fergus put his foot in the way.

"You need to go," Ade said, all of his effort on sounding calm and assertive, though he was quaking. "Now."

But Fergus didn't leave. He smiled and moved, slowly but surely, into the hallway of the apartment. Ade backed off. The front door closed. Fergus turned, raising his arms, an action to which Ade was so thoroughly conditioned that he reflexively flinched. Fergus let his arms drop into a lazy shrug. It was a gesture conveying surrender, yet this visit, not to mention how he'd gained entry, showed how little intention he had of giving up. At a slender five foot eight, Ade was used to other men being bigger than he was, and Fergus was both taller and stockier. He worked out almost every day, and once upon a time, Ade had appreciated his defined musculature and rugged features. Once upon a time, he'd thought Fergus to be a handsome, loveable rogue. Now, those very same qualities repulsed him and made him nauseous with fear.

No, physically he couldn't challenge Fergus, but the few weeks' respite had made Ade strong in other ways. This was *his* apartment, and right at this moment, he was supposed to be in the pub with his friends, colleagues and boyfriend. No way was he missing out again. Just the possibility that he might made him angry, but if he could keep it together, he was the one in control here.

"You've got fifteen minutes," he said and turned, leading the way to the living room. He sat in the middle of his new sofa, knowing that Fergus wouldn't sit next to him because he was long-sighted and used eye contact to intimidate.

Fergus sat in the armchair, leaning back, legs crossed, relaxed. He smiled, but it was false and smarmy. "New shirt?" he asked. Ade didn't answer. "Come on, Adrian. I'm trying my hardest." Still nothing from Ade, Fergus tried, "Do you want me to just say it?"

Ade lifted an eyebrow noncommittally. Fergus took it as permission to state his case.

"We've had a good break, and I'm sure you'll agree, it's been a much-needed opportunity to think through the way we treated one another."

Ade didn't mean to sigh, although time was ticking by, and he wanted to get to the pub.

"Am I boring you?" Fergus asked.

"Not boring, no. But you are holding me up."

"Why? Where are you going? On a date?"

Ade glared. "It's none of your business."

Fergus nodded slowly. "Fair enough. But, you know, you cannae blame me for all of it."

"Who said anything about blame?" Ade gave up on concealing how tedious he was finding this and rubbed his eyes. "Is there anything else you wanted to say?"

"Nothing important. Or certainly not important to you."

"Fergus." Ade paused and thought carefully about his words. He didn't want to antagonise, but he needed to make it as clear and unambiguous as he could. "You *were* important to me, and we have some great shared memories, but our relationship was over a year ago. We tried again, and it wasn't to be. Now it's time for us both to move on."

"You've met someone."

"It's irrelevant whether I've—"

"Of course it's relevant!" Fergus uncrossed his legs and shifted forward. He was riled. "If you're seeing someone else, then you've given up on us. Correct?"

"Which means you gave up on us first."

"Meaning?"

"Isn't it obvious?"

"Are you accusing me of cheating on you?"

"Did you?"

Fergus gave a small, supercilious laugh. "Our relationship was finished a year ago. You just told me that."

"Yes, but you were all for making a fresh start. As far as I was concerned, that meant we were trying to work it out. The fact you were screwing around—"

"One guy. One night. That's all."

"It doesn't matter if it was one or one hundred. And you brought whoever it was here, to my apartment. To my bed!"

"*Your* apartment now, is it?"

Ade shook his head in exasperation. He was on dangerous ground. It always began like this, but he refused to back down.

"I'm sorry, Ferg, but I'm late." Ade got up and waited for Fergus to do the same, which he did, intentionally stepping into Ade's space. It set him on edge.

Fergus gave him a sad smile. "For what it's worth, I'm sorry."

It was so difficult to play tough, but Ade had to. He couldn't let Fergus's long-awaited apology get to him because it was just more lies. Or maybe...it wasn't. "Me too."

"So it's really over for good?"

Ade nodded. "Yes."

In a flash, Fergus switched from humble to furious, shoving Ade hard with a palm against his chest. Ade staggered, his back slamming into the wall. He panicked and lifted his arms to push Fergus away, but Fergus grabbed his wrists and twisted.

"Get off me!" Ade hissed.

"Not until you've heard what I have to say." Fergus stopped twisting, but kept his grip tight, waiting for Ade to stop struggling. "Are you ready?"

"Let go."

Fergus gave Ade a pitying look.

"Or I'll scream."

"Scream away. If anyone hears, I'll just tell them you like it rough. Because you do, you filthy slut." Fergus released one of Ade's hands and grabbed his face, pushing his fingers into the flesh as if it were dough.

"Last chance," Ade squeezed out. Fergus's hand slid down, and he pressed his thumb to Ade's Adam's apple. It was impossible to swallow, and as Ade drew in the breath, preparing to follow through with the scream, there was another knock on the door, followed by Mary's voice.

"Ade? Are you in there, lovey?"

30: Boyfriend

Ade

"FOR FUCK'S SAKE," Fergus muttered darkly. A mania flashed across his face, which was quickly checked, but Ade had seen it, and it terrified him. Fergus leaned in and stared into his eyes at close quarters, a warning not to raise the alarm. He let go of Ade and moved towards the door.

"Don't!" Ade warned. He followed Fergus along the hallway, in no rush to stop him, yet at the same time dreading what came next. There was only one way that he would get Fergus out of the apartment, or only one where Ade also got out alive, and even then there were no guarantees. For now, it was safer if Fergus believed Ade was on his side, and so he stopped him from opening the door. "She'll call the police."

Fergus clenched his fists and turned back. "So? What are they going to do? We're just having a wee chat, aren't we?"

"Yes, but..." Ade was starting to wonder himself. What *would* the police do? He was still waiting for a court date for the restraining order, and while that was officially on record, they'd been through this a dozen times before and Ade had always refused to press charges. Even if Mary did call them, they might decide it wasn't worth following up, but maybe he could persuade Fergus to leave before it came to that.

Persuade him to leave and never return? Unlikely, not the way he was acting, with that crazed emptiness in his eyes. Behind the brave façade, Ade was a shivering, frightened mess, and it was taking all of his willpower and concentration to keep at the forefront of his mind that Kris was waiting for him.

"Tell Mary all's well," Fergus said.

It took a few seconds for the words to filter through. Ade stared at him in bewilderment. "I think it's time for you to leave."

Fergus shook his head, his face fixed in a tight-lipped, arrogant sneer as he used his body to steer Ade, until he was once again pinned to the wall. "We're not done here."

"I am," Ade asserted bravely. If this was the end, he was going down fighting. A shadow forewarned of the blow and Ade braced himself.

"Damn you, Adrian. You make me so fucking mad." Fergus flexed the fingers of the fist that had put a dent in the wall millimetres from Ade's left cheek.

"No. You make yourself mad and try to blame me. That's how it's always been. That's why we're over. This rage that you direct at me—it was never meant for me, yet you choose to try to destroy me rather than face the truth. We're finished for good, Ferg, and I truly am sorry. But it doesn't change the fact that you need help so you can deal with whatever happened to turn you into this."

"Don't you dare blame me," Fergus snarled. He reinstated his grip on Ade's wrists. "I was never good enough for you. Everything I wanted, you threw back in my face, but you still made your demands."

"What are you talking about?" Ade's eyes were watering from resisting the urge to cry out at the pain in his wrists. It felt like his hands were going to burst.

"Kids, Adrian. Kids and houses and a fucking dog. All that time, I paid out so you could work for nothing, and still you wanted more. Yet you wonder why I'm angry? It must be fucking fantastic inside your little bubble, thinking the world revolves around you. But it's never your fault, is it? It's always fucking mine."

This time, the fist made contact just below Ade's shoulder blade, winding him. He doubled up and Fergus's knee rose, but Ade's reflexes kicked in and he grabbed Fergus's leg, pulling it sideways and sending him crashing to the floor. Ade was out of his apartment before Fergus had a chance to move never mind retaliate. He banged on Mary's door. It opened, and she pulled him inside.

"Call the police," he gasped, still breathless from the punch.

"I already did, lovey. And Kris."

On those words, Ade bolted.

"Ade! Come back. It's safer here."

"Need to warn him," Ade said, hurtling down the stairs, out of the external door and straight into Kris.

"Whoa!" Kris grabbed him by both arms and kept hold.

"He's...Kris...I..."

"All right," Kris said calmly. "Slow down for me, Ade. That's it. Take a breath."

Ade was struggling to breathe at all, let alone deliver his warning, but it was too late. The door flew open, and Fergus stormed out of it, ramming into Ade and Kris hard enough for Kris to be thrown backwards, lose his footing on the kerb and fall into the road. Brakes screeched, and Ade screamed.

"No! Oh my god. No. Kris!"

He jumped in front of the stopped car, vaguely aware of movement around him, people running, blue lights. The car reversed and sped off, taking the blue lights with it.

"Mr. Simmons?"

Ade heard but wasn't listening, his thoughts only on Kris. He crouched next to him, swiping away the tears blurring his vision. "Are you OK? Babe?"

"I'm OK. Are you?"

"Yes." Laughing in relief, Ade held out his arm. Kris grasped his hand but then saw the burns around Ade's wrist and let go, bearing his own weight. Once he was on his feet again, the two of them embraced and cried like babies. Mary and Benny had made it down the stairs and were standing in the doorway, watching.

"What a pair of pansies," Benny said in a very loud voice.

"Benny!" Mary shouted.

Ade lifted his head from Kris's shoulder, all set to give Benny a piece of his mind, soon discovering that Mary was already on the case and had clamped a hand over his mouth. Ade started laughing.

"Sorry to interrupt, Mr. Simmons…"

Ade turned to look behind him. "Oh. Sorry. I didn't see you."

The police officer smiled swiftly. "Can you tell me what's happened here this evening?"

Ade nodded resolutely. "Yes, I can. Fergus Campbell forced his way into my apartment and physically assaulted me. I would like to make a formal statement, please."

*

ONCE THE POLICE were aware that Ade and Kris had been on their way to a night out, they took enough details to make the arrest and arranged for Ade to give a full statement the following morning. He and Kris made it to the pub before everyone moved on to a club. Not one person commented on Ade's shirt being gaudy or out of fashion, though plenty took the time to tell him how great it was that he was able to come and how healthy and happy he looked. He was exhausted but determined to enjoy himself and drank and danced the whole night away.

At four in the morning, Ade and Kris staggered up the stairs to the apartment and flopped into bed, too drunk and too tired to consider anything more than sleeping.

A few hours later, they were up again, showered, dressed and talking to the police. Fergus had been held overnight and released on bail, on condition that he made no attempts to contact Ade, but it wasn't enough. The phone calls started while the police were taking Ade's statement, and they listened in, making a note of what was said before advising Ade to block Fergus's number. This time, he did.

After the police left, Kris made tea and they sat in silence. Ade was trying not to think about how close he'd come to letting Fergus destroy everything again, but he was struggling.

"Do you want to talk about something else?" Kris asked.

"Yes, please."

"OK, well, I'll tell you again when you're paying attention, but…after what you said about me auditioning for TV stuff, I asked my agent to keep me in mind if anything came up. She phoned yesterday to say that they're auditioning for a new crime series. The main character needs to be fluent in English and Swedish and good at regional accents."

"Oh, wow! That was written for you. Are you going for it?"

"I think I might."

"That's great, babe." Ade gave Kris a congratulatory kiss and tried to be enthusiastic, but it was tough. His smile faded. "I'm going to have to move," he said, finally resigned to the truth. The apartment had been his home before Fergus bullied his way into his life, but for as long as he knew where Ade lived, Fergus would never leave him alone.

"What will you do?" Kris asked. "Buy another place around here?"

Ade hadn't thought any further ahead, but his mind was spinning now. If he moved somewhere else, Fergus would come after him at work instead, and much as he loved his job, he'd already wasted too many years living in constant fear and wondering when the next attack would happen. He wasn't about to waste any more.

"I'm going to resign from the studio, go and stay with Jules for a bit until I get something sorted."

"OK. I can see the logic in that," Kris said diplomatically, because it sounded spur-of-the-moment, but it wasn't.

"Of course," Ade said, "that does depend on you to a certain extent."

"Me? Why?"

"Well, it's too far from Julia's place to yours to just meet up for a drink and go back again, even once I've bought another car." Ade paused, unsure if he could make the request. His common sense was telling him five weeks wasn't long enough to conclude he wanted to spend the rest of his life with Kris, but that was how he felt.

"If you want to look for somewhere together, I'm OK—" Kris started to say, but Ade cut him off.

"No. Or at least, maybe, one day. I've seen how happy you and Shaunna are sharing your house, and I'd rather take it slowly, which isn't to say I don't think we'll stay the distance. I want to be with you, Kris."

Kris took Ade's hand, kissing it over and over, doing a sterling job of ignoring the red ring and blossoming bruises around Ade's wrist.

"So, what I was going to suggest," Ade continued, "is—"

Kris pressed his finger lightly to Ade's lips. "Can I just tell you this first?" Ade nodded mutely. "I love you, Ade Simmons." Kris removed his finger, but Ade was speechless. "Carry on," Kris prompted.

For several minutes, Ade remained still and quiet. He'd lost track of what he'd been saying, which all seemed so inconsequential now, although he did have big plans. For a while, he'd been considering setting up in business as a touring production company for gay performers. The only stumbling block had been the set-up costs, and if he sold the apartment, he could use the proceeds to get the business up and running. If it failed, he'd be homeless, but if Julia and Kris would support him, he stood a reasonable chance of succeeding. Kris's love declaration simultaneously guaranteed his support and complicated matters, unless Ade felt the same way.

Unless Ade owned up to feeling the same way.

Get some balls, Simmons!

"Ade?"

"Yes, babe?"

"What were you going to tell me?"

"Apart from 'I love you too'?"

"I didn't say it with any expectation for you to say it back. You've been through a lot lately."

"And you've been through it with me. You've scooped me up from the floor—literally—and you've been shoved in front of oncoming traffic—again, literally. When I was walking home last night, I remembered what I'd said to you about still loving Fergus, but it's not love, it's obligation." Ade took both of Kris's hands and looked him in the eye. "I don't ever want you to feel that kind of obligation to me."

"That won't happen."

"What I mean is, don't give up your life for me like I did for Fergus. I want to start my own business, and I'll be relying on you because it's the only way I can do it, but if we don't work out, then—"

"I want you," Kris said, no disguising his desire.

"What, now?"

"Yes, now. Right here, on your sofa."

Ade's eyebrows rose. "What happened to *is this OK?* and *if it's what you want…?*"

Kris shrugged and pushed Ade onto his back. "You were right. It should be good for me."

"And this is good for you?"

"*You* are good for me."

"I am?"

Those were Ade's last words before he once again succumbed to the charms of the handsome Scandinavian actor who had helped him find the strength to fight back and start to turn his life around. Whether it worked out or not, he had to admit that Kris was good for him too. For the first time in a long time, Ade felt optimistic, ready for the challenge. He was looking forward instead of watching his back. Cliché that it was, it was as if he had been roused from a deep, nightmarish sleep—or maybe this part was the dream because it all felt just a little too good to be true.

"Babe?"

"Mmm?"

"Pinch me."

Kris lifted on his arms and stared at Ade in horror. "Never."

Ade smiled up at him. "I suppose a kiss would work just as well."

"I beg your pardon?"

"Just k—"

The rest was lost to that kiss, the much-needed confirmation that it wasn't just a hopeful dream.

Ade was, finally, awake.

Acknowledgements

The cover for this second edition of *Crying in the Rain* includes elements from an image generated by DALL·E. I have not used AI for my covers before now and don't intend to make a habit of doing so intentionally (image-editing software uses AI, so it's hard to avoid). While there are countless arguments against using AI, I have spent countless more hours during the past ten years searching for a licensed cover model who looks even remotely close to how I wanted to depict Ade. Finally, AI has reached a point where it was able to create something decent I could work with.

The final version of the cover has undergone significant manual revision and re-composition, application of filters and effects, colour grading and so on, by me, using Adobe Photoshop. As I design most of my own book covers, I have not directly denied an artist work by doing so on this occasion. I do, however, acknowledge that the data used to train generative AI systems include creative works used without creators' permission. This is why I've been honest about how I constructed this cover, as I could not have done so without the work of those artists, therefore it is theirs as much as it is mine.

I still owe huge thanks to Natasha Snow for the first edition's cover, which was striking and undoubtedly resulted in many people picking up the book for its cover alone.

Inspiration from films (quoted or paraphrased):

- *Back to the Future* (1985, directed by Robert Zemeckis)
- *Bridget Jones's Diary* (2001, directed by Sharon Maguire)
- *Dead Poets Society* (1989, directed by Peter Weir)
- *It Always Rains on Sunday* (1947 film adaptation of novel by Arthur La Bern; directed by Robert Hamer)
- *Star Wars Episode 5: The Empire Strikes Back* (1980, directed by Irvin Kershner)
- *Thelma and Louise* (1991, directed by Ridley Scott)
- *The Wizard of Oz* (1939, directed by Victor Fleming)

DV Support (UK)

Galop

Tel: 0800 999 5428
galop.org.uk

Helpline for LGBT+ people experiencing abuse or violence, such as hate crime, domestic abuse, sexual violence, so-called 'conversion therapy' or any other kind of abuse.

Men's Advice Line

Tel: 0808 801 0327
mensadviceline.org.uk

Men's Advice Line: confidential helpline for men experiencing domestic violence from a partner or ex-partner (or from other family members).

24-hour National Domestic Violence

Tel: 0808 2000 247
nationaldahelpline.org.uk

Freephone 24 Hour National Domestic Violence Helpline, run in partnership between Women's Aid and Refuge.

Respect

Tel: 0808 802 4040
respect.org.uk

UK charity stopping perpetrators of domestic abuse.

About the Author

Debbie McGowan is an author and publisher based in a semi-rural corner of Lancashire, England. She writes character-driven, realist fiction, celebrating life, love and relationships. A working-class girl, she 'ran away' to London at seventeen, was homeless, unemployed and then homeless again, interspersed with animal rights activism (all legal, honest ;)) and volunteer work as a mental health advocate. At twenty-five, she went back to college to study social science—tough with two toddlers, but they had a 'stay at home' dad, so it worked itself out. These days, the toddlers are young women (much to their chagrin) and Debbie teaches undergraduate students, writes novels and runs an independent publishing company, occasionally grabbing an hour's sleep where she can.

Social Media Links

Website: debbiemcgowan.co.uk and hidingbehindthecouch.com
Newsletter Signup: eepurl.com/b8emHL
Blog: deb248211.blogspot.com
Facebook: facebook.com/DebbieMcGowanAuthor and facebook.com/beatentrackpublishing
Twitter: @writerdebmcg
YouTube: youtube.com/deb248211
Instagram: instagram/writerdebmcg
Tumblr: writerdebmcg.tumblr.com
LinkedIn: uk.linkedin.com/in/writerdebmcg
Goodreads: goodreads.com/DebbieMcGowan
Books2Read: https://books2read.com/DebbieMcGowan

By the Author

I'm not a single-genre author, for which I make no apology. Nor do I write stories of a specific length; I believe a story should be as long as it needs to be.

Thus, to assist you in navigating my catalogue, I've also included the closest-fitting genres and types of publication.

Hiding Behind The Couch Series
(Contemporary/Literary Fiction)
The ongoing story of 'The Circle'…
Nine friends from high school;
Nine friends for life.

The Story So Far…
(in chronological order)

* *Beginnings* (Novella)
* *Ruminations* (Novel)
* *Class-A* (Short Story – also in *Take a Chance* anthology)
* *Hiding Behind The Couch* (Season One)
* *No Time Like The Present* (Season Two)
* *The Harder They Fall* (Season Three)
* ***Crying in the Rain* (Novel)**
* *First Christmas* (Novella)
* *In The Stars Part I: Capricorn–Gemini* (Season Four)
* *Breaking Waves* (Novella)
* *Chain of Secrets* (Novella – also in *Love Unlocked* anthology)
* *In The Stars Part II: Cancer–Sagittarius* (Season Five)
* *A Midnight Clear* (Novella – also in *Boughs of Evergreen* anthology)
* *Red Hot Christmas* (Novella)
* *Two By Two* (Season Six)
* *Hiding Out* (Novella – CHO Crossover)

- *Those Jeffries Boys* (Novel)
- *The WAG and The Scoundrel* (Gray Fisher #1)
- *Perfect Tenor* (Novella)
- *The Lost Mitten* (see 'Children's Stories')
- *Reunions* (Season Seven)
- *Tabula Rasa* (Gray Fisher #2)
- *Breakfast at Cordelia's Aquarium* (Short Story)
- *Reverberations* (Novel)
- *To Be Sure* (Novella – also in *Never Too Late* anthology)
- *What A Scorcher!* (Flash Fiction)
- *Goth of Christmas Past* (Front of House #1)
- *The Advent of Reason* (Novella)
- *Not My Christmas* (Novella)
- *Highlights* ~ co-written with A.M. Leibowitz (Short Story – Notes from Boston meets Hiding Behind The Couch)
- *Distractions* (Gray Fisher #3)

Checking Him Out Series
(M/M and LGBTQ Romance)

- *Checking Him Out* (Book One)
- *Checking Him Out For the Holidays* (Novella)
- *Hiding Out* (Novella – Noah and Matty – HBTC Crossover)
- *Taking Him On* (Book Two – Noah and Matty)
- *Checking In* (Book Three)
- *The Making of Us* (Book Four – Jesse and Leigh)

Seeds of Tyrone Series
(M/M Romance)

~ co-written with Raine O'Tierney

- *Leaving Flowers* (Book One)
- *Where the Grass is Greener* (Book Two)
- *Christmas Craic and Mistletoe* (Book Three)

Stand-Alone Stories

- *Champagne* (LGBTQ Historical Novel)
- *'Time to Go'* (Contemporary Short in *Story Salon Big Book of Stories*)
- *And The Walls Came Tumbling Down* (Sci-fi Novel)

- *No Dice* (Sci-fi Novel)
- *Double Six* (Sci-fi Novel)
- *Sugar and Sawdust* (M/M Romance Short Story)
- *Cherry Pop Valentine* (M/M Romance Short Story)
- *Coming Up* ~ co-written with Al Stewart (LGBTQ Short Story)
- *Of the Bauble* (LGBTQ Fantasy Romance Novella)
- *So Long, Little Black Diamonds* (True Short Story)
- *The Pastor's Last Drop* (Ongoing Historical Novel – Wattpad)
- *When Skies Have Fallen* (LGBTQ Historical Romance Novel)
- *A Snowy Ball* (When Skies Have Fallen Novelette)
- *The Great Village Bun Fight* (LGBTQ Comedy Novella – also in *Seasons of Love* anthology)
- 'Oh No She Didn't!' (LGBTQ Short Story in *Upstaged!: an anthology of women who love women in the performing arts*)
- *The Great Pretendo* (Flash Fiction)
- 'Nina, Pretty Ballerina' (Short Story in *Play On…: a collection of short stories, poetry and prose, inspired by the songs of ABBA*)
- *Meredith's Dagger* (Contemporary/Historical Feminist/LGBTQ Novel)

Audiobooks

- *And The Walls Came Tumbling Down* – Narrated by Hannibal Mills
- *Checking Him Out* – Narrated by Tim Larkfield
- *Of The Bauble* – Narrated by Jack Hardman
- *The Great Village Bun Fight* – Narrated by Jack Hardman
- *When Skies Have Fallen* – Narrated by Tim Holbourne

Children's Stories (written as J.S. Morley)

- *The Lost Mitten* ~ illustrated by Sofia Oxelstrand
- *Chompy the Velociraptor* ~ illustrated by Kate Andrew
- Zoom the Pterodactyl

www.hidingbehindthecouch.com
www.debbiemcgowan.co.uk
www.beatentrackpublishing.com/debbiemcgowan

Beaten Track Publishing

For more titles from Beaten Track Publishing,
please visit our website:

https://www.beatentrackpublishing.com

Thanks for reading!